Night Swimming

DOREEN FINN

MERCIER PRESS

For Emily and David, and for Mark

MERCIER PRESS

Cork

www.mercierpress.ie

© Doreen Finn, 2019

ISBN: 978 1 78117 627 6

A CIP record for this title is available from the British Library

Printed and bound in the EU.

Prologue

My father was disappeared. He didn't disappear himself; it was done to him. He had no control over it, and he was gone before he knew about me, before he had a chance to meet his only child.

His name was Felipe and he was Bolivian. My mother met him in art college in Dublin and they fell in love. Felipe was a photographer – a brilliant one, apparently. He'd left Bolivia because of the junta and because he was on a list of some sort, a list of wanted people, the ones who went against the military, who spoke out about atrocities, who stood up publicly for what was right. Men and women, no one was spared. Felipe was marked because he had photographed protests by the miners and had them published in foreign newspapers. His father had publicly criticised the president. Before I was born, he went back to Bolivia. He took photos of military brutality, of mothers whose sons had been taken away. *Los Desaparecidos*, they called the ones who vanished. The Disappeared. Gone, into thin air, never to be seen again.

Except they weren't anywhere near thin air. They were buried, in spots around Bolivia. No crosses marked their resting places, no flowers were laid. And families spent the rest of their lives seeking the truth.

A bit like me, I suppose.

My mother never told me any of this, mind you. In fact, she never told me anything at all about Felipe. Instead, it was left to me to find out about him, to sort through the pieces of the puzzle and complete the picture. Clues dotted our house. Photographs. Paintings. Books. Old cuttings from newspapers, brittle and yellowed.

It wasn't easy; I was only nine that summer. Up until then I hadn't worried too much about my father. We lived our lives without him, and it didn't matter to me. I was a child. The patterns of my life were set, the rhythms slow and undemanding. My mother, my grandmother and I lived together, and we were happy, mostly. Fathers didn't really figure, until Beth arrived. Beth Jackson, with her questions and curiosity, making me think about things that hadn't bothered me up to then. Beth with her New York sensibilities and her bohemian parents. The changes that were wrought.

The Americans brought us many things that summer. New food. Cocktails. Quesadillas and margaritas, frittatas and mimosas, our tongues tied on the unfamiliar sounds. They bestowed upon us new music that made my mother's small record player judder in the swelter of those white, heatwaved nights. Led Zeppelin. Pink Floyd. The Ramones. The Doors. Such a change from the music we habitually listened to up to then. They gave us new ways of looking at the world, broke us out of our Irish slumber. The Americans gave us truth, though we may not have liked it at the time.

The truth has a funny way of outing itself, especially when we go to extraordinary lengths to hide it – even from ourselves. Like the heat during the relentless sunshine of those months, the truth emerged, vapour-like and shimmering. Like the heat, it was insistent, pressing itself on us, demanding our attention. It could no longer be ignored.

And we were never the same afterwards.

JULY

1

The ad in the evening paper was short and to the point: *Self-contained garden flat, two bedrooms, close to city centre. Available immediately.* I wondered why it didn't mention the fresh white paint on the walls, the tiled hall floor, the new front door. Jim, our handyman, had replaced our old, splintered door with its peeling paint, and in its place was a door he'd salvaged from somewhere else. Jim had sanded it, replaced the broken pane with new bubbled glass, and painted it bright red. Claret, it said on the tin. My grandmother, Sarah, said she had paid for the ad by the letter, so anyone interested in the finer details of the house could see for themselves when they came to view it.

At nine, I had no interest in thinking about letter counts in the small ads. It was far too hot, anyway. The heat palpitated, wrapped tightly around the still, summer days. Sarah made me wear a sun hat, a ridiculous thing made of leather that my mother had been given as a present from South America years before. It was a farmer's hat, or a rancher's, designed to keep the sun off while galloping across grassy plains. Definitely, it wasn't meant for an Irish child. The crown was too big for me, the brim wide and flat.

My mother liked South America. She had faded newspaper photos on her studio wall of miners' strikes in Bolivia, pictures of the Andes, a painting of a *cholita* in national dress. A line of small paintings of tango dancers she had done years before, blurred to show their movement across the page, hung on the wall. They had been there since I was a baby, and even though they were kept out of the light, they were starting to show their age. Edges curled, the red of the girls' dresses less vivid than it had been. Alizarin crimson, the paint was called. My mother, Gemma, still had a tube of it, well squeezed now, the remaining paint drying inside the small metal casing. Felipe's mother was Argentinian, a dancer. Felipe taught my mother how to tango. I imagined her, dark hair in a bun, a rose between her teeth, tapping out rhythms on a wooden floor with hard-soled shoes. She didn't much like to talk about any of it – Bolivia, South America, the tin mines – so I didn't ask her. Instead, I looked it up in the encyclopaedia. Bolivia was in the southern hemisphere, so they had their winter when we were in the middle of summer. It was famous for its salt flats, for having the highest capital city in South America, and for being the place where Che Guevara died. Gemma had a poster of him on the back of the attic door, all cigar, black beard, blacker beret. Felipe had met him once, Gemma said. The details were fuzzy and though I pestered her, she never had much to say about it. It was hot in Bolivia, but it couldn't have been as hot as it was in Dublin that summer.

Sarah got up extra early each morning to do the gardening, and was back in the house by breakfast time, dabbing her forehead with a tea towel. She said the heat made her feel like an old woman, but she didn't look that old. Her hair was going grey, but she still wore it in a bun at the back of her head. Her skin was brown from all the garden work, and her eyes looked bluer than ever. I got used to sweat trickling down my skin, gathering in the creases at my elbows and knees. I tasted salt on my fingers, on my lips. My eyes hurt from squinting. Sleep did not come easily, despite open windows and a single sheet draped across my big bed.

Heatwave was a new addition to my vocabulary. We were in the middle of a heatwave. If I concentrated hard enough, I could almost see the heat in the still air, zigzagging in jagged lines around me, mixing with the smell of petrol and dirty fumes in the wake of passing buses. Women fanned themselves with folded magazines. Children soaked each other with garden hoses. Tar melted blackly on the roads. Dire warnings were given on the news, in the papers, on radio bulletins, all saying the same thing: *water is in danger of running out.* Sarah forbade my mother and me from having baths unless it was absolutely necessary. She decanted all used water into a special bucket kept outside the back door. This she poured over the plants each evening. My mother remarked that Sarah was indeed being a good citizen. My grandmother replied that caustic comments should be kept out of the conversation when young ears were pricked. I was just surprised that Gemma even noticed the bucket. Maybe it was the crazy weather, the torpor driving her out of her attic, downstairs to where it was marginally cooler.

Heat made people funny. That's what I heard Sarah say to Mrs Brennan in the shop one day as she handed over money for our groceries. We're better off in the rain, was the woman's reply. At least we know where we stand. I began to observe people around me, my attention tuned to the slightest change. Miss Buckley, the retired teacher across the road, stopped going to daily Mass. Our family doctor took to wearing sandals to work. Mrs Doherty next door did no housework. Instead, she lay on a blanket all day and read books, offering her husband sandwiches when he came home from work. The husband, in turn, dug a huge trench the length of the garden and filled it with unsuitable plants – eucalyptus, dahlias, sunflowers – that Sarah said would die with the first hint of cold weather.

But the biggest change was in our family. I don't know if I can blame the heatwave, or if the Americans were the reason it all happened. Maybe we were just biding our time, and they were the catalyst we had been waiting for.

✧✧✧

The Americans made an appointment to view the flat. Within five minutes of their wandering around the whitewashed interior, admiring the two small bedrooms with their white linens and quilted bedspreads, the red sofa and mismatched armchairs, the tiny kitchen and the hot sunlight that poured onto the wooden floor, we had new lodgers. The French doors had been thrown open in the kitchen, but the white voile curtains hung listlessly on either side of the doors, cotton folds unmoving. It was equally hot inside and out.

It was just the mother and daughter that afternoon. Judith and Beth. A double act that didn't seem to work – even then, on that first encounter. Judith touched her daughter constantly, chattered too brightly when including her in the conversation. Beth, beautiful and tanned, kept her gaze on the garden, the walls, anything but her mother's face. She was older than me, her hair like bleached silk lying obediently down her back. Words streamed from Judith as she looked around, her Americanisms and inflections incongruous in the unmoving Dublin afternoon. Sarah stood to the side, allowing this pleasant stranger to peek behind doors, test light switches, peer into cupboards. Judith was older than Gemma, her skin less smooth, her long hair shot through with silver. This was nothing unusual; most mothers were older than Gemma. Judith's voice was gentle and I could have listened to her speak all day.

Judith twisted the knobs on the cooker. It was ancient, enamelled white with an oven door that stuck when the temperature inside got too high, but it was kept clean by Sarah, scrubbed so hard that the enamel was lucky to survive. So said Gemma.

'Are there saucepans?' Judith asked. She opened cupboard doors, taking stock of what was stacked in neat piles inside.

Sarah showed her where the pots and pans were kept, in a cupboard beside the cooker. Like cups, they were stacked inside each other, the lids placed neatly beside them.

'I cook,' Judith said, almost apologetically. 'It's what I love to do, and I'm always in the kitchen.' Her hands stilled on the countertop. 'I don't know what I'd do without it.'

She was the first person I had ever met who confessed to loving cooking. Cooking, like so much domestic work in those days, was a chore for most people's mothers, drudgery to be got through and tolerated. Food tended to be unchanging. Roast chicken on Sundays, leftovers on Mondays. The rest of the week was a steady stream of stew or shepherd's pie, lamb chops and potatoes, and fish on Fridays. I rarely thought of food. I neither liked it nor disliked it. It simply was.

The Americans were in Ireland for a year. Judith's husband was a professor of literature, taking up a post in Trinity College. She was leaving their furniture in their apartment in New York. They were subletting it to a friend of theirs, so there was no need to worry about anything. Was the heat always this intense in Ireland? Didn't it usually rain all the time? She hoped the grocery store wasn't too far away. Beth was going to start school in September. *Sixth grade.* I tried it out, but it sounded wrong. What was a grade? And so it began, the introduction of new words, the burgeoning of vocabulary. Over the summer I would test out these new sounds, see how they fitted alongside all those I already knew. As Judith spoke, Sarah smiled at times, made sounds of agreement, shook Judith's proffered hand when it was decided that they would return the following morning with her husband. Chris.

'So, Beth, how do you like Ireland?' Sarah asked the blonde girl.

Beth, leaning against the door frame, shrugged, her eyes fixed on the garden and Sarah's abundance of flowers. 'It's okay, I guess.'

Judith smoothed Beth's shoulders, her palms flat on the girl's skin.

Beth pulled angrily away from her mother. 'Would you stop doing that, Mom? Jeez.'

In the silence that followed, Beth jammed her hands into the pockets of her shorts. She sniffed and tossed her head. A wasp buzzed in a fold of the sheer summer curtain. Sarah knocked it to the floor and stood on it with the toe of her shoe.

'Oh my,' Judith said. 'I do hate those things. I'm allergic.'

'Nothing to worry about,' Sarah replied, picking the striped corpse up by a crushed wing and flinging it out the door. Nothing scared her. She left jars around, coated inside with jam and filled with water, enticing greedy wasps to their death. It worked every time.

'Why don't you show Beth the garden, Megan?' Sarah's hands were on my back, propelling me outdoors. It wasn't a request; it was an order.

✧✧✧

We stood, the American girl and I, on the hot, cracked slabs of the patio, among Sarah's plants that she kept in large, terracotta tubs. It was my job to water them each morning, before the sun got too hot and burned them. I knew all their names: lobelia, pansy, begonia, petunia, marigold, phlox, sweet pea. And the funny names: Tumbling Ted, Black-eyed Susan, Sweet William, love-in-a-mist. I liked painting them, their petals bleeding colour onto the page of my sketchbook, the paper wavy from watercolours, my fingers paint-stained, like my mother's. Usually the hose for watering the flowers snaked in loops around the pots, but now it was coiled neatly at the side of the garden, unused since the water restrictions had been announced. Hairline cracks spidered the sides and edges of the tubs. I loved watering the flowers because I could splash my bare legs and feet without being told off for wasting water.

Neither of us spoke for a moment. My hands hung by my sides. Beth chewed on a thumbnail. A few feet away, a bird pecked at a dry piece of earth that Sarah had turned over earlier. It crumbled and fell apart. The flowers drooped on their stems. The heat had sucked everything dry.

'I didn't want to come here,' said Beth, breaking the silence that had gathered around us. 'I'm supposed to be at camp now. With my friends. Not here in stupid Ireland.'

I felt compelled to defend the place of my birth. 'It's not stupid.'

Her snort was derisive as she walked away, plucking a bloom

from the clematis, dismantling it in one furious movement. The petals drifted to the ground, and she snatched another, demolishing it even quicker.

I glanced back at the house, but sunlight winked on the French doors and Sarah's face was hidden. Destroying flowers was forbidden, in the same way that stealing and smoking were forbidden.

At the end of the garden, the apple tree overshadowed the rambling rosebush, which scrambled over the back wall, smothering the grey bricks and the old wooden door. Sarah didn't like me scaling the walls. They were old, like the house, and in danger of crumbling. My friend Daniel lived next door, and he was forever climbing the wall that separated our gardens. Nothing ever crumbled beneath him, and he weighed more than I did.

I trailed after Beth, not wishing to seem as though I was following her, which I was. She pulled raspberries from the canes that grew at the bottom of the garden and pushed them into her mouth one by one. Juice wet the corners of her mouth, but I didn't worry that Sarah would see her. Berries were for eating. Flowers were for admiring, but any of the berries that grew in the long, narrow garden were available for consumption.

'These are so good!' Beth managed to say around a mouthful of raspberries. 'This yard is pretty cool.' She pointed at the house next to ours, where Mrs Doherty lay unseen on a checked wool blanket, sunglasses on, a book in her hand. I could see her from my bedroom window, but after a few days she wasn't that interesting any more. She wore her swimsuit and covered her skin in baby oil, and if she was lying close enough to the wall, sometimes I could smell the oil, its soapy sweetness at odds with the heavy scent of Sarah's summer flowers.

'Who lives there?'

'The Dohertys.'

'Are they old?'

I wondered. The Dohertys were older than Gemma, older, possibly, than Judith. It was hard to tell. 'Probably. I think so.'

'And who's in there?' Beth pointed at Daniel's house, shading her face with her hand.

'My friend.'

'What's her name?'

'He's a boy. Daniel.'

'Cool! How old is he?'

'Nine, like me. Why?'

Beth's shrug was fluid. 'Too young. Pity. Isn't there anyone my age around here?'

Curiosity bit me. 'How old are you?'

Beth shook her hair back. It flipped over her shoulder and settled into straight lines again. 'Twelve.' She made it sound like twenty-five. 'I'll be thirteen in November.'

The apple tree, which Sarah claimed was over fifty years old, shadowed the ground. Apples, tiny and rock hard, were beginning to form along the branches. The previous owners had planted it when their first child was born. I often wondered if they ever thought of the tree, if they even remembered it.

Sarah and Judith stepped outside.

Sarah called to me. 'Megan, is everything okay?'

'Everything's fine.' I waved down at her.

'Don't pick any apples.'

'I won't.'

Beth laughed for the first time. 'What are you, some kind of good girl nerd?' She eyed me more closely. 'Do you do everything your mom tells you?'

'Sarah's not my mother. She's my grandmother.'

Beth nodded as she yanked at a branch of the tree. The apples, tiny and hard and green, held on tight. A wind chime, hung by Gemma before I was born, dangled above our heads. Beth shook the branch again, then gave up, letting it spring back into place. 'So do you live here or are you just visiting?'

'I live here.'

'That's cool. I wouldn't mind living with my grandma. You must get to do plenty of stuff your mom doesn't like.'

I shrugged one shoulder. 'Not really.'

'I thought grandmothers were pretty relaxed about letting you do stuff. I know mine is.'

How could I have explained to Beth that Sarah was as strict as any mother? She expected me to behave and be good, and I tried as much as I could not to let her down. I was her only grandchild.

'So where's your mom today?' Beth reached up to make the wind chimes tinkle. They had barely moved since the heatwave started.

Gemma had gone out earlier and had yet to return. She bought all her paint from a wholesaler on the north side of the city, the father of a friend of hers from art college. He always gave her a good rate and she never went to anyone else. 'Getting paint.'

'Getting paint? What for?'

'She's an artist. She paints cards and people.' My mother's paintings were, quite simply, beautiful. Her studio in the attic was off-limits to me most of the time, but when I could, I went up and leafed through her pictures. I could never fully reconcile the pre-occupied woman with the joyful, brightly coloured paintings that she produced day after day.

Beth laughed again. 'You mean she paints portraits.'

I was slightly unbalanced by her tone. 'What?'

'You said your mom paints people. It's called portrait painting.'

She was beginning to get on my nerves. 'I know what portraits are.'

'I just don't think that people would let her put paint on them, which is what it sounds like when you say she paints people.' Beth pulled my plait. She leaned towards me. Her smile was mocking. 'Megan.'

I reclaimed my braid, moved away from her.

Sarah and Judith joined us by the apple tree. Judith fanned her face with a handkerchief. 'This heat! And all anyone told us about was the rain. All it does in Ireland is rain. That's what they say. All it does is rain, all day, every day, and that's why it's so green.'

Sarah laughed. 'Not this summer. I think the rain has forgotten about us.'

Judith touched the back of Beth's hand. 'Are you two girls having fun?'

'The greatest,' Beth muttered.

I glanced at Sarah. Her eyebrows were raised.

Judith's smile brightened. 'Oh good! It will be so lovely to have Megan living upstairs.' She put her hand on Beth's arm. I wondered how Judith couldn't see that her daughter retracted each part of her that her mother touched, as though she couldn't bear to feel the contact. The girl's anger hovered around her, hotter, almost, than the afternoon sun. 'Honey, are you ready to go get Daddy? We're going to move in tomorrow.'

'Dynamite.'

Judith's voice tightened. Her smile remained fixed, but it was a fake smile now, too obvious to be real. 'Now don't be like that, sweetie. We're going to have a fun time here and look, you already have a new friend.'

I wasn't sure I wanted Beth living so close. I liked things the way they were: Sarah, Gemma and me in our own, shrink-wrapped world. Daniel next door. New people could tilt the scales, disrupt our equilibrium.

2

There were ghosts in my mother's attic, she said, keeping watch. Protecting her. They'd lived there for years. Gemma had no problem working among them, but I couldn't bear to be alone with them. Late at night they came out to play. If I listened closely and was very quiet I could sort of hear them. Sarah always said it was nonsense to believe in ghosts, that there were none in the house, but I believed my mother.

I never looked among Gemma's things, even though the curiosity nearly killed me at times. Gemma kept an old trunk under a patchwork quilt she had made when she was a student. The trunk, which she kept in the corner behind her desk, was filled with things that I was not allowed to touch, and even though the urge to rummage was overwhelming any time I was in the attic, the threat of disturbing the ghosts was enough to keep the impulse to snoop at bay. Sometimes, I imagined pulling the trunk by one of its tin handles, dragging it out of the attic and bumping it down the stairs to my room, away from the ghosts. But I knew that even if I'd had the courage, the trunk was too big, too heavy for me ever to try.

It didn't stop me thinking about it, though. Any time I was in the attic, the trunk drew me in. Whenever Gemma was out, I resolved that I would at last venture to the attic, slip the patchwork quilt off, click the brass locks and uncover my mother's secrets. Once, when I told Daniel of my intentions, he had been horrified. You can't, he'd protested. It's your mother's. What would she say? How could she ever trust you again?

Daniel knew a lot about most things. He reminded me of the story of Pandora, which we'd learned in school. Pandora had opened the forbidden jar and by the time she was able to close it again, nothing was left inside but hope.

'Don't open the trunk, Megan. Once it's open, you can't put anything back in and you can't forget what you've seen.' We were walking back from the shop when I'd mentioned the possibility of snooping among my mother's belongings. Milk and bread were in a bag that swung from the crook of my elbow. Ice cream melted over our fingers. 'It'll just drive you mad, thinking about things you're not supposed to know about, and it's not like you can just ask your mum.' I supposed that he was really talking about his father, who hadn't been seen since he forgot to come home one day after work, years ago, when Daniel wasn't even one year old. Daniel believed he would never come back. It was easier that way, he said, just to accept it and not ask questions. No point in upsetting anyone or getting your hopes up.

It was a bit like the time the previous year when I lost a tooth. When I was in bed, supposed to be sleeping, Gemma had crept into my room and slipped a coin under my pillow. I hadn't wanted that, to know that the tooth fairy had been my mother all along, and I tried to forget that it had been she who'd given me the coin and not the fairy in whom I'd so fervently believed. I'd tried to convince myself that Gemma had only been checking that the fairy had indeed come to me, but I knew I was wasting my time.

Maybe Daniel was right and it was better to leave the trunk alone. But it was so difficult, and my hands itched to get at the brass locks under the quilt. Even the possibility of discovering things I should not know about did little to quell my curiosity.

✧ ✧ ✧

The Americans left Sarah in a happy state. As she closed the front door after we'd said goodbye to them, she turned to me and said, 'Let's go tell your mother.' Gemma had returned from collecting her supplies earlier, while we'd still been caught up in conversation with Judith and Beth. The Americans had stayed much longer than expected.

Music seeped from the attic as we made our way upstairs. If I'd been alone, I would have paused to listen. My mother played music to suit her mood. Sometimes it was Chopin and his soft études, the notes spilling down through the house, a gracious waterfall of sound. Other times it was Joan Baez, Bob Dylan, or Simon and Garfunkel. So far that summer it was mostly Carole King.

Ever aware of my mother's wish not to be disturbed, Sarah knocked softly and called her name before pushing the door inwards. I followed Sarah into the forbidden territory. In the late afternoon light, the attic gleamed. The sloped ceiling was set with skylights, and if I stood on Gemma's footstool I could see the chimney pots out on the roof, their red tiles glowing orange in the heat of the sun. The scent of charcoal and oil paints hung in the muted air, as familiar as the perfume my mother habitually wore. The attic was big and almost full of Gemma's things. Her art materials occupied the floor space. An easel stood in one corner, old paint dried into the wood. Half-empty canvases that she could not bring herself to throw away were stacked on top of each other in one corner. Watercolours were pinned to the wall and scattered on the floor, some in various stages of drying. Others were being flattened between the pages of the heavy art books that were heaped on the makeshift bookshelves that Daniel's father had hammered in before he disappeared. They sagged slightly in the middle, bowed under the weight of their heavy load. Gemma's collection of paint tubes, charcoal, pencils, inks, pens and brushes stood in jars, rows of them, lined up neatly on a small table that she had salvaged from a junk stall at a market in town. Now the table was sanded, smoothed and repainted in a bright blue that I loved. Cyan. Most people didn't know what colour cyan was, but Gemma loved it, and so naturally I loved it too. It was a natural companion to red, Gemma said, which is why the jars grouped on the table's surface were red jars painted by her. Her paintbrushes were grouped according to use and size: watercolours in one set of jars, oils in another, thin ones to the front, fat ones behind. A bottle of turpentine sat with folded rags. She didn't paint much with oils any more, not unless it was a commission. Watercolours were what she preferred, and pen and ink.

Big blocks of paper were stacked within arm's reach of her desk, where Gemma now sat, her head bent over her work. For a moment, she did not acknowledge our presence. The paper in front of her absorbed her attention and until she returned her paintbrush to the jar of cloudy water beside her, neither Sarah nor I spoke. The sun slanted through the room, hitting my mother squarely on the head. Her straight hair shone, the sun picking out strands of copper in her dark-brown braid. It almost reached her waist. On a small shelf behind her sat her camera bag. Gemma was a great photographer. At art school, she had considered pursuing photography instead of painting, and even now she still took photos. Albums of her pictures were stacked on the floor. Sarah had framed several of them and they hung downstairs. One of them, a black and white picture of me as a toddler, sitting on the piano stool, occupied the wall above the piano, a gentle reminder from Sarah to practise my scales and my exam pieces. Piano lessons did not enthral me, not in the least, despite promises of future success and ability. I was meant to practise every day, a fact I allowed to slip by. The heatwave was keeping everyone occupied, so much so that neither Sarah nor Gemma were paying too much attention to my distinct lack of musical compliance.

A creased paperback lay face down on the floor. Borges. My mother's enduring love affair with South American writers. She read them in translation, even though she had a pretty good level of Spanish. Her favourites were dotted around the house. Sabato, whom Gemma loved because he was also a painter. Lugones, especially for his poetry. Puig. Cortázar. Sarah never touched them, had no interest in what she called magical realism or existentialism. I didn't understand these terms, couldn't grasp what my mother meant when she explained them to me, but I liked their sound, how they felt on my tongue when I tried out their unfamiliar syllables.

Turning towards us, Gemma wiped her hands on the front of her painting shirt. She had a few, all of them my grandfather's, worn thin now from years of use, their fabric feathery and threadbare. Gemma's smile was wide as she held her arms out. I went to her, rubbed my cheek against hers, breathed her in – all her paint-filled, green-tea-scented gorgeousness. 'Well, what brings you both up here? What time is it? I'll have to get a clock up here.' Gemma rubbed her eyes, squinted at the open skylights. 'With all the sun it's impossible to tell when it's getting late.'

'It's almost six.' Sarah paused to look at a picture Gemma had left to dry. 'That's lovely, Gemma, it really is. Anyway, we have news.'

'Good news, I hope.'

The record player clicked, the stylus lifted and returned to the start position. It sat on the floor, records in a stack beside it. I loved the music my mother played. Often, I lingered on the stairs, listening to the songs through the door. I wanted to play the records myself, but I had to be very careful not to scratch anything. Sometimes, if Gemma was out, Sarah would put some music on for me and I would sit, listening. Mindful always of the ghosts, I preferred to sit on the top step outside the attic door and sing quietly.

I got off my mother's lap and wandered over to a book of Picasso's paintings that I loved. His misshapen women, the grotesque still lifes, the exploded space of *Guernica*. Using her bare foot, Gemma closed the lid on the record player. She reached her hands high above her head and stretched. Gemma knew yoga and was able to bend and stretch as though her limbs were elastic. I copied her sometimes, knitting my arms and legs into twisted poses, wobbling to keep my balance. Her shirt had a caterpillar of green paint on the pocket. For a moment, the only sound was that of the traffic outside, almost muted by the walls. I wiped my forehead with the back of my hand. Even the open skylights did nothing to relieve the thick heat in the room.

Gemma started to put away her paints. She handed me a silver tube of yellow paint, touched her fingers to my cheek. I closed my eyes, felt her stroking my skin. 'Do you want to do the lids, Megan?'

I jumped at any opportunity to be useful to my mother, to show her how good I was for her. At times, I felt responsible for her. If she hadn't had me, she could have been out in the world doing something else, being someplace else. I also knew that if I'd ever said such a thing to Gemma, she would have been horrified. We were a unit, she said. A package deal. Buy Gemma, get Megan for free. No bargaining necessary. That's what she said. But still, helping with her precious paints made me feel important and happy. I lined the tubes up in a row on the blue table, then sorted through the small hexagonal lids.

'Of course it's good news. The Americans who viewed the basement want to take it.'

'Excellent. I hope you've got a decent price from them.'

'Of course I have!'

Gemma stacked some books together. Miró, his strange shapes and lines, incomprehensible to me. Sisley, blurred landscapes, indefinite faces. Kandinsky, all angles and triangles, his foreboding of impending war. The sensitivity of artists. 'Mother, you'll understand my lack of conviction. Your idea of a fair price is way below everyone else's.'

'Gemma –'

'I just don't want to see you getting ripped off.'

Sarah sighed. 'I'm not daft.'

'And what are they like, these Americans?'

My mother said the word *Americans* as though it were something distasteful. I hoped she wouldn't start on about Vietnam when they were around. Gemma liked to talk about Vietnam any time American people were mentioned. There had been a huge war there, America versus Vietnam. It wasn't exactly clear who had won, but Gemma knew lots about it and loved to discuss it. She had a book of photos of the war, but I didn't like looking at them. I'd seen villages in flames, trees destroyed, children with their clothes burnt off. The Disappeared in Argentina, Agent Orange in Vietnam. There was no end to atrocity and Sarah hated that I knew about such things.

'I haven't met the husband yet, but Judith seems to be a very nice woman. They have a daughter, Beth. She's a bit older than Megan.'

'She's twelve,' I interrupted. 'She'll be thirteen in November.'

'What's she like, Megan?'

I paused in my lidding of tubes. What were the right words to describe Beth? Angry? Sullen? Impatient? 'She has blonde hair,' I concluded. 'And it's very long, longer even than yours, Gemma. And she's tall.'

Gemma took off her painting shirt. 'It'll be lovely for you to have a girl around.' She brushed the front of the T-shirt she had worn underneath my grandfather's old checked shirt.

'I don't need a girl. I have Daniel.'

'What does the husband do?' Gemma asked.

'Judith said he's a professor of something or other. Literature of some kind. They live in Manhattan.'

'And Beth is not happy that they're not there,' I interjected. Sarah and Gemma turned to look at me. 'She said that her friends were going camping for a month and she was going to miss it. She said Ireland was stupid and she didn't want to be here.'

'I think she's just a bit out of sorts at having to move to a new country where she knows no one,' said Sarah. 'I'm sure she'll be fine. The husband will be working in Trinity for a year.' She turned to me. I was looking at another book Gemma had left open on a shelf. Matisse. I touched a photo of one of his paintings, its bright colours, its beauty. 'What did she say his name was, the husband?'

I turned the page and didn't look up. 'Chris.' My fingers were stained with paint. I wiped them on my shorts.

'That's it. Chris. Chris and Judith Jackson. Don't put paint on your shorts, Megan. It's impossible to get it out.'

Gemma shrugged and finished her tidying away. We stood for a moment, watching her methodical routine. My mother's fingers were permanently marked with paint, despite her efforts to clean them. Secretly, I think she liked having stained hands, proof of her dedication to her art.

'Well, if you want to eat with us, it'll be ready in about half an hour,' said Sarah, turning towards the door. I wanted to linger a while in the warm attic cocoon and maybe catch a silvery shimmer of ghosts, but Sarah had her hand on my shoulder and steered me out the door.

'Thanks, Mum, but I'm going out.'

'Lovely,' Sarah said. 'Anything nice planned?'

Gemma fiddled with the corner of a book on her desk. *South American Politics of the Modern Age.* My mother loved current affairs. 'Some sort of gathering.'

'Where?'

'In town.'

For a split second Sarah's forehead furrowed, then as quickly as it had happened, it smoothed again. 'Be careful.'

Gemma's tongue clicked with impatience. 'There's nothing to be careful of.'

'I just worry.'

'Well, don't. It's fine. Just some speakers and a glass of wine.'

'Lovely,' Sarah said again, but she didn't really mean it. Occasionally, Gemma went to political meetings in unspecified locations. Awareness groups, she called them, where guests were invited to speak to those gathered, in the hopes of making the world a better place. Once it was about apartheid, another time someone came to lecture about the working conditions of children in factories in the Third World. The Third World was actually part of this world, but it was so poor that it was like a whole other world entirely. Another time there had been a meeting about Bolivia, and Gemma had been furious about that for days afterwards, which was why Sarah preferred her to stay at home or go to the cinema with her friend Ruth, whose father sold Gemma her art supplies at discounted prices. Ruth was nice, and worked as an art teacher in the city centre. Gemma said that maybe she'd like to be an art teacher herself some day, and Sarah said that if she wanted to then she should do it.

We closed the door behind us. The music started again before we reached the bottom of the stairs. Simon and Garfunkel. Ruth had given her *The Sounds of Silence* when I was born. Gemma said it occupied a very important place in her collection. The few other people who had given Gemma presents gave her baby clothes, but Ruth had said that Gemma needed something for herself.

I'd once heard Gemma say that she was lucky she'd been able to keep me. Sarah didn't like my mother saying such things. Gemma sometimes got upset with Sarah, said that it was easy for her. She wasn't the one who had doors closed in her face. Sarah hadn't lost most of her friends from school. Sarah wasn't the one who had left art college in her second year because it was too much, too exhausting to walk in each day and sit in classes after being up all night breastfeeding. I was her baby. She would take care of me. The art would work itself out. And it had.

People were funny about babies. They welcomed them, fussed over them, brought presents. They kissed them and told them how lucky they were. But there were words for them too, words for children like me, children with no father. *Bastards,* they called us. We who were born *out of wedlock*. Our mothers were whispered about. Our mothers who had brought shame on their families. Brazen hussies, letting themselves and everyone around them down. Then the cheek of them to complain. They made their beds, let them lie on them now. I never understood it, though. I was loved. Yes, my mother was tired, and sad sometimes, but she wasn't ashamed of me. Why would she be? My mother loved me.

3

Gemma was sixteen when my grandfather died, so he never knew me. He suffered a heart attack getting off the bus one day after work, the week before his fiftieth birthday. Gemma didn't talk about him too much because it made her sad, even twelve years after the fact. Sarah had carried on without him, because, she had often said, what else could she do? There were markers of him still throughout the house. His picture was in a silver frame on the sideboard in the dining room, another on the mantelpiece over the fireplace, and some of his books were on shelves, his name carefully scripted in fountain-pen ink. And, of course, there were the stairs.

My grandfather, helped by his friend Jim, built a set of wooden stairs leading from the garden to the kitchen when Gemma was little. The stairs were old now, and the bottom steps were broken, rotted through after too many winters of rain. The wood was black in places and splinters bared their teeth where the steps had fractured. The stairs ran up alongside the wall that divided our garden from Daniel's and ended in a deck, also built by my grandfather and Jim. A set of double doors led from the kitchen onto the deck, where Sarah kept pots of flowers, and where we often sat on warm days, birds in our eyrie. Neighbours had objected when the stairs were built and the doors put in the kitchen wall, but nothing was done about it and it was soon forgotten, petty neighbourhood squabbles laid to rest amid the natural rhythms of urban life.

After the bottom steps were deemed too dangerous to use, getting into the back garden wasn't as easy as it had been. Instead of descending the wooden stairs, we went through the garden flat. A door beside the kitchen opened onto the dark and narrow staircase to the flat. It was spooky, the light switch was stiff, and I always counted to ten before taking the steps two at a time.

Once the Jacksons had decided to take the flat, Sarah realised we would have to revert to using the wooden stairs to go into the back garden. We'll have to get Jim to mend them, she said to Gemma. We can't arrive downstairs on top of our new lodgers just because we need to go out into the garden. Sarah and Gemma were outside the kitchen as they discussed this, the doors thrown open to let the morning in. My grandmother touched the handrail with the feathery blooms of bougainvillea that twisted themselves around the wood. Your father would have been very impressed with his steps. I can't believe they've lasted this long.

The Americans arrived in a borrowed station wagon with all their stuff the day after the viewing. They made three trips from the house they'd been staying in since their arrival two weeks earlier, the car each time ejecting its contents onto the parched lawn. Initials and contents decorated the sides of boxes. *B clothes. C books. C books and papers. B shoes and books. C clothes. J clothes and shoes. C books.* How many possessions could one small family need? They seemed to own twice as many things as Sarah, Gemma and I, yet Judith had said they left most of their things in New York. Already they had borrowed an extra chest of drawers, and Judith asked Sarah would she mind if Chris put up some shelves for his books, the ones he wouldn't need for his office in the university.

That afternoon, Sarah and Judith sat in the shade, sipping iced tea from tall glasses. Already, change was taking place. Tea in a glass. Cold. With lemons. Later, it would be wine, chilled in the fridge, condensation wetting the label on the bottle. On other days there would be martinis, complete with olives lined up on a cocktail stick, or something else entirely: a margarita, with crystals of salt rimming the glass.

Now, I hovered at the edges of their conversation, reading a book. The sun had me in its full glare and my South American hat was nowhere to be found. Squinting made my eyes hurt and I put the book aside. A half-finished drawing of a bumblebee in a flower was wedged under me, and I pulled it out, smoothing its creases. It wasn't very good, and I disliked finishing anything that wasn't good. Normally, I loved drawing, and up in my room I had shoeboxes full of my pictures, all dated and signed, but lately I hadn't been doing much art. It was the heat, I suspected, and the difficulty that accompanied sitting still in the sunshine. It was too hot to be indoors, and the patience I usually had for sketching had abandoned me. I crumpled the bee picture and threw it to one side.

Sarah's gardening hat lay on the grass by the loganberry bush. Her transistor radio was wedged in its habitual daylong position in a fork in the apple tree. The dial was broken, stuck on Radio One, which was all Sarah listened to anyway. Something, a serial or drama, played to the quiet air. Someone called Johnny was having an argument with his mother over the girl he wanted to marry. Johnny's mother disapproved of her because the girl was English, and Johnny asked his mother not to make him choose. No one was listening. I would have switched it off if I'd had the energy to get up and walk over. The heat lingered, paralysing us with its intensity. My mouth hurt from thirst. Judith offered me iced tea, but I refused. I never drank tea, not even the hot kind, and I certainly didn't like the look of the brown liquid in the women's glasses. It was like something Sarah would use to pour over the houseplants, a fertiliser or feed. The offer was not made a second time. Ice clinked in the jug as glasses were refilled. Presently, I began to regret turning it down. Out on the main road a car honked, the sound muffled by the houses.

I rolled over on my back, my hands covering my eyes. A dragonfly darted above me, its shadow flitting across the latticework of my fingers. I felt sorry for the insects, scrambling desperately for water. In the mornings and evenings, when I soaked the tubs of flowers, I splashed extra water around, trying to find shady spots where it wouldn't dry out as quickly. It was old water anyway, so I didn't feel guilty for wasting it. Daniel was always helping insects, and he didn't think it was a waste of water. He left saucers of water around the garden and watched tiny creatures hover.

The doorbell jangled, distant inside the house. Sarah heaved herself out of her chair.

'I'll get it,' I offered. Anything to escape the heat of the unmoving afternoon, the dust so thick on the dry air it was catching in my nostrils and making me want to sneeze. I wondered how my mother could stand the heat in her attic.

'No, I'll go,' Sarah insisted. 'It's probably Jim.'

Jim was enlisted for all the jobs our small household of females couldn't do. That afternoon he was coming to fix the steps.

✧✧✧

The hammering of wood broke up the stillness. Judith gathered her things and disappeared into the hush of indoors. Cooking smells soon filled the air, new smells that were hot, spicy, different. Sarah picked up her hat and pulled on her gardening gloves. The radio drama ended, its signature tune fading into the news bulletin. A man read out something about Belfast, a car bomb, a British soldier. Dozens of bombs had exploded in Northern Ireland so far that year. Bombs in bins, under cars, outside shops. Bombs thrown at soldiers and soldiers shooting the bombers. Agents and double agents, spies and snitches. Sarah hated when I listened. A shadow crossed me, blocking the sun. I opened my eyes. Beth stood over me.

'Hey,' she said.

I pulled myself up onto my elbows. Beth didn't wait for me to say anything. She flopped down on the ground beside me.

'It's really hot here. Not as hot as New York, but much hotter than they told us.'

'What have you been doing?'

I wasn't bothered, but felt I should ask her. Sarah always reminded me to be interested in what people said to me.

'Oh, nothing, just putting my stuff away, but I got bored. My mom's cooking chilli. She had such a job finding kidney beans. In the end, she just bought a tin of baked beans and washed them in the sink.' Beth shuddered. 'Ugh. All that tomato sauce mixed with water was gross.' She shaded her eyes with her hand. 'What a racket.' She pointed at Jim. 'Who's he? Does he live here too?'

I followed her finger. Jim had paused in his hammering. His blue shirtsleeves were rolled to his elbows and he wore a hat to keep the sun off his face. Jim was as old as Sarah, but he didn't look it. His hair wasn't even grey and he was stronger than anyone I knew. He'd been my grandfather's friend their whole lives. They'd lived next door to each other, gone to school together, and had remained firm friends as adults. After my grandfather died, Jim helped us with jobs around the house. Now he wiped his forehead with the back of his wrist, drank from a glass of water Sarah had left for him and resumed his work. 'That's Jim. He's our handyman.'

Beth smirked. 'So he's not your dad?'

An ant tumbled over my thigh, followed by another. In their hardworking jaws, they carried crumbs we had carelessly strewn around. Crackers, bread, the odd biscuit. They scrambled on my hot skin, unaware of being watched. I let them. They distracted me. I pretended not to hear Beth when she repeated the question, but I knew she wouldn't let it go. Already, I could see the kind of girl she was. Insistent. Confident.

She prodded me. I moved away, reclaiming my arm.

'Jeez, Megan, it's only a question. He either is or he isn't. God.'

'Jim is not my father.'

'Okay, so he's not your father. Big deal. I mean, there's no need to just, I don't know, disappear like that.'

Two more ants climbed across me, followed by three more. 'I didn't disappear.'

'Yes, you did. You just got this funny look on your face and said nothing.' Beth frowned in imitation, pursed her mouth in the way I knew I did, because Sarah mimicked me sometimes, if I was annoyed. Beth was teasing me, I could see that, but I wasn't used to it, not by someone close to me in age. I had no sister and I hardly knew this American girl, this tall stranger with hair that glowed white in the crazy light of the early afternoon.

I didn't say anything. The father question drove me mad. It was like the first time at school that the teacher asked us our fathers' occupations. When it was my turn, I said I didn't have a father. It was the truth, and it hadn't meant anything to me until that moment. The teacher went pale and said not to be silly, of course I had a father, everyone did. She moved on to the next girl before I could protest. Other girls' fathers were bankers, shopkeepers, dentists, plumbers, teachers, doctors, policemen. One girl's father was even dead. But nobody except me said they did not have one.

'Want to get an ice cream?'

I shrugged one shoulder.

'Come on, I have money. I don't want to sit here all day.' Beth tugged my arm. 'Come on, Megan. Show me your neighbourhood.'

Jim was finishing a step. He slapped it with the heel of his hand.

'That one shouldn't give you any more problems,' he said, winking at me. 'Just a couple more to do and you'll be running up and down like no one's business.' He pushed back the bougainvillea that clustered beside the base of the staircase and wound its way around the handrail all the way to the top. My grandfather had planted it for Sarah after they'd been on holiday in Italy. Sarah said she had laughed, told him bougainvillea would never survive an Irish winter. It's a Mediterranean plant, she told me. It thrives on sunshine and dry heat, not rain and cold dampness. But somehow, miraculously, it had survived, and it still grew, thicker each year. Now its blossoms covered the branches that wove themselves around the handrail, making themselves firmly at home among the pale wood and new, shiny nails.

'Come on.' Beth tugged again, this time at the sleeve of my T-shirt. I allowed myself to be propelled towards the house.

4

Heat rose off the pavement as we walked. Grass was yellow in the gardens. Flowers wilted in weary rows. Up ahead, the surface of the road lifted in a silver shimmer, like water. A mirage. We often saw mirages in the intense heat of day. Gemma said they were an optical phenomenon, which is something that your eyes think they're seeing, only they have been tricked by the sun. Each time I watched out for mirages I was disappointed, yet they had a habit of appearing when I least expected and they were always a surprise, like this one. By the time I turned to Beth to alert her, it was gone.

The shop was twelve doors away from our house, at the end of the terrace. It had a name, News and Food, but no one used it because it wasn't a very good name. Everyone just called it The Shop, and there was never any doubt as to which shop was being referred to. We went there every day to get the newspaper. Beth rattled the coins in her hand. I pushed against the hot metal handle of the shop door. The bell over the door jingled as we entered. The interior was dark after the mica-bright dazzle of outside. Mrs Brennan, the shopkeeper, wiped her forehead with the back of her hand, the fingers of her other hand pressed to the small of her back. Despite the dim light, it was oppressively warm inside, the smell of sugar overlaying everything. Sugar, with an undernote of newspaper ink and dust.

On every wall of the small shop were shelves, all of them old, painted over several times so that if you looked closely enough you could see the brush marks in the paint, and sometimes a bristle or two shed by the brush. Behind Mrs Brennan, the shelves held sweet jars, rows of them. Pear drops, bullseyes, cola cubes. Sherbet pips and lemon sherbets. White mice, pink, white and yellow bonbons. Humbugs and imperial mints. Boxes of chocolate bars, rows of sweets in tubes. Lollipops, chewing gum, penny sweets. Everything you needed to rot your teeth, Sarah said. Other shelves held dry goods, tins of beans and peas, packets of soup and custard, jars of jam. Bottles of lemonade in crinkly orange cellophane. Balls of string, clothes pegs, boxes of nails and screws. Stacked on the floor were newspapers, some still tied in bundles.

'Hi there!' Beth stepped forward. 'We'd like two ice creams, please.'

Mrs Brennan squinted at us. She smoothed her blue shop coat with the palms of her hands before slipping them into large square pockets. Mrs Brennan's hair was combed neatly, her roots a grey inch along her parting. On her lapel was a Pioneer pin.

'Is that yourself, Megan?' she asked.

'Hello, Mrs Brennan.'

'Fierce heat, isn't it? I think I'm going mad. Don't know what to be doing with myself.'

A large fly buzzed on the counter. Mrs Brennan smacked at it with a rolled-up newspaper and missed.

Beth dug into the chest freezer and produced two wrapped ice pops. 'How much are these?'

'Three pence each.'

'I'll take two.' Beth laid the coins out on the counter. Six pennies in a neat row. Beside the cash register were the cigarettes and matches, the pouches of tobacco. Mrs Brennan also sold individual cigarettes, for which she charged a whopping five pence each, plus a penny for a match. Sarah said that was just Mrs Brennan's way of ripping people off.

Beth plucked a single cigarette from an open box. Players No. 6. The blue and green stripe on the white box, the gold lettering. No one in my family smoked. Sarah said it could kill you. 'This too, please.' My mouth must have fallen open slightly, for I saw Mrs Brennan look from me to Beth and back again.

'Is that for your mammy?' she enquired. 'Or your daddy?'

Beth swatted the question away with an impatient hand. 'Oh, it's for my mom. She's trying to quit.'

'Well now, isn't it well for her to try? Will she take a match with that?'

'I'm sure she will,' Beth said, and took the proffered match.

'That'll be another six pence, so, on top of the six for the lollies. Anything for yourself, Megan? The paper, a pint of milk?'

'No, thank you.' I preferred to avoid conversation with the shopkeeper. She liked to ask after Sarah, always with a tilt to her head, as though bad news were expected.

'How's your granny?' There it was, the expectant pose, hand on hip, head tilted ever so slightly to one side. She ran her fingers over her Pioneer pin.

Sarah hated the word *granny*. 'She's fine, thanks.'

'She's a great woman, all the same. It's not easy for her.'

Beth said thank you and moved towards the door. I followed.

'Tell her I said hello, now, won't you?'

I mumbled something inconsequential while biting the top off my ice pop. It was so cold it hurt my front teeth.

✿✿✿

'What was she talking about?' asked Beth as soon as we were outside. 'What isn't easy for your grandma?'

I shrugged. Mrs Brennan was only one of many women who felt my mother had ruined her life by having me, and that we had both dragged Sarah into our fallen lives. For that reason, Gemma was a source of conversation, most of it not good. There were things I wasn't meant to know, things my mother kept from me. Girls without husbands were sent to homes and their babies were taken away. Sometimes the babies were sold to rich Americans, and the priests and nuns kept all the money and bought new things with it, candles and chalices and things. The girls were then slaves in the homes and in laundries. No one really knew about the laundries and that's why they were behind high walls, so that no one could see the slaves and their shame. That's what happened if you had a baby too young. You got what you deserved. Bringing shame on your family. Getting your comeuppance.

It didn't make sense to me.

A priest had visited our house once, when I was an infant. Gemma told me the story last year. He knew someone, he said. Someone who wanted a child. Who could give a baby a good home. Two parents. Good people. Catholics. Gemma shouted at him to get out of her house. The priest pointed out that it was her mother's house, not Gemma's. Gemma stood up, with me in her arms, and said to the priest that if he didn't leave that very minute she would ring the police. He insulted her then, called her a name. *Jezebel.* The priest was like the women who gossiped about my mother. A holy person who wasn't good. That was why I didn't go to Mass on Sundays, why none of us did. Sarah stood up for us. Her girls, she called us. *My girls.*

My mother had wanted me. She could have given me up, sent me away, gifted me to strangers. But she kept me, kept me close, and I was glad she had. So even when she looked sad, or if she was annoyed with me for not finishing my dinner, or being too slow with my homework, or not practising the piano, I held on to that little fact. My mother kept me. She loved me and she kept me. And it never failed to lift me.

'Is it because your dad isn't around?' Beth licked a trail of melted ice pop from her hand. A red stain inked her skin, transferred itself to her tongue. 'Hey, is my tongue red?'

'Yes.'

She stuck it out at me and I laughed.

'Is mine?'

'Definitely! Anyway, is that about your dad?'

I frowned. 'I suppose.'

'Why does anyone care?' Beth dropped the uneaten part of her ice pop in the bin that was attached to the bus stop. She then placed the Players meant for Judith between her lips, scraped the match off the wall beside it and lit the cigarette. Her movement was fluid, almost graceful. This was not Beth's first time to light up.

'It's to do with sin. That's what my teacher said.' It was never very clear what the sin actually was, but it was something big. Something unforgivable. Adam and Eve in the garden. And because of that we were all poor children of Eve and spent our lives wailing in the Vale of Tears, wherever that was.

'Who cares? My dad says that sin is all stupid anyway. He doesn't even believe in God, but I'm not meant to know that.'

I pointed at the cigarette. 'Won't your mum kill you?'

Beth considered the glowing tip of the cigarette. 'What, this? My mom doesn't smoke! I only said it was for her so that woman would let me buy it.' She nudged me. 'Come on, race you.'

She took two quick drags, then threw the cigarette on the ground and took off down the street. Laughing, she turned back to me. 'Last one's a chicken.'

Where we were going I had no idea, but I ran after Beth. She didn't care that I was a fatherless child, the half-orphan other mothers didn't want their children playing with. Beth pushed my fatherlessness to the side, laughed at my mother's sins. It made me light inside, dizzy almost. In some small way, it freed me.

She remained stubbornly ahead of me, her hair like yellow streamers on the hot air. We stopped intermittently, gasping for breath, before taking off again. The shops were a blur: the butcher's, with its display of blood-reddened meat and the smell of iron that tightened the hot air; the draper's, with the window covered in yellow cellophane to prevent the clothes inside fading. Another newsagents, where comics curled at the edges in the heat of day and rolls of newspapers were wedged into a metal display outside the door. We ran past the small Protestant church with its meeting house, a tiny park hidden from view behind a high stone wall. Gardens awash with flowers, bedsits filled with students and poor people who couldn't afford to live anywhere else. The old railway bridge that they'd never got around to tearing down, despite the fact that the last train had travelled the tracks of the Harcourt Line back when Gemma was my age.

When we finally stopped, at the canal, I leaned forward, my hands on my knees. Sweat glued my T-shirt to my back. My mouth was paper-dry and I craved a drink of water. Before us, the water of the canal was dark and peaty. Boys queued on the wooden lock and took turns flinging themselves into the murky gloom. They wrapped their arms around their knees and dive-bombed, vying with each other to send the most water splashing in every direction. Their shouts bounced off the flat surface of the canal and hovered momentarily on the hot air before bursting, like bubbles, into nothing.

Beth dropped down on the bank and plunged her bare feet into the water. Her sandals lay where she had dropped them, a tangle of white straps and shiny silver buckles. 'This is great!' She reached up, twitched the hem of my shorts. 'Come on, Megan. Sit down. Cool off.'

Sliding my trainers off, I slipped my toes into the water. A rush of cold. My feet clouded in the murk. Around us, the boys' shouts echoed. The grass, sun-yellowed and scratchy, left textured indents on the palms of my hands. Beth lay back, propped on her elbows. Her arms were brown, slim, her shoulders filled with tension. Her hair spread itself like a shawl on the ground behind her. She reminded me of a cat, watching the boys, most of them older than she. She seemed ready to spring.

'Can you swim?'

I was a so-so swimmer. Lessons were torture for me, rows of children hanging onto the bar, kicking and splashing, chlorine making my throat hurt and my eyes smart. Gemma had ended up teaching me; it was easier with her. She had held her arms out and I splashed my way over to her.

'Can you?'

I nodded.

Beth kicked up water with her feet. 'I love swimming. My dad taught me.'

I had yet to meet Chris. He was busy, Beth had said; something about papers and getting ready for conferences. He had left the business of unpacking to Judith. Beth turned to me. 'My dad grew up in Georgia, where it's really, really hot in the summer. Much hotter than anywhere and it gets so dusty that people have to shake their clothes out the window when they take them off. When my dad was young, he used to sneak out of the house at night and meet his friends to go swimming. There was a creek near his house and that's where they all used to go.'

'Swimming at night?'

She nodded and swung her eyes back to the water. 'Night swimming. That's what it's called. Night swimming, when everyone else is asleep and no one knows you're gone. You don't even have to swim. Just being out at night, in secret, is enough.'

There wasn't any chance that I could so much as open a door at night without either Sarah or Gemma hearing me and coming to investigate. Leave the house to go swimming? Or just to go outside? Impossible.

There was a swimming pool a few doors away from our house. It was empty, had been for years. The house was rented and the owners lived abroad. They had moved when Gemma was still in school, and no one really knew where they were. Daniel and I had tried to find some way of filling the pool the previous summer, but we realised we had no way of running a hose from my garden, which was closer than his, over the walls in between and into the pool itself. There was also a lot of cleaning to be done, because the pool was clogged with old leaves, clay, the general debris of an unkempt garden.

Beth nudged me. 'We could try it some night. Here.'

I shook my head. 'I couldn't. I wouldn't be allowed.'

Her laugh was a loud burst. 'No one's allowed. You're not meant to be allowed. That's why it's done. You have to do things you're not allowed do.' She tossed her head. 'Otherwise, what's the point?'

I was dismissed, silenced, like the child I was. Those boys jumping off the lock didn't look as though they cared about what their mothers thought, or even whether they were supposed to be in the canal in the first place. They just did it. Acted first, reflected later – if, in fact, they reflected at all. The heatwave was affecting them too. Surviving in this burning city meant disobeying orders. Who could blame them?

'I can't stay here long,' I said, swinging my feet onto the parched grass of the bank. I reached for my shoes. Already I missed the cool of the water.

Beth broke her gaze from the boys to glance at me. 'Why?'

'I'm not allowed down here. I'll be killed if I'm seen.'

'What's wrong with being here?' She returned to observing the diving boys.

'It's too far. Too dangerous.' Aware of how young I sounded, I tried another tack. 'Someone drowned here when my mother was a child. A girl from her class.'

I'd caught Beth's attention again. 'Drowned? How?'

Details were not within my reach. 'I think she fell. Tripped. I don't know. But she drowned.'

I recalled Gemma's voice when she told me about the child. Sally, her name was. Sally, who ran away from her mother and somehow managed to slip and fall into the canal. Gemma's class had been given the day off school for her funeral, and they'd never been allowed to mention Sally in school again. She lingered, Gemma said, like a ghost. Reminding everyone of what happened when you didn't do what you were told. But her name wasn't spoken again.

The thrill of the ice pop, the freedom of running all the way to the canal, the surge of energy that stemmed from disobeying Sarah and Gemma had dispersed, and I was left with a cold feeling of guilt. 'We have to go home,' I said. The light was too strong in my eyes. Squinting made my head throb. The dead heat of day, the sun a fireball in the platinum sky. 'Please. I'll be in awful trouble if I'm seen.' Had Sarah noticed I was gone? Maybe she was out looking for me, asking neighbours if they'd seen me. Gemma wouldn't notice. She'd be in the attic till evening, but Sarah would know I was gone.

Sighing, Beth picked up her sandals and stood up. 'I do this sort of thing all the time back home. I ride the subway, go to the park, take the bus uptown.'

'What's a subway?'

'It's like this train that goes all over the city, mostly underground, and it's all dark outside the windows, even when the sun is shining. It's very cool. Everyone uses it.'

'I don't go off on my own around town. I'm not allowed.'

'I'm not either. But I do it anyway.'

'But what do you tell your mother?' I thought of Judith, her arms claiming her daughter. A shadow of anxiety on her face.

Beth shook her head. 'Nothing.'

'Nothing? But what if she sees you?'

She laughed, another sudden shout of sound. 'Sees me where? It's New York City. You don't see people you know. Ever.' She turned her gaze once more to the whooping boys. 'That's what I like best about it.'

New York was familiar in the way that famous cities are – from books, from photos of skyscrapers and snatches of song – but I had no means of imagining a city so huge, so unknowable that it was possible to travel all day by bus and train without meeting someone you knew. I wanted to ask Beth more, hear about solo trips on public transport, but I knew Sarah and if she thought I'd strayed further than the shop, there'd be trouble for sure. I touched her arm. 'We should go now.'

Beth rolled her eyes, dragged on her sandals. I thought we'd race back home again, but her mood had changed, become quieter, and she resisted my efforts to hurry our journey along.

It seemed to take all afternoon, that walk home. The heat hindered our progress, slowed us. I needed a drink, badly. The ice-pop wrapper crinkled in the pocket of my shorts. My shoelace repeatedly came undone and turned grey from being trodden on. I pulled leaves from hedges, retied my ponytail as Beth stopped to stroke three dogs. The afternoon smelled of wilting flowers, dry leaves and the heat that came off the road. Tar melted visibly in the sunlight.

✿✿✿

Sarah was in the front garden, talking over the hedge to Daniel's mother. She smiled when we turned onto the drive.

'There you are! I was wondering where you were.'

Beth spoke before I could fumble for something to say. 'We just went for ice cream and then Megan showed me around a bit.'

'Good girl,' Sarah said to me.

That was it? I'd been gone ages, hours possibly, and she believed Beth's lie? I cast around, looking to catch Beth's eye, but she had sloped away and was ringing the bell to the garden flat. It shrilled in the sudden lull. I heard Judith greet her daughter, close the door softly.

'Megan, your nana was telling me all about your new friend.'
Daniel's mother beamed at me from across the hedge. Mrs Sullivan.
She always referred to Sarah as my nana, even though I'd never
called her anything but Sarah. Mrs Sullivan had her own name too.
Bridget. Named after a saint from over a thousand years ago, who'd
since become the patron saint of babies and children of parents who
weren't married. Maybe that was why Mrs Sullivan was so good
and kind to me, and to Gemma. Mrs Sullivan was devoted to her
religion, but even though her house was full of statues and holy
pictures, and even though she wanted Daniel to be a priest, her
kindness shone through it all. Mrs Sullivan wore headscarves and
went to Mass every day. She subscribed to missionary magazines
and sent money to a priest in Africa. Father Bob. She had never met
him, but spoke of him as though he were a friend. Father Bob wrote
letters of thanks, which were pinned to the wall near the statues Mrs
Sullivan prayed to each day. I was very fond of her.

Gemma laughed at her, said how ridiculous her devotion was.
As though God would give Mrs Sullivan preferential treatment.
Gemma liked to say things like that sometimes. Sarah always
shushed her, told her not to say anything unless it was something
good. Gemma laughed at that too, but not in a good way. When
she laughed at religious people, it was anger-tinged, broken, sad.
Nuts, she called them. Religious nuts. Daniel's father hadn't been
religious. After he forgot to come home, Mrs Sullivan didn't allow
anyone to mention him. Daniel said it was because she was too sad.
I wasn't supposed to know that Mrs Sullivan had inherited money
from her parents, which is why she didn't have to make curtains
like Sarah, or paint cards like Gemma. It wasn't a huge amount of
money, but Sarah said that Mrs Sullivan lived frugally, so she could
survive very nicely. The house had belonged to her mother's family,
so there was no chance of himself coming back to take it. Whenever
a man was referred to as *himself*, it wasn't a good thing, I'd noticed.

I see himself is out again. Himself is drunk again. Himself thinks he's above taking his children to the park. That sort of thing, the things women said to each other when little ears weren't meant to be listening.

I tugged at a leaf in the hedge. 'Is Daniel coming out?' A dragon-fly darted between us, an iridescent flash of blue. I remembered how thirsty I was.

'Later. He's doing his reading.'

I couldn't understand it. School had finished for the summer, but Daniel was kept indoors to practise reading every afternoon. He read from a book about the saints. Daniel didn't want to be a priest, but his mother wanted it. She liked to push his long fringe off his forehead and kiss him. You'll be a great priest, my love, she would say. They'll be lucky to have you.

Daniel had no intention of being a priest. I knew that, but he didn't want to upset his mother, so he played along. Daniel was going to be a pilot. Or an animal scientist. I was the only one who knew that. He told me in secret one day, as we filled a sticker book with pictures of planes. Daniel knew all the airlines, could recite them one by one. Alitalia, Lufthansa, Cathay Pacific. Iberia, Sabena, KLM, Delta. Pan Am, United, Qantas. There were so many of them, the names exciting and unknown. We found their countries on the map in my grandfather's big atlas. Huge blue oceans, candy-coloured countries, vast stretches of land. Daniel was going to fly over all of them. He also kept insects in jars, wrote about them in his notebook and cried if any of them died. He read about the saints' lives because it made his mother happy. He was her second boy, her youngest and favourite child. He had a brother who was thirteen, and twin sisters who were ten, but Daniel was the one his mother reached for first.

My head ached from the sun. 'I need a drink of water,' I said to Sarah. A few houses up, a dog barked, but it was a defeated sound, a protest more than anything aggressive. The dog sounded like I felt: hot, tired, parched.

'You must be roasting out here,' Mrs Sullivan said. A heavy silver crucifix sat on a chain around her neck. She zipped it from side to side. 'It's too hot.'

'Go on inside and get a drink. I'll be up in a minute,' Sarah said, her hand on my arm.

The back of my neck was damp. So were the palms of my hands. I dragged them down the front of my T-shirt, leaving a grimy trail across my stomach. I thought of the boys in the canal, how their whooping had echoed off the water's surface. How they had glistened like seals.

5

Gemma was painting a portrait of me. It had been Sarah's idea, but Gemma agreed almost immediately, which meant that I had to sit for half an hour each day in the attic. I didn't mind, except that I wasn't allowed to talk. There was to be no movement of any sort from me, unless my mother asked for it.

The ghosts kept watch as I sat on the chair. Gemma had pushed it into the centre of the room and then made me sit with my hands in my lap, my ankles crossed. It was early, but the heat had already risen, languidly stretching itself across the morning. I'd already completed my watering outside, the plants limp from days of minimum water. The windows in the low attic ceiling were open, but the air didn't stir. A car engine sputtered outside on the main road. The canal was out of sight, but I knew it was there. Since my trip with Beth the day before, it had burned in my mind. I saw the mercury splashes of water, the bare backs of the boys as they dive-bombed, heard the flat smack of skin on water.

My mother wore her usual old shirt that had belonged to my grandfather, paint-spattered, frayed at the cuffs, too large for her.

'Would my granddad have liked me?' The question fell between us.

Gemma took ages to answer. She always did when she was working. 'What?' Her voice was vague, faraway.

'Nothing.'

Eventually her face cleared. 'Sorry, Megan.' She wriggled her fingers, then picked up a blade and started sharpening her pencil. The scraping was the only sound for a few seconds. Blade on wood. 'What did you say?'

I waved away her question, accidentally swatting a fly that had come in the open ceiling window. 'Nothing. It doesn't matter.'

She looked up. 'Sure?'

'Sure.'

'Music?'

'Carole King.'

That was the album I loved most that summer. It wasn't new, but I hadn't heard it before then. Carole sitting at the window on the cover, her feet bare, a striped cat her companion on the window seat. Gemma crossed the floor to the shelf where she kept the record player. Albums were bundled beside it. She selected Carole King and clicked on the record player.

Gemma resumed her sketching. She never liked me to look at what she was working on, couldn't stand being inspected. I was used to it, never bothered asking her to show me anything unfinished. I listened to the first side of the record before moving. The sun inched slowly overhead, shortening the shadows in the attic. Gemma's pencil scratched against the paper.

Sarah's knock was soft, a triple rap on the closed attic door. She poked her head around. 'Sorry for disturbing. I won't be long.'

Gemma laid her pencil down, flexed her fingers. 'Don't worry about it.'

Sarah stayed where she was, resting her shoulder against the door frame. 'I was talking to Judith and she wants to mark their national day tomorrow. Are you available?'

Gemma leaned back in her chair, stretched her hands above her head. 'What are they planning?'

'I've no idea. Judith said they usually have a barbecue with some friends.'

'A barbecue?' Gemma laughed.

I chimed in. 'We don't have a barbecue, Sarah.'

Sarah turned to me. 'I know, love. They'll have to do something else. Anyway, will they include you?'

My mother had already picked up her pencil again. 'Sounds nice. Why not?'

'That's all I wanted to know. I'll make something, a salad or something, although God knows what they'll think of it. The things Judith cooks! And all she seems to talk about is food, and where to buy things. She asked me if I had any cilantro yesterday. Cilantro!'

Gemma's mouth edged into a smile. 'What did you say?'

'What could I say?'

'That you hadn't a clue, mother!'

Sarah folded her arms. 'I couldn't say that!'

'Why not?'

'Because I don't want her thinking I'm even less sophisticated than I already am.'

Sarah surprised me. She never worried about what others thought, and was forever reminding me that it wasn't what people thought of me that mattered, it was the kind of person I was.

Gemma laughed. 'You're very sophisticated, Mum. Don't let a few Americans put you down.'

What's sophisticated, I wanted to know.

Gemma explained. 'It means you know things.'

'About what?'

Gemma tapped her pencil on the table. 'I don't know, like things about art, or food, things like that. You know what wines to drink with dinner.'

'But Sarah hardly ever has wine.'

Gemma gestured. 'I know, but it's that sort of thing. It's hard to explain.'

I was no more enlightened than I had been before.

'So,' Sarah said. 'I'm still no clearer on what cilantro is.'

'It's coriander.'

Sarah laughed. 'That's all? I was imagining all sorts of exotic things.'

'Can I go now?' I asked. I was thirsty. The record had finished, the ghosts hadn't appeared and I wanted to go outside.

My mother nodded. 'Go on. Just leave the door open on your way out. It's too hot in here.'

I made for the door. Sarah went out ahead of me.

'Megan?'

I turned back. Gemma's hands were stretched towards me. 'Hug?'

Her shoulder was strong under my cheek, and I rubbed my face against the fabric of my grandfather's faded shirt. My mother stroked my arms, my back, pulled me onto her lap.

'My angel.' She sat back, put her hand on my face. 'You're my little angel. Do you know that?'

I nodded. This was when being with my mother was best. When it was just the two of us and she held me to her. She always used to do that, back when I was little, and sometimes I caught tears silvering her skin. Then she'd kiss me extra hard and hug me a little bit tighter and not let me go for a long time.

'I'll see you later, Meg.'

I hugged her once more. 'See you later, alligator.'

'In a while, crocodile.'

Not a ghost stirred as I exited. The attic looked as it always did: the books, the stacks of supplies, the line of dancers caught in the slipstream of an eternal tango. The smell of linseed and turpentine heavy on the late morning air. As I stepped onto the landing, I heard the record player click back on again. Bob Dylan, his harmonica whining. The banister was cool to touch. I trailed my hot palm along its curved surface and thought of the decades of hands that had worn it smooth.

6

It was their voices I heard first. The apple I'd grabbed from the bowl on the kitchen table cracked against my teeth. Juice leaked down my chin. Stepping out of the kitchen, onto the wooden deck, a man's voice shouted, 'Careful!'

Jim was back. Sarah had said he would be in. He had to replace some cornicing in the hall, paint the architraves and repair a ceiling rose in the front room, but the big job for now was fixing the garden steps. The new steps lay neatly in place. All the old, rotting wood was piled at the side of the garden. Rusty nails poked their heads out. Jim had also put in new posts, making the deck stronger. Sarah wanted to put the chairs outside again, so we could sip our tea and watch the morning gather its strength. Maybe we could even have a table, a small one, and eat all our meals there. The heat was too intense for eating much, but it would be nice to sit out anyway. I was beginning to forget what cold weather was like. I hoped the summer would last and last.

Jim had sandpapered the steps, the railings and the decking the previous day, and now he was painting it all. Sarah had chosen green, a pale sage, and Jim's brush was deft, quick, the dry wood swallowing the paint without delay. He had managed to paint the entire handrail without splashing the bougainvillea too much. Now, he smiled up at me, the morning sunshine making him squint.

'You'll have to use the other stairs. There's to be no walking out here until tomorrow. Do you hear me?'

I said yes.

'It'll be dry in no time in this heat, and then I'll put on another coat and it'll be right as rain. You won't know yourselves, with your fancy green steps and deck.' He laughed. 'The neighbours will all be jealous of you.'

He rattled the rail to show how firm it was. 'See that? Nothing short of an earthquake is going to dislodge this staircase.'

Sarah waved at me from the end of the garden. She pointed to the garden flat. 'Just come down the stairs inside. I've left the door open for you. It's only for today.' Shading her face with her arm, she called over to me again. 'Where's your hat?'

I pretended not to hear her. Not for any reason was I going to appear in front of Beth with that ridiculous hat. A *campero*, Gemma called it. Worn by all the best *gauchos*. No way was I wearing it. A headache was infinitely preferable. Why they couldn't just buy me a normal hat made of cotton or straw, I would never understand. Sarah's standard response did not sit well with me: why waste money on a new hat when there's a perfectly good one there for you?

When I stepped out into the garden, Daniel and Beth were sitting on the wall. It was over six feet high, and I used irregularities in the brickwork as footholds for climbing. Daniel kept an old chair on his side, saving himself from the scraped knees and scuffed shoes that I frequently suffered as a result of scrambling up to sit beside him. Beth's clogs were tumbled together on the grass. Her legs hung long from her white shorts, her hair like a spill of cream down her back.

Why was she talking to Daniel? How had she even met him? He was my friend. Not hers.

'Hi, Megan.'

Beth's drawl irritated me in that moment. It sounded affected, put on. I bit my apple, considered ignoring them both. I hadn't seen Daniel in days, and now here he was, sitting on the wall with Beth. Over the wall, I could hear Stevie, Daniel's older brother, kicking his ball against the brickwork. He knew it annoyed Sarah, but he did it anyway. Stevie liked to irritate. Besides fighting with Daniel and destroying his things, he enjoyed getting in everyone's way. Gemma said he was insecure because his father left, that he liked to remind people that he existed. She said he was worried that if he wasn't annoying people, they'd forget he was there. I wasn't so sure. I think he just liked tormenting Daniel and, by extension, me. Gemma said I should be nice to him, to make him feel better about himself. I thought Stevie was feeling just fine about himself. It was others he needed to be nicer to.

'Here!' Daniel threw me something and I caught it with my left hand. Something slimy stuck to my palm, but I kept my hand closed around it. It wouldn't do to recoil, to be spooked, not in front of Beth. I knew what it was.

Daniel had thrown me a snail. He loved animals, all creatures, even the glutinous kind. I opened my hand, peered at the snail. My apple I discarded. The birds would eat it. The snail had retreated inside its shell, a tight spiral of flecked grey. Beth recoiled, as I'd presumed she would.

'Yuck. Gross.' She waved her hand in front of her face. 'Keep it away from me.'

Daniel collected creatures and kept them in jars, on beds of grass that we pulled from the garden and minuscule bits of sticks that we dropped in. Often, they died; other times they escaped. I preferred it when they got away. It was cruel, somehow, keeping insects imprisoned in old jam jars, even if they had been scrubbed to perfection. Between the airline sticker collection and his insects in jars, not to mention *Lives of the Saints*, Daniel was kept busy. I helped him, but my own interests lay elsewhere, between the pages of books, in drawing, and in the mysterious hieroglyphics of sheet music that I was beginning to conquer. But these were individual pursuits, things I did when it was time to be at home.

I placed the snail on a twist of clematis and we watched it nudge its way upwards.

Beth swung herself off the wall. 'You guys are so weird.'

'Why?' Daniel asked, turning to face her.

Her shrug was graceful. 'You just are. I mean, bugs and things.' She shuddered. 'Horrible.'

Then Beth looked beyond me, towards the house. Her face changed, brightened. I turned and saw a man cross the grass towards us. He looked a bit like a man off a cover of one of Gemma's records: tall, sun-browned, wearing denim from head to toe.

'Daddy!'

She put her arms around the man's waist, laid her cheek against his chest. The man poked Beth in the side, the soft fleshy part below her ribs, but gently, as though he might hurt her if he did it any harder. She squealed and sprang back from him.

'Guys, this is my dad. Daddy, this is Megan and this is Daniel.' She turned to us. 'You can call him Chris. Everyone does.'

Chris's hand was firm around mine. His hair was blond, almost like a woman's hair in the way it fell, thick and straight and all the one length, past the collar of his blue shirt. Three pens stuck out of his shirt pocket. His tanned feet were bare inside his sandals, the nails clean and square. I think I noticed his feet because I'd never really seen men's bare feet close-up before and imagined them to be vaguely distasteful, grubby and unkempt. His teeth were the whitest I'd ever seen. So this was the night swimmer. He looked vaguely like the Greek gods from my history book at school. We'd read some of the myths and I'd loved them. Chris was Apollo, or perhaps Helios, all golden locks and burnished skin. I'd never seen a father like him before. Like mothers, fathers had a pattern of familiarity to them when I was a child. Mostly, they were absent, at work all day in jobs that required a suit. They came home, sat in favourite chairs, had things handed to them. They doled out physical punishment to their children and were the last word on discipline, even though mothers were the ones who spent all their time with their children. It baffled me, and more so because I didn't have a father to compare. It's not that I missed having one. I didn't. It made no difference to me. Our small, female world was fine just as it was. Fathers distorted things, tilted the balance.

Chris was saying something to me. I blinked. His laugh was like Beth's, shouty and sudden. I smiled and he turned to Daniel, enveloping his hand in his own big one. It gave me a moment to draw breath.

Chris's voice was slow and oozy, like honey. Words took their time, easing themselves into the spaces between us. He grinned a lot, called us *y'all*, took pleasure in tickling Beth. *Bethy*, he called her. *Li'l girl.*

'Where's Mama?'

'Gone to the store. What are you doing, Daddy?'

Chris raked his hair, his fingers separating the strands into shades of blond. Dark and light.

'Just in from work, baby. Just in.'

'But I mean what are you doing now? What do you want to do?'

This was a different Beth unfolding before me. The pouting lower lip, the offended silence that watermarked our slow walk home from the canal were gone. In front of her father she was a new person, someone who laughed, who greedily sought his attention. She reminded me of a bird, preening her bright feathers, needing to be noticed. She was Phoebe, vying with the mortals for her father's attention.

A huge bee bounced on the air between us. Beth shied away. Stevie shouted on the other side of the wall, something inconsequential, unimportant. I rubbed my arm where the skin was turning pink. Jim's paintbrush kept up its scratching, the dry wood swallowing the paint. Swatting at the bee, I noticed my mother standing at the kitchen door.

Something shifted in that instant. I was too young to under-stand, and maybe no one there in the garden in that sunlit moment fully understood but, looking back, that was the second that things tilted. Everything had run along its own lines up to then – our lives, our routines, our home. Our female family. But that all changed with Gemma's appearance at the kitchen door, her bare feet touching the newly painted wood of the deck, her hair falling out of its topknot, my grandfather's old shirt splotched with paint, and that split second of awe on Chris's face. The shift on Chris's features was infinitesimal. If pressed, I couldn't have sworn it happened. When I glanced back at Chris, his face was normal again; he was smiling at something Daniel had said and I was left wondering if I'd imagined it all. Until he did that thing again with his hair – the raking of fingers. This time he did it with both hands, and he cast his eyes in my mother's direction, without moving his face.

Gemma saw him, and she seemed to understand, though I had no idea what it was that she had detected in his furtive glance. At nine, I had no real understanding of what happened between men and women. My mother floated down the wet steps, like one of her attic ghosts. She ignored Jim's squawk of protest, paid no attention to the sage green paint that coloured her soles. She appeared to glide the remaining distance to where we huddled, Daniel coaxing the bee onto a clematis bloom, Beth laughing at her father, who appeared now to be pouring all of his concentration into what his daughter was saying. He made no move to acknowledge Gemma until I reached out my hand to her. The other hand I kept closed around another of Daniel's snails, this one smaller and more curious than its relative, who had disappeared among the clematis petals. Its head nudged invisibly against my clammy skin. The urge to drop it was too much, and I opened my palm and flung it over the wall.

'Hey!' Daniel turned to me. 'Why'd you do that? It was only a little one.'

Chris saved us from further confrontation. He held his hand out to Gemma. She dropped mine with a gentle squeeze.

'Chris Jackson. Your new tenant.' He smiled. 'Good to meet you, ma'am.'

Gemma took his proffered hand. 'Gemma. Welcome.'

Never had I seen my mother so at ease with a stranger, so smooth in her exchanges. Usually, she kept a distance between herself and new people, especially men. She allowed conversation to evolve around her, rarely putting herself in the centre of it. Always hovering, watchful. Gemma knew what it was to be talked about and she trusted few people.

'I hear y'all are joining us for a little celebration for the Fourth,' Chris said. With a gesture, he included the three of us children, but he really meant Gemma.

'I believe we are,' Gemma replied, as though invitations to Fourth of July parties were a common occurrence.

'Wonderful.'

I glanced at my mother as she tucked a strand of hair behind her ear. Her topknot had all but fallen out, the pencil that she used to keep it in place dangling precariously at the back of her head. A streak of paint was smudged on her cheek, yet still she managed to look utterly beautiful. I knew it. Daniel knew it, Beth knew it. And Chris Jackson, with his suntanned face and his straight white teeth, knew it too.

In that moment, Judith stepped through the French doors. Chris turned casually towards her as if nothing had happened.

'I'm sure I'll see you soon,' he said, touching his forefinger to his temple in a somnolent salute. His eyes didn't leave Gemma's as he tugged Beth's hand. 'Coming, baby girl?'

Beth said no, not yet.

Chris strolled over to his wife, hands in the pockets of his jeans. He disappeared into the darkness of indoors, Judith following him. The voile curtains stirred in their wake, and came to rest again.

For the rest of the day I wondered if I had imagined it all.

7

The next day was the Fourth of July. Sarah explained that it was like St Patrick's Day for Americans, their national day. That year, 1976, was a big one because it marked two hundred years since the Declaration of Independence had been adopted. All over America there would be fireworks, parties, barbecues and parades. Americans were very proud people. They loved their country and knew their history. They had no problem hanging flags outside their houses, or putting stickers on their cars saying they were proud to be American. Sarah told me all this during breakfast on our newly painted deck. We sat with our bowls on our laps, watching the early sun burn the haze off the garden. I'd already done the watering, slopping dishwater into the tubs and over the plants. There hadn't been enough water, though, and I was feeling guilty for leaving so many flowers thirsty.

Church bells chimed. All over the city, Mass-goers were putting on their best clothes, mindful of the heat. The very organised would be at early Mass, the rest of the day open to them, like a clean sheet of paper. Then the tardy would troop to the church later, children whining, mothers determined. It was always the same. Observing them from the window in the front room, I watched families, some in cars, most on foot, beating the same path to Mass every Sunday in the local church. Daniel's mother went to the Latin Mass at seven on Sunday mornings, then again at half past ten, her children in tow. The routine never changed. Sometimes I wished I could go too, just so we could be normal. I didn't bother asking, though, because I knew what the answer would be. Any place that rejects your mother, Sarah liked to say, rejects you and me as well. It wasn't always easy, being on the outside.

From our deck, we could see into the neighbours' gardens. That was why some of them objected when my grandfather had built it. He'd meant it to be just for going down to the garden, to save Sarah from having to go through the garden flat, back when they first started to rent the flat out. Then he expanded the structure into what we now had. We loved it. It was our lookout on the world behind the house. We could see the low walls of the piggery down the lane that stretched behind the back gardens, the stench of pig sometimes too much to bear. On that morning, though, the piggery was quiet. No snuffling or oinking, no mad dashes for freedom as there often were. Next door, Mrs Doherty was already on her blanket, sunglasses on, her book held up against the sky. Of her husband, there was no sign. Three doors down was the swimming pool, a cobalt oval at the end of the garden, almost completely hidden from view by the overgrowth of trees. Gemma remembered it being lowered over the back wall by six men, then sunk into the ground. We didn't know any of the people who leased the house, a revolving door of students and short-term renters. The pool had remained dried out, neglected, and until Beth had recalled her father's episodes of night swimming, I hadn't thought about it in a long time.

But now a plan was hatching in my head, a means of bringing the swimming pool back to life. Surely no one would notice? Daniel's mother said that the house was empty for the summer. I'd overheard her telling Sarah. She said that maybe it would be suitable for Beth's family, would give them more room than our garden flat, but Sarah said that the house three doors away was in no fit state for anyone to live in, not even students. Nothing worked, she said; the windows at the back were cracked and she was sure the place was full of mice. She wouldn't want anyone to live there. I also knew that Sarah didn't want the Jacksons moving out because we needed the money from their rent.

But the pool. In my mind it loomed – large, blue, deep. I could almost feel the cool water as though I were submerged, washed clean of the summer dust that coated my skin.

I would need help in restoring it.

Daniel's mother appeared and began hanging washing out on the line. That was unusual enough in itself. She was so religious that she never did any work on Sunday, except for cooking a simple dinner. No cleaning, no laundry, nothing. She was fond of quoting the Bible on Sundays. She was fond of quoting it any chance she got, but especially on Sundays. *And God blessed the seventh day, and declared it holy, because it was the day when He rested from all His work of creation.* Nothing was so important that it made her work on Sundays, not even gardening. And there she was, only in the door from Latin Mass and she was hanging out washing. But, as Sarah said, heat made people funny, made them do strange things. And that was a hot day, even though it was early, only just gone eight o'clock.

Sarah fanned herself with a handkerchief. I sipped water from a glass. On the chair beside me were my sketchpad and a new box of pencils that Gemma had bought for me when she went to get her paints. I touched their sharpened tips, ran my thumb over the impressions they left in my fingertips. A ladybird landed on my knee and crawled speculatively around before opening up its curved wings and taking off. The sky was drenched in colour, the day thick with possibility.

8

It wasn't until much later that day that we saw the Americans. Sarah, Gemma and I took the eleven o'clock bus for Dun Laoghaire to spend the day escaping the stupor of heat that was dragging the city under. The bus was packed with day trippers making for the shore. Families with children and an abundance of buckets and spades, teenagers in groups and couples. There were some individuals in their Sunday best, maybe destined for church or an early Sunday lunch. Not having a car meant it wasn't as easy to drive off somewhere cooler, find a river miles away and drop a fishing line in, or a field to throw down a rug and have a picnic. The sea was the best we could do, but it always worked. Sarah had packed sandwiches and a flask of tea, Gemma folded rugs and swimming things, and everything had been stuffed into a couple of oversized bags.

When we arrived at the tiny beach at Sandycove, the sun was high and it glinted off the sea. The water was green and mild, and there was enough room to spread out. Splashing with my mother was the best bit of all. I ran and she chased me, while Sarah sat with her back to the stone wall, the tiny cove a perfect crescent around us.

I swam underwater, my waterlogged ears muting sound. Down there, everything was darker, greener. Sand was kicked up by my thrashing limbs. Seawater swirled past my eyes, a billion minuscule bubbles set in motion by my movements. My mother's legs were dark shadows ahead of me. I kicked off, grabbed her, pulled her under. We both surfaced, spitting water, laughing. Water ran in rivulets down her face. Her long dark hair was plastered to her shoulders, down her arms. She blew water off her lower lip and kissed me.

Later, eating our picnic, I thought how lucky I was. I didn't need anyone else. I had Gemma and Sarah to care for me.

Sometimes, rarely, Sarah suggested that Gemma should meet someone. By someone, she meant a man. Sarah wanted Gemma to have someone to take care of her, to keep her company. My mother had gone out with men, but it wasn't a regular occurrence. Gemma preferred to be with me, with Sarah and me. Men didn't really want to be with her, I heard her say once to her friend Ruth. They just wanted to see what they could get for themselves. I had no idea what they wanted, but Gemma was convinced that it was only one thing. That was another thing I heard her say. *They only want one thing, and they're not getting it from me.* That sort of thing made her sad and a bit angry. I was glad she didn't want a man, a husband.

Beth had asked me again, more than once, about my father. What could I say? He was a closed book. It's not that he had gone to work one day and forgotten to come back, like Daniel's dad. He simply didn't exist any more. There was no dad, no man who had been around at the beginning. What there was, was an unmarked resting place, a mound of earth under which Felipe reposed. I didn't know where it was, and nor, I assumed, did Gemma – not that I asked her.

Beth liked secrets. She liked whispering about things, liked talking behind her hands, behind closed doors, liked beckoning me to sit with her while she told me things, things like night swimming and why her parents were sad. I didn't want to hear her secrets. There were a few in my own life and I didn't have space in my head for anyone else's. Gemma's attic ghosts for starters. They swirled above my head, kept things in the attic safe. Kept my mother safe. Beth wanted to tell me about her father, and why they'd moved to Ireland. Something about a girl at the university, a line Chris overstepped. She tried to tell me about her mother. Sometimes Judith sat with bottles of wine, Beth confided, and only stopped drinking them when they were empty. Sometimes, but not all the time.

I didn't know what to do with other people's secrets. They were secret for a reason — so that no one else could know them. Secrets were for keeping, for guarding and making sure they stayed unknown. You couldn't decide to pass them around like a box of sweets at a party, with everyone being allowed to choose which one they wanted. Maybe that was why I liked being Daniel's friend. He didn't pressurise me the way girls did. He knew me and accepted me as I was. There were no conditions with him. He was my friend. I was his. It was very simple.

Gemma snapped her fingers in front of my face. 'Earth to Megan.'

I looked at her. The stone wall was warm against my bare back, the sand cool and damp under my legs. The remains of my sandwich flopped between my fingers. I stuffed it quickly into my mouth. 'What?'

'Ice cream?'

I nodded.

'With chocolate?'

'Please.'

Sarah looked at her watch. 'We should get moving soon after that. That way we won't have to rush back. It's not fair to be late.'

Judith had said she wanted to start the party at six. She had managed to borrow a barbecue for the evening from another American family living nearby, and she was spending the day leading up to the party making food.

'Who's going to this party besides ourselves?' Gemma asked Sarah as she rummaged in one of the big bags for her purse.

'I'm not sure. She's asked the Sullivans, but I can't see them going.'

'Is Daniel going too?' The possibility of having him there lessened my apprehension about spending the long evening with only Beth for company.

Gemma dug through her purse, shook change onto her towel. 'Her nibs might lead us in a decade of the rosary. To keep the sin away and all that.'

Sarah was gently admonishing. 'Not in front of the child.'

'She's not stupid, Mother. She can see for herself.'

'See what?' My mother and grandmother often did that, spoke over me when I was sitting right there with them. 'What can I see?'

Gemma shushed me. 'Nothing, don't worry about it. Now, three ice creams and then we'll make tracks for home.'

She walked over to the striped van that sold ice cream, her wet ponytail swinging. The van was parked where it always was, up on the footpath. It was the only van that we ever bought ice cream from. The man had been coming to this spot since Gemma was a child, and there was always a queue.

As Gemma waited in line, I struggled into my T-shirt and shorts while Sarah held a towel around me. Once dressed, Sarah and I packed up our things. I gathered our towels and shook them hard. Sand flew into the air. It settled on my legs, my arms. Walking to the water, I rinsed my skin. Tiny waves sucked at my feet. The sun dried my arms, leaving shadows of salt on my skin. I stooped to pick up some shells for Daniel. Then we stacked the buckets inside each other, wrapped our wet swimming things inside the towels, and threw the remnants of our picnic into the bin. My hair I yanked into a ponytail. I was sticky from the salt water and it was an effort to get the elastic around it.

'A bath for you when we get home,' Sarah said. 'Just a small one. We don't want to waste water.'

The walk to the bus stop was punctuated by the slap of our flip-flops on the hot pavement. My ice cream melted in the hot sunshine. I licked it off my fingers. Around us, people lazed on blankets, boys threw Frisbees, dogs sat panting, tongues hanging out. Old people sat on benches along the seafront, pointing out things to each other. A sailboat, perhaps, or the staggered walk of a toddler on the shoreline. The sun was relentless, burning my eyes. Gemma had sunglasses, large dark discs that obscured her face and in the same instant made her look like a film star. Not for the first time, I noticed men noticing her. Not in the subtle way Chris Jackson had noticed her, but in an open, gaping way. Stop it, I wanted to shout. Don't look at her. She's my mother.

Gemma finished her ice cream, wiped her fingers on a tissue, brushed cone crumbs off her sundress. Catching me watching her, she smiled at me, pinched my nose.

'Everything okay?'

'Fine.'

She slung her arm around my shoulder, kissed the top of my head. 'You're getting taller, do you know that?'

I didn't know, but it thrilled me. Beth was so much taller than me; maybe soon I'd catch up.

Gemma rubbed my bare arm. 'Don't grow up too quickly, do you hear me?'

I smiled up at her. 'I won't.'

'What would I do without my baby girl?'

I pressed my face to my mother's middle. She smelled like she always did – of warm skin, cotton and the faded scent of her green-tea perfume. I didn't even know what green tea was, but it smelled wonderful.

Sailboats were triangular flashes of colour far out in the bay. Seagulls spiralled overhead, wheeling like bits of discarded paper. Flowers wilted in beds. The sea moved imperceptibly, layered in blue all the way to the horizon. I wanted to catch the afternoon, spin it out for as long as I could. The heat, the sun on my skin, and Gemma and Sarah on either side of me. We were in no hurry to get home. There was still plenty of time.

9

Being late for a party in your own garden is strange. By the time we arrived home, washed, changed, went downstairs and rang the doorbell of the garden flat – like proper visitors, as Sarah had insisted – everyone else was already in full party mode. Daniel was standing by a small table, his hand in a bowl of crisps. Stevie skulked behind him, his face cloudy. Mrs Sullivan stood with her twin girls gathered at her legs. She held a glass of orange juice in one hand, the other hand fiddling with her silver crucifix. Despite the heat, she was dressed as though for Mass, her good blouse fussy and out of place in the simmering late afternoon heat, her skirt in rigid pleats to her knees. Her hair was held back with a tortoiseshell clip. A wide grey streak ran from her forehead and disappeared into her clip. She was staring off into the distance. Probably thinking about Father Bob and the next letter she would write to him. She smiled when she saw me, touched my cheek with her fingertips.

'Hello, pet. Did you have a nice time at the beach?'

I nodded, accepted the kiss she placed on my head. The back of my leg itched with sunburn and I scratched it with the strap of my sandal. Gemma had tried to insist on my wearing sandals and a dress. I hated dresses and so we'd compromised – I was allowed to wear shorts, but with a sleeveless top that Ruth had brought me from Spain. It was white cotton, with tiny figures embroidered across the front. Judith was directing Beth towards a long table draped with a white cloth. Food was piled in dishes in a straight line down the centre of the table. Bunches of flowers in small vases were dotted at intervals. Unlit candles squatted in jam jars all over the garden. A black grill smoked in a corner. Chris stood with a long fork, poking periodically at whatever was being cooked. There were other adults I didn't recognise standing around, glasses in hand. Shouts of laughter punctuated the various conversations as exotic smells that I hadn't encountered before filled my nostrils.

I glanced around for Sarah, spied her carrying two bowls of salad to the table. She smiled at something Judith said, then shook hands with a tall woman in a short, lime-green skirt and bare feet. I strained to hear their conversation, but they were too far away. On the patio near the French doors, a record player belted out The Doors.

My mother hadn't appeared yet. She had some things to do before joining us. I knew what she wanted. A bath, with plenty of water and no Sarah around to object. Gemma would wash her hair, lie back in the lavender water and have a short burst of time to herself. Sometimes I watched my mother in the bath. It was always the same. Lavender oil, smoky steam spiralling, water almost spilling over the edge of the cast-iron, claw-footed bath. Her hair swirled on the surface, her eyes closed. Unobserved, I had seen my mother cry in the bath once, as though the heat and the steam and the privacy of our large bathroom allowed her sadness to seep out. Gemma wasn't given to sitting around swamped in sorrow, but there was something that made her sad and at times it just had to be let out.

'Where's your mom?'

Beth was so close that I could feel her breath whisper on my cheek. 'I thought she said she'd be here.'

'She's getting ready.'

'Cool.' A stack of plates was thrust into my hands. 'Here, put these there, will you?'

Taking great care not to drop anything, I placed the plates where Beth pointed. 'This is the longest table I've ever seen.'

Beth rolled her eyes. 'That's my mom. She always has to have everything bigger than we need.' She dropped a handful of cutlery with a careless clatter on the white cloth. 'This is just a bunch of tables put together. It's not like it's even a proper long table.'

Once again I marvelled at Beth's constant irritation with her mother. How she publicised it was new to me. It wasn't the done thing in my family to be openly critical of each other. Resentments were few and guarded. Even if I'd wanted to declare annoyance with Gemma or Sarah, I wouldn't have dared. Something – a sense of justice or loyalty – kept me from considering it.

Beth slid off, over to her father. I joined Daniel at the crisp bowl. He immediately launched into an idea he had for building a tree house. All we needed was wood. And a tree.

'Forget the tree house,' I told him. 'We need a swimming pool.'

Daniel opened his eyes wide, pointed his index finger in the direction of the pool three doors down. 'What about that pool?'

Around a mouthful of salty crisps I said, 'But we can't fill it, remember?'

'I know that, but maybe we could try, properly this time?'

'But we'd need an extra-long hose and where would we find one of those? Plus, hoses are banned.'

Daniel looked deflated.

The house was only three gardens away, but that was a long distance to try and drag a hose that was attached to a tap. Besides, Mrs Doherty next door would hear us, and then she'd be sure to tell Sarah and that would be the end of that.

'But Megan, it'd be brilliant. No one would have to know.'

'No one would have to know what?' Beth had rejoined us, smelling of charcoal.

'There's an empty swimming pool three doors down,' Daniel told her. 'But we can't fill it because there's a ban on hosepipes, and besides, there's no way of getting a hose that long.'

'Why not?' Beth leaned towards us, her voice hushed. 'Of course we can do it. Nothing is impossible.'

'But there's a water shortage,' I reminded her.

She made a dismissive sound. 'So what? One small swimming pool isn't going to make any difference.'

'But every drop makes a difference,' I said, echoing Sarah.

Beth sighed. 'Megan, I like you, but sometimes you're just too obedient for your own good. You know?'

I didn't know. I was only doing what everyone was asked to do: to be careful with water. Without water there's nothing, I had read on the front page of the paper.

Stevie had sauntered over while we spoke, drawn by our hushed, urgent voices. 'What's going on?' Stevie liked to keep his light-brown hair as long as he could without his mother insisting he get it cut. That summer, it reached his collar. He had a habit of tucking it behind his ears, to keep it from falling in his face. Like Daniel, his eyes were the brightest shade of blue.

Beth turned to him. 'So it turns out that there's a swimming pool a few gardens away.'

Stevie dug his hands into the pockets of his jeans. 'So? It's filthy and it's empty. It's not a proper pool. You can't swim in it or anything.'

Beth leaned closer to him. 'But we could get it clean and filled. Couldn't we?'

The implication that this was something that Beth and Stevie could do together, and possibly alone, caused Stevie's eyes to widen, his face to flush. Beth nudged him.

'Why don't we at least give it a shot? There has to be a tap somewhere, and we can borrow Sarah's hose.' Beth silenced me with a look when I opened my mouth to object. 'It's not like she's using it, Megan.'

I hushed her. Daniel's mother sat near us, on the edge of a folding chair, her glass having been refilled by Chris. Her tights were wrinkled at the ankles. My own feet were bare with streaks of white skin where my flip-flops had kept the sun away. My shorts were too short, but Sarah said I'd have to wait for the sales before I got new ones. I wondered how Mrs Sullivan could wear tights in weather like this. She must have been melting. Daniel's sisters were in their Sunday dresses. They stood beside their mother. Occasionally, she reached a hand out to them, caught a stray piece of lint on their shoulders, smoothed their clothes. For someone so holy, she was always quick with affection.

Two American couples stood in a huddle, furiously discussing something. Snatches of their conversation drifted to me above The Doors and the sweeping laughter of Sarah and two other women who were seated at the table, a jug of something pale and cloudy between them. Margaritas, Judith had said when Sarah asked. Try one, Judith urged my grandmother. You won't believe how good they taste. The smoke from the barbecue was making me weak with hunger.

'Ford is a moron,' one of the American men was saying. 'A fool. What has he achieved? No, I really mean it. What exactly has he done?' The contents of the glass in his hand splashed onto the grass, but he paid no heed.

'But with Nam,' the other man began.

'Forget Nam. Nam is over. Over. Finished. Kaput.' He made chopping motions with his free hand. I wondered where my mother was. She used to love talking about Vietnam.

Chris materialised out of nowhere, rubbing his hands together. 'Right, I need helpers. Who's on? Megan? Daniel? I have tons of food to bring to the table. Who'll help?'

We followed Chris over to the grill, took plates from him as he filled them. Judith began asking people to sit down, anywhere they wanted. She put her hand on my arm. 'Megan, is your mother coming?'

'She said she was.'

'Good, good. I just don't want her to miss dinner.' Judith weaved among her guests, touching their elbows, directing them to the long table.

✧✧✧

I sat at the end of the table with Beth, Daniel and Stevie. Daniel's sisters sat with their mother, far enough away from us so that we didn't have to spend the whole time watching what we were saying. Mrs Sullivan liked to correct us, to tell us to pronounce our words clearly, not to slouch, not to speak with our mouths full. I was invariably included, as though my crimes warranted equal attention to those of her offspring. Daniel was just relieved that she hadn't suggested we say grace before the meal. She always insisted on grace, even at birthday parties. Daniel was slow to criticise his mother, but saying grace at a birthday party was guaranteed to get your friends giggling.

We ate hot, sticky, spicy meat from the barbecue. We used our fingers, burning our skin and our mouths. It was the most delicious thing I'd ever eaten. I said so to Beth. She shrugged and dropped a rib bone on her plate before reaching for another one.

'It's my mom. She's from New Mexico and she's all into spicy stuff. She puts green chillies on everything. Plus hot sauce, Tabasco, whatever.'

The world was getting a little bit bigger every time I was around the Americans. So many new words, their sounds exotic, untested. Chillies. Tabasco. The careless shrugging off of Nam. Margaritas. Beth lifted a charred, shrivelled thing from a plate with a fork, dropped it on her own plate. 'You have to try one of these. Not with your hands, though,' she chided as Daniel reached for one. 'You get this stuff on your fingers and then you rub your eyes, you're spending the night in hospital.'

'What is that?' Stevie asked, mistrust curling his lip. 'It looks like a cooked sock.'

Beth shouted with laughter. 'Don't tell my mom that. This is a green chilli. Very hot, totally delicious.' She broke it up with her fork and ate it.

Little of the food was familiar to me, but I ate with gusto. Flavours, textures, everything new. The adults were absorbed in their own conversations about Vietnam, about Pol Pot, Northern Ireland, and South Africa. Sarah sat beside a man with a beard who kept her glass filled with margaritas. Sarah, who hardly even drank wine, sipped avidly. Keep it flowing, she laughed. Keep it flowing, whatever it is. Mrs Sullivan kept her hand over her glass of orange, as though the bearded man might lean over and refill her glass with alcohol. Only Communion wine ever passed her lips. Judith chatted with another American woman, the wife of the man who hated Gerald Ford. They were discussing Dublin, how difficult it was to get proper ingredients here, how long the buses took to arrive, a woman they knew whose husband had left. The woman lingered over her wine, sipped it slowly, said how delicious it was. *Excellent pairing*, she said more than once. *Amazing choice*. I kept an eye on Judith to see if she was drinking all the wine, but she barely touched her glass. Maybe Beth had been lying.

The seat beside Chris was vacant. He sat with his elbow resting on the back of the empty chair, his chin in his hand. His hair was gold in the dipping sunlight. *Gilded*, my mother would have said. She still hadn't turned up. Disappointment prickled my throat. I'd wanted Gemma to be here, to have fun with us. She deserved to have some fun. I knew she was lonely. She didn't need to say it.

The man who sat on the other side of Chris, the man who had lent him the barbecue, was talking about a book he was reading, but it was clear to me that Chris wasn't listening any more, his attention suddenly elsewhere. The man didn't notice and kept up his dissection of the novel about the deep sea, but I turned to see what it was Chris was looking at.

My mother stood on the wooden steps, halfway down to the garden, looking for all the world like one of her attic ghosts. Her hair, dry now and brushed, hung down her back. Her white floaty dress was new, a gift from a friend whose child Gemma had painted. Her feet were bare. Her hands clutched at each other – a sign, I knew, that my mother was nervous.

I glanced back at Chris. He was a panther, ready to pounce, tension in his arms and in the stillness of his shoulders. The man talking about the book spoke on. Snatches drifted to me. *His prose is good. Tension sustained. Descriptions of the ocean realistic enough. Movie rights already sold. It'll make millions.*

I waved at my mother. Extricating myself, I wound my way around the snake of tables and went to her. Her green-tea perfume hung between us on the warm evening air.

'Come on, you're really late. All the food will be gone.'

Gemma reached out, stroked my face. 'Sorry, sweetheart. I had a few things to do.' She stepped down onto the grass. 'What am I missing?'

I plunged in, telling her about the chillies that looked like socks, the hot sticky ribs, the people we'd never met before, The Doors. 'I saved you a seat too, over with us.'

Gemma slid onto the folding chair. Before anyone could say a word, the bearded man leaned over, his hand extended.

'Brad Zimmer. I work with Chris back home, and now in Trinity.' Gemma shook his hand. 'So, where do you fit in here, Gemma?'

'I live here.'

'She's my mother,' I explained. Was I imagining it, or did Brad Zimmer's face fall ever so slightly at this?

Chris moved into the empty seat beside him. One place closer to my mother. A woman on the other side of Gemma introduced herself as Holly, Brad's wife.

'Have you just arrived? There's plenty of food left.' Holly

splashed wine into her own glass. She looked around the table. 'Is your husband here?'

Did I imagine the sudden intake of breath around the table?

No one ever asked my mother about her husband. No one ever asked her because everyone already knew the answer: Gemma didn't have a husband. She was famous for not having a husband but still having a child, for being out in the world with her child and her shame, and not caring. My heart pounded so loudly I was sure everyone around me could hear it. The voices of the guests dimmed, it seemed to me, conversation lulled by Holly's audacious inquiry. Further down the table, Sarah piled salad on her plate, passed the bowl to her neighbour, laughed at something someone said. Not a single person seemed to understand the import of the question Holly had just posed, as casually as if she'd been asking Gemma to pass the water. *Is your husband here?* As though to have a husband was the most normal thing in the world.

Gemma sipped from the glass Chris had passed her. White wine, ice cold. Her favourite. She touched her necklace, a silver fish on a chain, and looked at Holly. 'I don't have a husband.'

Holly laughed. 'Good for you! Who needs one anyway?' She blew a kiss at Brad. 'Sorry, sweetie!' She winked at Gemma, and my mother smiled at her and, as though by magic, the din picked up again and everything was restored.

Gemma accepted a plate from Beth. Judith passed down a knife and fork wrapped in a star-spangled napkin. Gemma spread the serviette on her lap. Chris stood and made his way to the record player, and put another record on the turntable. The Rolling Stones. I loved the thump of sound, the energy and Mick Jagger's voice. Further down the table, Sarah smiled at Gemma, raised a glass. Gemma winked at her mother. I relaxed into my seat.

✧✧✧

Later, as night bruised the sky and the conversations had slowed to clusters of drawled murmurs, I lay on my back on the checked rug, Daniel beside me. Our shoulders touched companionably, his T-shirt sleeve soft against my bare arm. His mother had left and taken his sisters with her. Daniel and Stevie had to be home in twenty minutes and Sarah had promised to deliver them to their door. I tugged at my too-tight shorts. Tiredness congregated along my limbs, lay heavy on my eyelids. It was a struggle to stay awake.

From near the apple tree, someone asked what time it was. Late, was the answer. Gotta love these Irish nights, right? And the reply was murmured too softly for me to hear, but it elicited laughter and the clinking of glasses. Beth lit the candles in the jars and they flickered in the darkening garden. Judith cleared away the plates. Chris refilled glasses, ignoring protests from the adults that they'd had enough. I propped myself up on my elbows, glanced around for my mother. The garden, our garden, so unfamiliar now in the inky light. The white line of tables pushed together to create the illusion of one long buffet, the chairs occupied by people I'd never met before, the tiny candles in jam jars. It was as if I had been dropped into someone else's home, someone else's life for the night. Over by the French doors, balanced on a stool, sat the record player, more muted now than earlier, but still loud enough to be heard. Bob Dylan whined about being tangled up in blue, his mouth organ sawing through the night. Unseen, a blackbird called out its final song of the day. From a few houses down, another answered its call.

Beth and Stevie sat behind us. For the first time ever, Stevie wasn't picking on Daniel or trying to annoy me. Beth laughed out loud at almost everything he said, and even I knew that she had to be faking it because little that Stevie had to say was interesting, let alone funny. Beth shook her hair around a lot as she laughed, letting it settle down her back each time, before doing it again. No matter what way she flicked it, it always came to rest in obedient sheets. Mine never did that. It did little, in fact, and until Beth entered my life, I hadn't given it any thought. But now I was beginning to understand the power of hair. I'd seen it with my mother and now with Beth. Other people noticed. A swing of a female head garnered more attention and a quicker response than almost anything.

My ponytail had unravelled during the party. Not breaking her conversation with Brad, Gemma had gathered my hair in her hands, combed her fingers through its length and braided it, snapping on an elastic around the ends, then dropped a distracted kiss on my head and sent me on my way. Gemma had been kept busy since her late arrival. She sipped from her wine glass, ate the new food with a confidence I hadn't felt, engaged in conversations. Brad offered her a top-up every time she drank, it seemed. Chris had hovered at the edges, joining in momentarily in the exchanges. Judith had many jobs for him to do and any time he looked settled, she called him and asked him to see to someone's glass, put more meat on the barbecue, fetch a plate from inside. I observed Judith in quiet moments, but she didn't look sad and wasn't drinking wine by the bottle. Maybe she was saving that for later.

A match zipped along the side of a box, a small blue flame spurted, a cigarette was lit. Shaking the match, Holly offered Gemma the cigarette box. Gemma shook her head. No thanks, I never smoke. Holly's eyebrows arched in surprise. Really? Yes, really. The tip of the cigarette was a firefly in the darkness. I followed its movements. Beside me, Daniel was asleep. Stevie and Beth were still talking.

'Do you want a cigarette?' Beth offered him.

'Definitely!' came the reply.

Beth got up, sauntered over to the table, removed a cigarette from a box and palmed a plastic lighter someone had left there. 'Come on,' she said, and Stevie followed her. I got up off the blanket and went too. At the bottom of the garden we gathered, Beth hunched over the task of lighting up. The apple tree cast its tentacled shadow over us. The wall behind us was warm when I touched it.

Stevie glared at me in the glow of the lighter flame. 'What are you doing here?'

Beth sucked at the cigarette, then coughed.

I knew Stevie too well to let him push me around. 'I live here.'

'Go back to your boyfriend.'

'He isn't my boyfriend, and anyway, he's asleep.' I pointed at Daniel on the rug.

At the top of the garden I heard Sarah call Stevie and Daniel. *Boys, time to go home. Come on now.*

'Off you go,' I said to Stevie. 'Bedtime.'

'Fuck off, Megan.' He took the proffered cigarette, dragged on it and coughed louder than Beth.

'Hey,' Beth said. 'Watch your language.'

Sarah called the boys again.

'I have to go,' Stevie said, still coughing.

'Oh come on, stay a little while longer.'

Stevie wanted to, I could tell, but he also didn't want his mother calling him from their garden, embarrassing him.

One more drag on the stolen cigarette and Stevie turned to go. 'See you soon.'

'Night night, Stevie,' said Beth.

Stevie pulled at a branch on the tree, then let it spring back with a snapping sound. The unripe apples were small hard spheres, too green and bitter to eat. In the warm night air, their scent was sharp, undiminished by the cigarette smoke.

Stevie sloped over to Daniel, shook him roughly by the shoulder. Eventually they both disappeared.

'If we stand around like this, can we call it night swimming?' I asked Beth after a moment's silence, while she impressively pulled

on the cigarette. She offered it to me, lit end first. I declined. Gemma
didn't smoke and neither would I.

'No, too many people about.'

'But it's night time.'

Beth shook her head again. 'Night swimming is done in secret.
You can't do it if anyone's around. It has to be when everyone else
is asleep.'

'What if your mother sees you smoking?'

Scorn dripped from Beth's features. 'My mother! She hasn't a
clue. And besides, what can she do to stop me?'

Many things, I would have thought. No pocket money, no
sweets, no going out. Lists of punishments would be prepared for
me should the temptation to smoke ever arise.

'Hey, so …' Beth spoke around a mouthful of smoke, 'what do
you think of Stevie?'

'He's a pain in the neck.'

Laughter, muffled by a coughing fit. Beth considered the cigarette in her hand, then stubbed it out against the apple tree. Tiny
sparks jumped. 'No, he's cool. I like him.'

'I don't.'

'He could be your brother, you know that?'

'What? Stevie? How?'

A languid shrug, which I was beginning to know well. 'Just.'

'Just what?'

'My mom said that you have the same hair, and she's right.'

I tugged my plait over my shoulder. 'This is nothing like Stevie's
hair.' Mine was long, thick. Stevie's was lighter in colour, summer-
streaked, almost girlish. Daniel wore his hair quite long too, but his
curled at his neck. It was much nicer.

'But look at the colour. You could be twins!'

I didn't reply. It was late. I was tired and arguing never left me
feeling anything but hollowed out inside. Besides, my father was

Bolivian. One day I would go there and find the place where they'd buried him.

Beth leaned against the wall, one foot behind her. 'I'm too hot.' She spread her arms out, splayed her fingers against the dark bricks. She pulled away and turned to look at the wall. 'What's this?'

There was a door in the wall, old, unused. Sarah had planted a clematis beside it and now it obscured the green painted wood. All the gardens had doors to the lane, from when the houses were built, during the time Queen Victoria was on the throne, so deliveries could be made from the dairy, the mill, the slaughterhouse. Now, most of the doors were unused. Ours was locked. It was hardly ever opened. The only person who needed the lane was the man who ran the piggery. People sometimes left waste food outside their lane doors for the pigs. When Gemma was a child, they called him the Skinsman because of the amount of potato peelings he gathered for the pigs.

'Can we open it?' Beth pushed against the door. The old wood creaked.

'Stop it! Sarah will hear.'

Beth pushed again. 'No, she won't. She's too busy.' She slammed the palms of her hand flat against the green paint. 'We need to open this door.'

'Why?'

She faced me. 'Megan, I swear, sometimes you really are the most unimaginative person I've ever met. This door could be life changing. We could use it to come and go at night, and never worry again about waking anyone up.' She knocked on my head with her knuckles. 'Earth to Megan. Night swimming.'

I had an idea where this was leading. 'No.'

'What do you mean, *no*? There is no *no*. There's only possibility.'

Beth moved too fast for me. I no longer felt safe, even from myself, my traitorous self that wanted to follow her, that wanted to swim at night, to explore beyond the confines of my own life. But too much change scared me. Everything was charging ahead too quickly and I needed time to adjust.

Beth turned abruptly away from the door. 'Anyway, I'm going to change the music. Coming?'

She walked back towards the party without waiting for a response. I followed her. Her hair swayed like a white veil in front of me, platinum in the darkness.

☼☼☼

Back in the dying embers of the party, Sarah and Holly scraped leftovers into a plastic bag and stacked the plates in piles to be carried inside. The contents of glasses were thrown into the shrubs. Conversation, punctuated by the clatter of silverware being gathered, was quieter now, a contented murmur under cover of darkness.

One by one, the visitors got up to leave, patting their shirt pockets for glasses, checking around them for handbags and cardigans, cigarette boxes and silver lighters, discarded shoes. Goodbyes were exchanged, along with promises to meet up soon. Gemma was nowhere to be seen, at first, and Sarah called my name before I saw my mother over by the record player, flicking through the stack of records piled to the side. Beth busied herself slipping discs out of their paper sleeves.

Sarah held her hand out to me. 'Come on, Megan, it's far too late. We'll go upstairs now.'

'Are you coming?' I asked my mother. Even though it was late, she looked lovely, her dress gathered at her knees, her face bright and happy. She held an album in her hand. Carole King.

'I'll follow you on up.'

'Can I do anything else?' Sarah called to Judith, who was just inside the French doors.

'No, thank you,' Judith said, walking towards us, wiping her forehead with the back of her wrist. A tea towel was draped, waiter-like, on her left arm. 'My, it's warm.' She laughed. 'I hadn't expected to hear myself saying that quite so much here.'

I thanked Judith for the party.

She touched my face with fingers soapy from dishwashing. 'Oh, you're welcome, sweetie. I hope it wasn't too boring for you, with all those adults.'

I allowed Sarah to steer me up the green steps, her hands light on my shoulders. The kitchen door was wide open. The house was still hot when we went inside, a close heat that we moved through as though it were a fog. Lying on my bed shortly after, too warm even for a sheet, I tried to stay awake, to run through all the new things from the evening. An oblong of moonlight, almost too bright not to be sunshine, illuminated the floorboards. I thought I heard Beth outside in the garden, but maybe it was just a record playing.

10

Thirst woke me, but it was the laughter that I heard. Soft, muffled, it travelled the silence of the night. At first, I thought it was one of the attic ghosts, but then I heard it again and it seemed to come from downstairs. There was a voice behind it. A man's voice.

I rolled out of bed. My feet touched the wooden floorboards without a sound. The door creaked when I pushed it open and I stopped for a moment, ever mindful of waking Gemma or Sarah. Nothing stirred.

I stood on the carpet outside my bedroom, placed my hands on the banisters and looked down. The long staircase ran like vertebrae up through the house. On the first return was the bathroom, on the second my bedroom and Sarah's, then up six steps to Gemma's room, then on up to the attic. The stairs were cobwebbed with shadow, light from the street thrown in fractured splinters through the fanlight above the hall door. In the kitchen, as I reached for a glass, I heard the laughter again, closer now. A woman's laugh this time.

The kitchen door was open. Outside, the fleeting darkness was complete, an ebony sheet resting over the gardens. Sarah's night-scented stocks breathed their fragrance into the empty air. Tiny lights flickered at intervals around the garden below me. Beth's candles in jars. Again, the laughter, stifled. A low murmur of conversation.

My eyes adjusted to the lack of light. At the foot of the wooden steps, two forms were visible. A white dress, a curtain of dark hair. My mother. Gemma and someone else. I squinted, trying to bring a face to the unfamiliar outline. Then it spoke. I knew those soft, drawling vowels, those elongated syllables. By now, the slow drag and pull of how Chris spoke wasn't so new to me any more. The first time I'd heard him, it was difficult to understand exactly what he was saying, but soon his accent had ceased to mystify me. Southern, was how Sarah described it. A Southern boy. Only Chris wasn't a boy at all. He was forty-five, Beth had confided. Forty-five. Such an age was almost incomprehensible to me. Beth had then whispered that Judith was five years older. That made her fifty. What an age. She didn't like anyone knowing her age, was ashamed of being older than her husband. That's just silly, Sarah said when I told her. Age is no one's business but your own.

Liquid glugged. Glass chimed. They laughed, clinked their glasses, swallowed. I crouched behind the largest of Sarah's pots. A huge rosemary plant obscured me, blunting the other scents of night. The sky was clear, with only a glitter of stars shaken across its vastness. A quarter moon hung at an odd angle. The heat of day had receded, but a warmth lingered, even outside.

'You want some water?'

'I'd love some.'

'Ice?'

'God, yes!'

Chris disappeared, only to materialise again in seconds, a jug of water in his hand. Ice jangled as he poured some for Gemma, then sat down beside her on the step.

'So, you're okay with living here? You know, with your mama and all that?'

Gemma turned away from him. 'Sure. Why wouldn't I be?'

Chris shrugged. 'I couldn't wait to get away from mine. Soon as I was finished high school, I was gone.'

An edge crept into Gemma's voice. 'I have a child. It's not about upping and leaving. I can't do that.'

'Hey, I wasn't saying that. Your mama seems like someone I wouldn't mind being around. She's sweet.'

Gemma gazed down the garden. 'Believe me, I couldn't be without her. Not with Megan. I wouldn't be able to do it on my own.'

'That hard, huh?'

'Harder than you'll ever know.' Gemma ran her free hand through her hair. 'The great moral majority have had me tried many times over.' She sipped again from her glass. 'The indignation of the righteous.' She laughed, but it wasn't a proper laugh. It was more of a shout and it managed to be sad at the same time.

Chris said something, but his voice was too low and I couldn't catch it. Gemma shook her head. 'I wouldn't change any of it. Not really.'

My foot was starting to fall asleep. Pins and needles threatened. I eased myself into a seated position. I was getting bored. Night swimming wasn't as enthralling as Beth had made it sound. I'd imagined adventure, a chance to move beyond the everyday and sample the forbidden. But this – my mother sitting at the foot of the steps, with Beth's father beside her, the night so inky it made everything near-invisible – was barely interesting.

I wondered where Judith was. Was she sleeping? Did she not hear my mother and Chris, did their softened voices not reach her where she lay indoors?

Gemma leaned her elbows on the step behind her, let her head fall back as she looked at the indigo sky. 'I can't believe how warm it still is.'

'I know, right? It almost reminds me of home.'

'I haven't slept well in weeks, ever since this heatwave began.'

Chris scrabbled in the jug of water and extracted an ice cube. Without asking my mother's permission, he slid the slippery frozen cube the length of her arm. Gemma's intake of breath was sharp, and she started. But she said nothing and, after a pause, Chris did it again. Gemma kept her eyes on the sky; did not once look at Chris until the ice was melted and only tracks of water glistened on her skin.

The rosemary was making me feel sick. My bed suddenly seemed like the best place to be. The kitchen was a few feet away. Would I make it without being rumbled?

Gemma stood up. Her dress settled in ghostly folds around her legs. 'It's late. I need to go.'

Chris didn't rise. 'Stay.'

'I can't.'

'Stay.'

'Really. I should go.'

I knew Gemma. She didn't sound in the least bit anxious to leave.

'Come on. A few more minutes.' He laughed. 'I can't finish this on my own.' He held up the wine bottle.

Gemma hesitated. She glanced up the steps at the house. I prayed that she wouldn't see me. She shrugged, a fluid motion I knew so well, and sat back down. 'All right, five more minutes. But only five, okay? I have to get up early.' She said nothing about the ice cube and Chris had left the jug on the ground, out of arm's reach.

'Scout's honour.'

Chris held up his fingers in some three-fingered salute I had never seen before. He tipped the remains of the wine into my mother's glass. I seized the opportunity and escaped back into the house. The heat that seemed to hide in the walls of the house, in the floorboards, eased itself into the empty darkness. It followed me up to my room, which seemed hotter than it had been when I woke up. Without thinking of the night swimmers below me, I shoved the sash window up. It creaked in resistance, then groaned as it rose. Outside, all was suddenly silent once more.

11

The following day, I helped Sarah pick raspberries. The canes lined the wall at the end of the garden and stood in rows, bowed under their burden of fruit. My campero kept the sun off my face and out of my eyes. Thankfully, Beth was nowhere to be seen. No way did I want her to see me wearing such a horrible thing.

Sarah's radio was wedged in its habitual place, the fork in the apple tree. Black streaks marked the bough. Beth's cigarette, stubbed out in a hurry the night before. Men's voices sombrely discussed a loyalist paramilitary attack over the weekend. An ambush on a deserted country road. Three o'clock in the morning. A family man, father of six, shot twice in the head. Execution style, the presenter said. The loyalists were making a point. What point, I wondered? Once Belfast or any part of Northern Ireland was mentioned on the news, Sarah usually reached for the switch. She didn't like me listening to reports about violence. The same happened with the riots in Soweto, the killings in Cambodia. The merest reference to any unrest and the radio was switched off. My grandmother firmly believed that there was no reason for me to know anything about man's inhumanity, about what human beings were capable of doing to each other. I understood her desire to shield me, her need to protect me, but I also knew it wouldn't work. No matter how quickly she drew my attention to something else, or distracted me by pointing out the window, it was impossible. I knew about the war in Belfast. I knew about the rioting in South Africa, about Pol Pot. It was impossible to hide that summer. There was violence everywhere and the news leaked into our lives. Not even the heat could mask it. Headlines screamed at me from the newspapers, radio bulletins on the hour every hour delivered the latest atrocities. Because I wasn't meant to hear any of it, I heard it all.

Sarah wanted to protect me. That's why we didn't have a television. Sarah said television made people stupid, stopped them thinking for themselves, but I knew she wanted to keep the world's sadness out of our home. If I was exposed to all the wrong in the world, it meant that Sarah, my grandmother, was unable to do her job. Stop worrying, I wanted to tell her. Don't fret. But I couldn't find the words to tell her, and I hardly understood her concern myself.

At that moment, Sarah was too preoccupied by the garden to pay much attention to political uprising. I dropped berries into a basket at my feet. The wasps were going crazy, crawling over the raspberry canes, diving into my basket. Sarah swatted at them with a rolled up newspaper, but it was a pointless battle. The wasps were too determined and there were too many of them. I just hoped we wouldn't be stung.

Paramilitary activities were still loud on the airwaves when suddenly Sarah heard what was being discussed and nearly twisted her ankle trying to reach the radio. Before she could turn it off, the discussion ended. A thin stream of music rose into the quiet garden. Opera. Sarah loved opera. I hated it, all those awful songs that went on forever, and everyone dying at the end. The high voices carried an echo of sadness into the stillness of the summer heat. Berries kept piling up in the basket. Sweat gathered under my ridiculous hat, making my head itch. I craved a drink of water.

At the end of the garden, the door to the lane was almost invisible behind the clematis. Beth was right. It threw up endless possibilities. A chasm was opening inside me, the urge to move on and explore doing battle with staying safe, quiet, out of trouble. I needed to keep Sarah and Gemma from worrying about me, and the only way to do that was to behave. I suspected that they had enough to worry about.

Judith materialised as Sarah and I were finishing. She balanced a tray with a jug of something opaque and three glasses. 'Good morning, ladies! You look like you're in need of refreshment.'

She poured lemonade. Ice chinked. Thin slices of lemon floated on the surface. 'I hope you like this. I make it all the time back home.'

'This is delicious!' Sarah said, taking a sip. 'I don't know what I did to end up with you living downstairs, but I'm certainly glad you're here.'

She and Judith laughed.

Judith looked at me right as I yawned. 'Tired, Megan?' I covered my mouth quickly. 'It was a late night for everyone,' she added.

'A bit,' I conceded.

I told her how Daniel had fallen asleep on the blanket, omitting the part where Beth and Stevie had stolen the cigarette and smoked it, how they hadn't been night swimming because so many people had been around.

Judith said she and Beth had gone to bed after everything was cleared away. 'Chris stayed up a bit. He does that a lot at home.' She shook her head. 'A throwback to childhood. I just want to go to bed, but he insists he sleeps better if he sits outside a while on hot nights.' I liked her accent. Its cadences were different to Chris's, less drawled. New Mexico. I needed to find it on the map. Land of green chillies and Tabasco and marinating meat.

I leaned my back against the apple tree. The sky blistered with heat, cloudless and a blue so pale it was almost white. The grass underfoot was yellow. I felt sorry for it, so faded and tired-looking. I wanted to drench it with the hose, just once, though I knew Sarah would refuse. Not for any reason could we waste water. But Gemma was on my side; she said we could do it next time Sarah went out, as this withholding wasn't fair on the grass.

Judith told us that it was almost bright before Chris got to bed.

'He needs so little sleep, just four or five hours and he's set. Not like me!'

'And what does he get up to? There's nothing to do, surely?' Sarah was a firm believer in early nights and equally early mornings. No time to waste lounging around in bed.

Judith shrugged one shoulder. 'Who knows? Nothing, I'm sure. Probably work, preparing lectures, that sort of thing. He says it frees up his daytime hours.' She said it as though all men sat around their gardens at night, as though all men spent hours night swimming alone while their families slept.

Except Chris hadn't been alone the previous night. He hadn't been sitting, planning his summer lectures and thinking about work. Chris had been pouring wine into my mother's glass. Chris had been drawing her out of herself, asking her questions no one ever asked, persuading her to stay a little longer, to elongate the time they had without their attention being claimed by their families.

'Gemma seemed to enjoy herself,' Judith said. She wiped drops off her glass, rubbed her fingers on her apron.

'She had a great time,' Sarah nodded. 'It was good for her to get out. Away from the painting!' She said that as though it were a joke, as though Gemma deliberately avoided social contact in order to keep painting. If Sarah had her way, Gemma would go out a lot more, meet more people. Meet a husband.

'I think Brad was quite taken with her.'

'Which one was Brad?'

I remembered Brad. The bearded man whose expression had changed ever so slightly when I said Gemma was my mother.

'He's quite the ladies' man!' Judith laughed. 'I don't know how Holly puts up with him.'

Sarah's humour seemed to fade a little. 'Well, he should just behave himself. There's no excuse for that sort of carry-on.'

Judith refilled our glasses. 'Oh, you know these academics.'

Sarah watched her closely. 'No, I don't, actually. Know what?'

Judith rattled the ice in her glass. 'They're not like other men, the ones who go to work in a suit and spend their days in an office. They're …' She searched for a word. 'Freer. They're freer than most. All that time spent in their own heads.' She laughed again. 'It gives them notions.'

Sarah placed her empty glass on the tray. 'Well, I know what I'd give them if they tried any of their notions on me.'

Judith put her hand on Sarah's arm. 'They wouldn't dare.' And they both laughed, my grandmother and this American woman. They laughed and then they laughed some more.

Sarah wiped her eyes. 'Bloody right they wouldn't,' she said. 'They wouldn't get far with me.'

I thought about Brad being taken with Gemma, but I knew Judith wasn't being quite honest. It wasn't Brad who had watched her, or refilled her glass, played the music she liked. It had been Chris. Chris had made sure Gemma had enough to eat, had moved into the seat near her, had asked her what records he should put on the turntable. Judith had found countless ways to distract her husband, and it wasn't because Brad Zimmer, with his beard and his wife, Holly, was entranced by my mother. Judith didn't want Chris near Gemma, but she could never say that because it was only a hunch. The same way I had a hunch.

Something wasn't quite right.

12

My mother was sitting at her dressing table, trying on lipstick. The late morning light worked its way through the half-open shutters, burnishing the bedroom, illuminating Gemma's skin. Gemma was beautiful in a way that didn't need enhancing with cosmetics. Her face just worked. She smacked her lips together, blotted them on a tissue and then applied more. Some sort of dark red, it made her mouth look huge, bruised. She lifted her brush and dragged it through her dark mass of hair over and over. On the little table beside her bed, the radio played. The DJ announced three in a row by John Lennon. Gemma and I loved John Lennon. His songs moved me in a way that I couldn't explain at the time. My mother was a real fan, even when he was shouting about his mother and I found it difficult to understand him.

'You won't ever scream like that about me, will you?'

Gemma had cupped my cheek when she asked me that one day, while she painted and I sat on the overstuffed armchair, reading. Not fully comprehending her question, I had shaken my head. Why would I scream about her? She had then lifted the needle on the record player and let it drop softly onto another, happier song. Sometimes music made me sad and my mother knew this and anticipated it.

This wasn't like Gemma, examining her face. Painting was her thing, what consumed her fully. Gemma was happiest when she was in her attic, working on her pictures. She also loved reading, and her books dotted the house. Here in her room she had piles of books, most of them creased and thumbed to fragility. She read novels, usually in translation from Russian or Spanish – dark, heavy stories of oppression and denial. She loved poetry too, and kept volumes on the small table beside her bed. Poetry helped Gemma sleep at night.

Lorca, Bécquer, Borges. Clara Janés, when only a woman's poems would suffice. Bishop, Plath. Yeats, when she needed something Irish to think about, and some Heaney and Kavanagh when Yeats was too much. Gemma read in cycles, phases. Inexplicable to all but us. Poetry informed my mother's art, she told me once. All art is related, part of one big movement of the soul. It didn't matter how you expressed your art. You could be a painter, a writer, a photographer, a sculptor. You could write poetry or music. You could see the world in a hundred different ways, and create something out of a piece of stone or nothing more tangible than your thought. There was no right or wrong, Gemma said. Everything was relative. The only real truth in the world was art.

My mother had changed out of her painting shirt. The top she wore was pale green with narrow straps over her shoulders. Her skin was turning brown. She wore a skirt she'd made a couple of months before, all bright colours bleeding into each other. It looked like all her paint tubes had exploded on the material. It was long and diaphanous, and trailed on the air when she moved.

She caught me watching her. Turning to me, she smiled, held out her hand. 'What's going on?'

I squashed in beside her on the rectangular seat. 'Nothing.' I touched a blue glass bottle. 'What's this?'

Gemma picked it up, removed the glass stopper. 'Perfume.'

'Is it new?'

She shook her head. 'No. I've had it for ages but I don't wear it. I prefer the other one.'

Somehow, I doubted she was telling me the truth. I had definitely never seen the blue glass bottle before. 'Can I have some?'

She tipped it against her fingers, dabbed them to my neck. The scent was new, different to the fragrance she habitually wore. It smelled of midnight, of whispery taffeta, of navy velvet. I imagined a man in a dark suit, elbow crooked, his arm offered to a woman.

'I prefer the other one.'

'The green tea? So do I. This is just for a change.'

But I don't want you to change, I thought. I like the way you smell, even when you don't wear perfume. I like you without red lips and I like you in your painting shirts.

'Are you going out?'

'No.' My mother picked up a mascara wand and began to blacken her eyelashes.

'Why are you doing this, then?'

She kept her eyes on her reflection as she blinked her lashes against the sticky black wand. 'I'm not doing anything, Megan. It's just nice to look nice sometimes.'

'You always look nice.'

Her laugh was unexpected. She nudged me.

'What?' I asked.

She shook her head again, screwed the lid back on the mascara again. 'Nothing. You're just funny, that's all.' She put her arm around me, dropped a kiss on my forehead. 'Don't change, Megan, do you hear me? Make sure you're always this sweet.'

I rested my head on my mother's shoulder, trailed my fingers over the tanned skin on her arms. 'Do you like Beth?'

Gemma picked up her brush again and ran it through her hair. Her nails were a dark red, the polish shiny and new. 'She seems nice. A bit sulky, I think.' She divided her hair in three and rapidly plaited the strands together. Her fingers worked the sections into a braid, snapped an elastic around the ends and flicked it over her shoulder. I lifted it and let it fall. My mother's hair entranced me.

I twisted the lid off a bottle of cleanser, poured some of it into my palm. 'What about Judith?'

Gemma made a face in the mirror. 'I don't know. She seems nice.'

'Beth says that sometimes she drinks a bottle of wine by herself.'

My mother laughed. 'Good for her!'

'Judith is fifty.' I liked having information to pass on to Gemma. It made me feel important, her equal.

'Fifty? No way!'

We were both laughing now. 'Beth told me.'

'Well, well, well. She doesn't look it.'

'And Chris?'

I busied myself with a tissue, wiped my hands clean of lotion. I knew that if I looked my mother in the eye as I asked her that, she'd know I had seen her night swimming with Chris. She would know I had observed how he was when she was around: quiet, watchful, a jungle animal ready to pounce. I wanted her to know that I had seen them night swimming, but I couldn't ever say it, so I thought that maybe if I hinted at what I knew, Gemma would understand.

A pause, a slight intake of breath. Then her voice, as normal. 'He seems nice.'

'He's nice to you.'

Gemma occupied herself with putting her small collection of cosmetics back in the zipped pouch she kept them in. 'Do you think so?'

I shrugged. 'I suppose.' He *was* nice to her. Even Gemma had to see that. 'Will you do my nails?'

Gemma held her hands out in front of her, fingers splayed. 'Maybe later.'

'No, do them now.'

I fanned my hands on the dressing table. My mother painted the varnish on in short, careful strokes. When she was finished, she screwed the lid back on and put it away. She returned the perfume bottle to the dresser drawer. Perfume should always be stored in a dark, cool place, she told me once. That way, it lasts.

'Let me see,' she said. I held my hands up for her to inspect. 'Perfect. Now let me do your hair and then you can go back downstairs. I have to finish something this afternoon.'

Gemma gathered my hair into a bun and stuck hairpins in it to keep it from falling out. The pins dug into my scalp, but I didn't want to hurt Gemma's feelings, so I said nothing. She turned me around to face her when she was finished.

'Lovely,' she declared.

I smiled.

Gemma stroked her thumbs across my cheeks. Our faces were so close that I could see the tiny amber flecks that stippled her green irises. Our identical eyes. 'They wanted me to give you away, you know that. But I didn't tell you that they said that, if I kept you, I should pretend that you were my sister, that Sarah was your real mother.' She shook her head. 'As though that would've worked, with my father dead.'

They were the nurses at the hospital where I was born, the woman from social services who visited us in the days after Gemma and I came home, the priest whom Gemma told to leave the house and never return. And probably others. People had a lot of opinions in those days, especially when it came to mothers without husbands.

'Why?'

Gemma stood and moved to the window. She pushed the sash until it opened. Warm air made the voile flutter. She sat on the sill, her arms folded. 'I don't know. To make it all seem acceptable, I suppose.' All the fun and lightness had left her, as though only minutes before we hadn't been painting our nails or putting on perfume. I didn't know how to put her mood right again. So I didn't try. I just listened to her. 'It didn't seem to matter how *I* felt about anything, or how you would be affected. It was all about making it all right for everyone else. Keeping the shame away. That sort of thing. They didn't even know me, but already they were planning out my life for me.' She bit her lower lip and shivered, as though it were winter. Then she waved her hand, stood up. 'Sorry, Megan. I don't know why I said any of that. It's not important any more.'

I didn't move from my position on the rectangular seat. I hated that my birth had made my mother's life so difficult, my grandmother's life so difficult. It wasn't my fault, I was often told, but always, over everything, there was this pervasive sense that somehow I was to blame for it all.

Sarah would have gone mad if she'd known that Gemma was talking to me like this. There was no point in rehashing everything, she liked to say. No point in dragging the past around with us. Let it go. Move on. Be in the present and look to the future. That's what Sarah did, and it worked. She didn't get angry or upset if people asked about Gemma and me, didn't worry about what others thought.

But Gemma did allow others to get to her, spent too much time locked away in her attic. Brooding, Sarah called it. Nothing good came of brooding. It was the same with the news. We didn't need to hear about Northern Ireland. We didn't need to hear about apartheid. Anything that diminished our lives in any way was not welcome. Hence, we didn't go to church. It was out there, all around me, around all of us, but here in this house life was for living and for being happy.

My mother moved towards me. She put her arms around me, laid her cheek against the top of my head. 'My little angel,' she whispered into my hair. 'You're my sweetest angel.' And I knew that, whatever had gone before, whatever decisions my mother did or didn't make, keeping me had been the right thing to do, for both of us. I tightened my arms around her, breathed in her scent. Green tea, coriander, lavender soap. Her new perfume an extra layer, different, unknowable. Her hair tickled my face. Outside, the heat continued unabated.

On the wall behind us, Gemma had framed a quote from Jorge Luis Borges, the writer she so admired. *So plant your own gardens and decorate your own soul, instead of waiting for someone to bring you flowers*. Gemma had written the words in black ink and painted over them in washed-out watercolours. It was difficult to fully understand what Borges meant, but Gemma said he was a genius and I accepted that. She was right about most things.

I'm sure that Felipe had admired Borges too, possibly had even introduced my mother to his work.

Gemma was doing just fine when it came to planting her own garden.

13

My knees were sore from kneeling but there wasn't enough room to stand up or stretch. Daniel fiddled with the lid on the huge Mason jar his mother had given him, oblivious to the cramped conditions of his hideout. Inside the jar, a ladybird tripped over a branch Daniel had dropped in earlier, along with a handful of withered grass and a blossom from the bougainvillea. The blossom curled at the edges, dark cerise with a white centre, and the ladybird ignored it. I angled my book to catch slants of light that slipped through cracks in the makeshift wall. Daniel made notes in his insect book, his neat handwriting sloping across the lines. My pencils lay in a neat row on the ground, my sketchpad open on a new page. Daniel liked me to draw pictures of his insects. He dated them, named them and stuck them in a scrapbook he kept with details of all the creatures he had captured. He said that he would write a book all about them when he was older.

We had built the hideout during the Easter holidays the previous year, after reading a book about a group of children who had one and used it as their crime-solving headquarters. Solving mysteries was something we were briefly interested in, but once our own HQ had been built, we sort of lost interest in being crime busters. Daniel's mother had let us use a corner of the end of their garden as our site, and we had collected various materials: bits of wood, some bricks, plastic and a sheet of corrugated metal that someone had abandoned in the lane behind the gardens. We dragged it through the door in the wall and wedged it in place as a roof. When it rained, the sound was like thunder right over our heads, ricocheting around the compressed darkness inside.

I hadn't been there since the previous summer, and until I'd ducked under the temporary roof, I hadn't realised how much I had grown, how much we both had. Mostly, Daniel used it to store his insect jars or to shelter injured birds. Once, a fox cub, lame and abandoned, had found its way into the garden and Daniel had carried it to the hideout, laid it on an old towel and fed it leftovers, bits of chicken, beef, bacon rinds. We never knew what became of the cub. After a week of careful minding, it disappeared. Sarah said it had got strong enough to leave, but Stevie had sneered and said dogs had got it in the night. Sarah had said not to pay any attention to Stevie, so we didn't.

That day the air inside the hideout stagnated, heavy with dust. Spiders' webs made our hands sticky, and the dry ground was as hard as cement. I shifted, pins and needles beginning to numb my legs. Dusty earth stuck to my skin and I brushed it off.

'Careful!' Daniel put his hand out. 'No sudden movements.'

'It's only a ladybird,' I admonished. 'She doesn't care what we do.'

'Ladybirds are very sensitive.' He stroked the outside of the jar with his finger.

We lapsed into our own activities. Pages flicked. Pencils rasped.

Eventually Daniel broke the silence. 'Stevie went out last night. After we were all in bed. I heard him.'

This caught my attention. 'Where did he go?'

'No idea. But he took his bike.'

I wondered if Beth had been with him. She was very interested in being around Stevie. She found him much more amusing and interesting than I ever had. Since the Americans' arrival, Stevie was suddenly around a lot more, visible, irritating.

'I think he was fishing.' Daniel leaned towards me, confiding. 'There was a jam jar of worms outside under the hedge. I bet he was at the canal.' He lifted the lid off the Mason jar, put his hand inside. The ladybird tumbled across his fingers. 'Mummy would go mad if she knew.'

'You have to stop calling her *Mummy*, you know that. You'll be ten at Christmas.'

Daniel sighed. 'I know. But she likes it. I don't say it in front of people.' He gestured at me. 'Except you, and you don't count. I mean, you do, but you don't mind.'

'I know.'

Daniel did everything his mother asked. I think he felt responsible for her, and in some way he felt that if he was good enough to her, she wouldn't think about his father and she wouldn't be lonely. He didn't even mind about the becoming-a-priest thing, and just smiled when she brought it up. It seemed as though he got better and better in increments, particularly if Stevie's behaviour seemed to worsen. Daniel said he was always fighting with their mother and their sisters, sneering at Daniel's insects. He had taken to slamming doors and stealing money for sweets. The only time he wasn't in bad humour was when he was playing football with his friends in the park. And lately, when Beth was around.

I let my sketchbook drop to the ground. My eyes were strained from squinting, and anyway, it was too hard to concentrate when Daniel returned to talking about the ladybird.

'They're really important in the garden, did you know that?'

I didn't know, and up to that point, I hadn't particularly cared.

'Ask Sarah. They eat aphids, which destroy plants.' He trailed a finger down the jar. The glass squeaked under his skin. 'I think I'm going to be an entomologist.'

'A what?'

'An entomologist. They study insects.' He said the word carefully, his enunciation slow under the weight of the new word.

'I thought you were going to be a pilot.'

'I am. And then I'll be an entomologist.'

'What about being a priest?'

I heard the sneer in my voice, didn't like how mean it made me sound, but I was irritated by Daniel, which was new for me. Daniel was my closest and best friend. He was part of me, like a limb. Shame prickled me. It gathered deep inside me and swelled. Daniel would never scorn me like that.

'You know I don't want to be a priest. It's what Mummy wants.' If he'd noticed the tone of my voice, he didn't let on. Instead he explained the finer details of entomology, how it was much, much more than just keeping insects in jars.

My left leg tingled and I stretched it out in front of me. It was hot in the shelter, too hot and too cramped. The fuzzy heat of the hideout and the cobwebbed darkness were more than I wanted. I didn't care about the ladybird in her jar, or about the other creatures that hid behind dried grass and broken twigs. The sounds of outside were muffled by the makeshift shelter. Traffic on the main road. The snorting of pigs. Sarah's radio. Daniel's sisters calling to each other, his mother's voice over them. A dozen or more ordinary sounds that made up the background of my everyday life, things I paid little or no heed to. Suddenly they constricted me. It was all too normal, too bereft of anything new, anything different. Up to now, I had loved the predictability of my days, especially since the heatwave had begun, but somehow things were changing and other possibilities were drawing me out. The hideout was too cramped, too hot, the sun seeming to double the temperature under the corrugated roof.

I heard Beth somewhere outside and suddenly I longed to be out in the sunshine, where I could at least breathe properly and move without fear of knocking something over. A beetle meandered over the back of my hand, its shell shiny and black. I flicked it away. It hit the corrugated roof with a ping and fell back down. It lay on its back, tiny legs bicycling crazily. Feeling sorry for the tiny creature, I set it on its feet again and watched it scurry away, trauma probably forgotten already. Insects were lucky like that. They didn't carry troubles around with them.

I crawled to the door at the side of the hideout. The murky heat inside was too much.

'Where are you going?' Daniel's voice sounded alarmed. 'I thought we'd eat in here. Mummy would make us sandwiches if I asked. And we could look at those new stickers I was telling you about.'

I brushed at the seat of my shorts. 'No thanks. I'm boiling. I'm going outside.'

'But what about the drawings?'

I turned back to him. 'What drawings?'

He gestured towards my pencils, lined up neatly. 'The insects. The ones you said you'd do. For my album.'

'I'll do them later.'

Something in his eyes, I couldn't quite read it – disappointment? Rejection? – flared briefly, then he returned his attention to his jar. A shrug of his thin shoulders. 'All right.' His pencil continued its scratching across the page of his notebook.

✿ ✿ ✿

Beth was bouncing a yellow tennis ball on a racquet in the back garden, her eyes fastened on the ball, her lips forming words. *Eighty-three, eighty-four, eighty-five.* When she saw me, she stopped. The ball rolled away and disappeared behind the green stairs. The bougainvillea was an explosion of colour, its vines wrapped firmly around the handrail, winding its way upwards. Its long life was a gardening miracle, Sarah often said. The plant was older than my mother, and almost as beautiful. Now, Beth scrabbled among its flowers, trying to locate her ball.

'How many can you do?' she said when she finally found it and placed it on the strings of her racquet.

I shrugged.

'You have to try. Here.' She handed me both, then watched as I faltered with the first attempt. 'The trick is to keep your eye on the ball. The rest will follow. Always watch the ball.'

I did as she instructed. Soon I was up to forty-three. Beth was generous with her praise, and I bloomed in the light of her encouragement. This was better than being cooped up in a ramshackle hideout with only Daniel's insects for company. Then I instantly regretted the thought.

Yet it was so different being with a girl, an older girl. I watched Beth bounce her yellow tennis ball, her shiny chrome racquet catching the sunlight. I'd never seen a metal racquet before, only wooden ones. The only racquet I had was Gemma's old one, a chipped affair with two broken strings. Beth had lots of shiny things and more clothes than I had imagined anyone could have.

'Let's go to the park,' Beth announced. 'There are tennis courts there, right?'

There were, but I had never gone without an adult. 'I don't know if I'll be allowed.'

'Sure you will. We'll just say we're going. Do you have a racquet?'

'I do, but I'm not sure where it is.'

Gemma's old racquet was finally located in a box of junk under the stairs. I dragged it out. It was heavy, the paint peeling, broken strings curling in stiff spirals.

'Yikes! It's ancient!' Beth's laughter wasn't mean, but I burned.

'I don't have anything else.'

'Whatever, it's fine. Let's just go.'

I walked from the hallway into the kitchen. Sarah was sitting at the kitchen table, peeling apples. The peel came off the big cooking apples in long green strands, like streamers. I caught one before it fell off the table onto the floor. It was bitter on my tongue, then the sweetness broke through. I reached for another one, but Sarah stopped me.

'Too much will make you sick.'

The heat in the kitchen was overwhelming. On the stove, a huge pot of loganberries simmered. I pushed the wooden spoon through the dark berry liquid. About twenty jars, all sterilised and sparkling, were lined up beside the stove. Sarah had cut out discs of waxed paper to be placed on top of the jam when it had cooled in the jars. These she would then store, or sell.

Sarah dabbed her forehead with a clean tea towel. Minuscule beads of sweat popped up on her nose. She smiled.

'I never thought I'd hear myself wish for a bit of cold weather, but I do.'

'We're going to the park,' Beth said from the doorway. She lounged against the door frame, her racquet slung over her shoulder. She reminded me of an advertisement for sportswear that I'd seen on the back page of a magazine. 'We'll be back by lunchtime.'

I was amazed by how she spoke to Sarah, as though they were equals. She presented our plans as a finished whole, not something to be interfered with or altered by a third party. No room for discussion.

'Does your mother know?' Sarah asked Beth.

Beth looked out at the garden. 'She won't mind.'

'That may be so, but you're surely not going off out without telling her, are you?'

A graceful, insolent lifting of one shoulder.

Sarah pointed at the stairs. 'Go down now and ask her if you can go. Megan can wait up here with me.'

Beth was back within a minute, a small bag in her hand. 'She says it's fine. I have to bring some water and a sandwich.'

'Good idea. I'll make you one too, Megan, that way you don't have to rush back.'

Minutes later, we descended the front steps. A wrapped sandwich and a glass bottle of water rustled in a paper bag in one hand, Gemma's ancient racquet in the other. As I listened to the slap and scrape of our rubber soles on the pavement, I thought of Daniel in the hideout, the insects in their jars and his mother inside praying for him. It was a relief to be out in the world, away from what I knew. Pollen stung my eyes and made my nose itch, the sun burned my bare arms, but our pace increased the further we got from home.

We had almost reached the park when Beth nudged me. 'I've worked out a way to open the door.' Without waiting for my reaction, she told me. Last night, after everyone was in bed, she and Stevie had managed to wiggle a wire into the lock. The door had opened without resistance. 'And get this,' Beth continued, 'this is the best bit of all.'

She paused for dramatic effect. Beth loved to drop extraordinary news.

'We found a tap in the lane. It's old and rusty, and I wouldn't drink the water from it, but it works. It works!'

She must have seen how mystified I was, how uncomprehending.

'We can fill the pool! We can fill it, Megan!'

She danced on ahead of me, miming swimming and diving. I ran to keep up with her, but she got in front of me again, still swimming, her tennis racquet and sandwich bag clutched in her hands.

14

The chestnut trees in the park were laden with cones of pale flowers. It was impossible, in the grip of heat, to imagine the fruit ripening and falling to the ground around the time when school began. It seemed as though life had become suspended, caught in the amber of the heatwave. Dictated by water usage, safe times to be outdoors, fear of overheating, the danger of dehydrating, I was beginning to chafe at the imposition of the heatwave, at how my very existence was becoming defined by it.

Beth loved it, of course. New York is like this all the time, only hotter, she enjoyed telling me. This is nothing.

She wasn't like anyone else I knew. The girls in my class were like me, caught up in their own lives, their own families. Routines were punctuated by swimming lessons, a trip into town, visits to cousins. No one took buses around the city while their parents thought they were somewhere safe. They didn't slip out at night, or smoke cigarettes with boys they had just met. They didn't address adults as though they were equals, or argue their points till the adults conceded defeat.

Beth was the first girl I had known with the power to entrance boys. Before she arrived, boys had just been boys. They were brothers, cousins, friends. They lived next door or down the road, we either played with them or we didn't. But boys weren't for impressing. They didn't exist for our amusement. Boys weren't a sport that we had to excel at. They were just people. They didn't matter more than anyone else.

Until Beth arrived. Beth, with her linen hair, her endless legs in denim shorts, her array of clothes. Beth, who made boys stop their games of football or tennis just so they could look at her.

The boys playing doubles on the court next to ours kept laughing, but it wasn't because they thought anything was funny. They just didn't know what else to do. Beth ignored them, sent ball after ball sailing from the shining chrome of her tennis racquet, over the net, past me. I stood at the baseline and waited, ran forward each time, and usually missed. She flicked her hair, pinned off her face with a shiny red clip, picked up another yellow ball and started all over again.

It didn't bother me, the fact that I wasn't as good as Beth. Tennis wasn't something I played particularly well, but I did want to get better. Maybe if I improved, Gemma could come here with me. I could impress her with all I'd learned. Before she had me, Gemma had played a lot of tennis. She'd even won competitions in school.

An ice-cream van played its music out on the road. Beth ran to it; once she reached it she called me.

'Want one?'

'No money.'

She gestured impatiently. 'I've got money. What do you want?'

Pocket money was a luxury in my childhood, something noted more for its absence than anything else. Sometimes Gemma pressed a coin in my hand, if I'd helped her tidy her paints, or stack her pictures on the shelves in the attic. Other times, Sarah dropped fifty pence in my pocket, but these were rewards for helping more than an allowance that I expected with regularity. Older girls got pocket money, older girls who shortened their skirts, tossed their hair, sucked on lollipops or coloured ice pops. Girls like Beth.

I waited on the court so we wouldn't lose it to the older girls who were waiting to play. We still had a bit of time left. On the adjoining court, the boys stopped their game of doubles. Their laughter stopped too. I scraped the wood of my racquet along the tarmac. The paint that marked the lines of the courts needed touching up and the nets all sagged in the centre. I picked up a ball and bounced it.

'Hey!' Then I heard it again. 'Hey! You with the ball!'

I glanced around. The biggest of the four boys beckoned me. He wore a red T-shirt with a faded picture of a guitar across the front. His long hair was dark and his eyes strayed over my shoulder. I stayed where I was. 'So listen, is your sister coming back?'

'She's not my sister. She's my friend.'

'Wardy's looking for her.'

'Who's he?'

One boy threw a tennis ball at the speaker's head. It struck him, then fell away to the side. They all laughed again. Their mirth was self-conscious, loud, and in it I heard them assert themselves, jostling for superiority in the eyes of the American siren. They looked about fifteen.

By the time Beth came back, the boys had started their game again. She handed me a cone, the heat already melting the pink ice cream.

'Hey, blondie! Wardy wants to go with you!'

Beth removed her hair slide, shook her hair and pinned it back again. Finishing her ice cream in a few quick mouthfuls, she picked up her shining racquet and stalked to the baseline. Without pausing, she picked up the yellow ball, threw it in the air and smashed a serve that flew by me while I licked melted ice cream off my fingers, my racquet lying on the tarmac. One of the boys whistled as Beth did it again with another ball.

'Go on, blondie!'

Beth merely smirked.

✿✿✿

When our time was up and the man in charge had called us off the court, Beth walked by the boys. One of them whistled, a long, low sound. 'Hey, blondie, next time leave your little pal at home.' He had a checked shirt with the sleeves cut off, his arms skinny and white.

Beth tugged at my T-shirt. 'Stop staring at them. Keep walking.'

But I wasn't staring at the boys. I had no interest in them. The cat and mouse games of attraction held no meaning for me. My sandwich was long since eaten, the water finished by Beth, and the heat had settled on me like a blanket I couldn't shrug off. Suddenly, I wished Daniel was with me. No one would have noticed us; there would have been no catcalls or remarks.

'Let's go home,' I said.

'I need water first.' Beth rattled her empty bottle.

We took a detour by the water fountain and refilled our bottles. Beth splashed me and I squealed, the cold drops a shock on my hot skin. We threw water at each other, free to do so without anyone warning us of water shortages.

The sun had bleached all colour from the day. A dusty haze lingered. Couples lay in patches around the park. Someone had a transistor radio and it played a song Gemma liked. *The boys are back in town,* the singer said, *the boys are back in tow-ow-ow-ow-ow-own.* The afternoon was heavy, soporific.

We were just at the park gates when a low whistle distracted us. Two of the boys from the courts were standing nearby, half hidden by the enormous chestnut trees. The one with the guitar T-shirt and another one, who wore sprayed-on jeans. His hair had been shaved off. Shaved Head had his fingers in his mouth, and he used them to whistle.

'Hey, blondie.'

I turned away, moved closer to Beth. 'Come on, ignore them.'

Beth turned to the boys. I sensed a change in the air, something mean and cruel surrounding us. I tugged her arm but she shook me off.

'Come here, blondie.' Shaved Head beckoned her with his finger.

Beth took a step towards them. The people lying on the grass were too far away from us, too absorbed by the heat and their music and each other to notice.

'Wardy wants to go with you.'

The boys' greedy, piggy eyes scared me, and they were bigger than we were, stronger.

'Beth, stop. I want to go.'

'Then go.'

I hung onto her arm but she shook me off again.

'Come on, blondie. We won't hurt you.' The boy whistled again. 'Or are you just a prick tease?'

Beth, for all her independence and self-belief, couldn't see that the boys were up to no good. She was like a mouse walking towards the claws of a cat. She went to the chestnut tree, leaned one shoulder against the ancient trunk, twirled a long strand of hair between her thumb and forefinger. I picked up her racquet from where she had dropped it on the ground. Part of me wanted to stay, another part wanted me to leave her there. I counted to ten and then twenty. I told myself that if I counted to one hundred and Beth still hadn't come back I would go and get her.

I'd got as far as fifty-four when she squealed, 'Stop!'

I ran towards my friend. The boys had pushed Beth up against the tree. Red Shirt had his hands on her stomach, her T-shirt ruched by his searching fingers. The other was trying to kiss her, his lips fat and rubbery. Beth twisted her face this way and that to get away from his seeking lips. Her hands pushed at his shoulders. 'I said stop!' The boys laughed, but they didn't stop.

Red Shirt pulled at Beth's top. 'An American, eh? Come on, baby, you know you want it. Aren't all Yankee girls gagging for it?'

'Leave me alone!'

Dropping the racquet, I shoved Shaved Head. I surprised myself with my vehemence, the fury that surged. 'Let her go!'

'Fuck off, you.' He elbowed me, his bone making contact with my ribs. I pushed him again, my hands flat against his back, and again he elbowed me. Stumbling, I lost my balance and fell.

Brandishing Beth's tennis racquet, I stood back up, stepped forward and swung wildly, with far more strength and confidence than I had felt all afternoon on the court. Metal hit bone and the boy fell back. His hands shot to his face, to his ear. His face was a still life of shock. Blood spurted from a gash I'd opened up under his cheekbone.

'You stupid fucking bitch!' he screamed. 'Look what you've done.'

Red shirt laughed. The injured boy turned on him, his hand holding his face. Menacingly, he stepped towards him. 'What the fuck is funny? What are you laughing at?' Blood seeped through his fingers and dripped onto his white T-shirt.

I dropped Beth's racquet, grabbed her arm, and we ran while the boys were distracted. Too soon, they ran after us, their footsteps gathering speed. We didn't stop. We couldn't. To stop would be the worst thing we could do. My breath burned in my lungs, blood pounded in my ears. My feet hurt from running, but we didn't slow down. When we got to the traffic lights at the big intersection, I ran straight out into the traffic. Beth screamed my name, but I didn't care, didn't stop. I couldn't. If I stopped running, I was dead. I knew that Beth had followed from the screech of brakes behind me. The blare of a horn. A man's voice, swearing at us out the car window. *Stupid bitches. You deserve to be run over.*

At the far side of the intersection, we stopped. Hands on knees, breathing over and over. We looked back; the boys were standing at the traffic lights. More cars were passing now than when I'd run out and they couldn't follow us. It didn't stop them shouting threats, though, and making obscene gestures at us.

'Beth, come on, let's go. We have to get home.'

Off we ran again. Houses, gardens, trees, all blurred past. We didn't stop till we were close to home and were certain that the boys were no longer following us.

'Not a word about this,' Beth said, when we finally ducked into the lane. We leaned against the wall, panting. 'Not a word, do you hear me?'

'Why?' I couldn't believe she didn't want to tell anyone. 'But they could have really hurt you. We should tell your parents.'

'And what, have them ground me for the rest of the summer? No way, Megan, and don't you dare think you're going to breathe a word to them. Got it?'

I wasn't a tattletale. In school, I never told the teacher about someone else's misbehaviour. But this, this was different. We could have been hurt. Killed, even. 'We have to. What if we see them again? Or if they find us?' Cautiously peering around the corner, I saw no one other than a family of three, an old lady with a shopping bag on wheels and a couple with their arms around each other.

The old Beth was reasserting herself again: the queen bee, first in the pecking order. Leaning into me, she squeezed my arm. 'I will never speak to you again if you say anything. Anything at all.'

My arm hurt under her fingers. 'But our racquets are still down at the park.'

'So? I'll send my dad down to get them when he comes home.' Beth released me, once again dismissive. 'We'll say we forgot them.'

'But what about the boys? What if they're still looking for us?'

Beth shook her head, her hair swinging. 'They're not.'

'But what if they find out where we live?'

My imagination was running riot now, seeing the boys breaking down the green garden door and finding us, smashing the locks on the house and forcing us out of our beds. I could still hear the crack of the racquet on bone, the slow-motion opening of skin and the gush of blood.

I turned away from Beth and threw up over a patch of weeds that had died in a corner of the lane. My hands on my knees kept me from falling over. Beth clicked her tongue and stalked off, leaving me there in the dusty heat, the afternoon light turning orange, the taste of vomit in my mouth making me sick again.

15

Dusk was slipping over the garden, a gradual purpling of the sky as the sun began to sink. The scent of phlox and evening primrose was heavy on the warm air. My eyes tingled with the stirrings of tiredness. Beth was teaching me how to play Scrabble. We were outside, on a blanket. The record player had been dragged out earlier by Beth, and now a Pink Floyd album circled in the fading light. Pink Floyd were new to me, their dreamy guitars swirling in the hush of the garden. My crayon rendering of the album cover had been discarded when we started playing Scrabble. It had been difficult to fill in the details with my stubby crayons, and the man with his suit on fire looked as if he was wearing an orange suit and hat. I needed better art supplies for detailed drawing. Some fine pens, something like that. Maybe I could borrow some of Gemma's when she wasn't using them. My art would never improve if I didn't have the right materials. My mother would disagree, of course, would remind me that talent isn't based on what you have in your hand, but what you have inside you. She said the same thing when I'd asked if I could get a new tennis racquet and not have to use her shameful relic that was almost too heavy to lift. Talent lies within.

I didn't agree fully with her.

Beth placed seven tiles on the board, lining them up with a z I had put in my star word, *jazz*. Pride had almost rendered me speechless as I'd laid my squares out. Pride, and a good amount of one-upmanship over Beth, who was far better than me at everything, it seemed.

Beth and I hadn't spoken a word about what happened with the boys in the park two days before. What frightened me was the possibility of what could have happened. Being pushed up against a tree and having a boy's unwanted lips on your skin, well, that was something that could be dealt with, walked away from. But it was what could have happened that scared me, the dark shadowed possibilities that looped themselves around in my head and didn't let go.

Beth's word didn't look like any word I had ever seen before. *Quetzal.* I tried to pronounce it. Beth shook her head. 'No, no, the sound is a hard *c*, as in *cat*. Quetzal.'

Her tennis serve may have been too good for me to return, and the amount of clothes she owned was more than my entire family added together had in our collective wardrobes, but I wasn't letting her get away with invented words. No way, José. 'That's a made-up word.'

'No, it's not! It's a bird.'

'Doesn't sound like any bird I've ever heard of.' Around us, robins and blackbirds rustled in bushes, perched on branches, trilled evening songs into the quiet air. Those were birds.

'Mom!'

She turned to her mother, who was reading a cookbook in a deckchair near the record player. Judith's hair glowed red in the dying light of the day. A drink of something clear sat within arm's reach. Her glass was shaped like an upside down triangle, with what looked like two olives on a cocktail stick inside. Her book was inches from her face. Sarah and Gemma never let me read in bad light. It will ruin your eyes, they always said.

Beth raised her voice. 'Mom! Tell Megan what a quetzal is.'

Judith put her book on her lap, the cover facing up. Something to do with southern cooking in the foreign kitchen, whatever that meant. 'It's a bird, Megan.'

I looked from mother to daughter, unwilling to believe them, unwilling to allow Beth to win yet another game with a word that I had never seen before.

'It's from Guatemala,' said Beth.

'It is, Megan.' Judith picked up her glass. 'It's the national bird of Guatemala, which is in Central America.' She drained the clear liquid.

'Is that water?' I asked.

Judith held the glass up. 'This? I wish! No, it's a martini.'

'What's a martini?'

'It's a cocktail.'

'Why do you put olives in it?'

Judith twirled the triangular glass on its stem. 'Because they suit the taste.'

'Can I have one?'

'An olive or a martini?'

I considered this. 'Both.'

Judith shook her head and laughed. 'Sorry, honey. No can do on the alcohol front. But an olive you can certainly have.'

Olives were another thing the Americans loved. They could be green or black, and sometimes they had orange things stuffed inside them. On second thoughts, I didn't really want one. They looked a bit strange. 'No thanks.'

'Anyway, the quetzal is Guatemalan. I'm sure we have a picture of one somewhere. I'll show it to you when I find it. Scarlet chest and shiny green wings. In New Mexico, Guatemalans often kept pictures of quetzals in their houses, to remind them of home.'

'They speak Spanish there,' Beth said.

I thought of the yellowed photographs on Gemma's wall, scissored years before from a newspaper, the line of tango dancers. I remembered a stack of photographs I'd seen once, when Gemma's trunk had been open. People marching, a banner held by many hands. *Liberación*. Mouths open in protest. Fists raised. Others of groups of men, their faces blackened from being underground. *Los mineros*. The miners, men who spent their working lives finding tin. They hadn't looked angry, not like the protesters in the previous shots. Instead, they just seemed resigned. Had Felipe taken the pictures? I imagined him, kneeling on one knee, lens aimed at his subject. His quest to take the perfect photographs and the price he paid for it. I had tried to decipher the words in the pictures, but it was impossible. Gemma had gently taken the photos from my curious hands, had closed the trunk. And I, wary of the ghosts, had not pursued the matter further. 'And in Bolivia.'

'Exactly,' said Judith. 'Clever girl.'

'I'm clever too.' Beth's voice, darkened with sudden sulkiness. 'She'd never even heard of a quetzal.'

Judith bent over and kissed the top of her daughter's head. Beth squirmed away, thunder in the set of her mouth and her furrowed brow.

Sarah appeared on the deck, watering can in hand. 'Beth, you'll have to turn that down. It's too late for music now.' Sarah's face was shadowed by the deepening twilight. Her silver hair, cropped close to her head, glowed white. She smiled when she saw Judith. 'I didn't see you there.'

'The music is my fault.' Judith went over and turned the volume down so low that I could hardly hear the swirling guitars any more.

Sarah made a dismissive gesture with her hand. 'Don't worry about it. I just don't want anyone complaining that we're keeping them awake.' She poured water over the parched pots on the deck. For a moment, the only sound was the sudden rush of overflowing water seeping through the wooden boards before hitting the ground below. 'Ten more minutes, Megan, do you hear me? It's bed time.'

Beth nudged me. 'Want to go night swimming?'

'What, now?'

She rolled her eyes. 'Not now, silly. Later. When everyone's asleep.'

Daniel's voice floated on the quiet air, calling to his sister. I hadn't seen him since I'd left him with his jars in the hideout.

'Can we bring Daniel?' I knew he wouldn't come, would not want to disobey his mother, but I didn't want to leave him out. Guilt nibbled at me.

'I don't mind, but he has to bring Stevie.'

I didn't pursue it further. Beth's interest in Stevie was inexplicable.

Judith moved beyond the French doors, her shape silhouetted against the gauze of the voile curtains. A lamp flickered inside. A moth flung itself against the glass of the door.

'Where's your dad?'

Beth shrugged. Her hair swayed, the colour of raw silk in the shadowy dusk. 'Out. He's always got something on. Or so he says.'

'What do you mean?'

Beth bit the nail of her index finger. 'He likes to be out. Faculty dinners, drinks parties. That sort of thing.' She swept the Scrabble tiles into a pile. 'It makes him feel important. He's teaching some summer class, even though he doesn't really have to. He's technically free till September.'

Beth leaned towards me. Her breath was ticklish against my neck. 'My father had an affair. That's partly why we're here.'

I pulled away slightly. 'What's an affair?'

There it was again, the language of adults, the terms they used to couch their own activities, make them less displeasing to themselves and others. It didn't sound like something good, though, and I glanced again at the French doors and the shadows the lamp threw against the curtains. Judith was nowhere to be seen. The record player was gone, back indoors on the sideboard, Pink Floyd silenced.

Beth laughed, then she pulled on my ponytail. 'Oh, poor Megan. Do you not understand?'

'It's just a word,' I snapped. 'So what if I haven't heard it before? I'm not American.'

Again, that laugh, the all-knowing mocking laughter of the upper hand. 'It's nothing to do with being American. My father had an affair with one of his postgrads. It means they had sex. And then it all ended and someone found out.'

I knew about sex. Gemma had told me the previous summer and had asked me not to discuss it in school, or with Daniel. 'I don't want to be branded further,' she laughed. 'But it's better that you know about it. It takes the sting out of finding out when you're older.'

It was disgusting, of course, but it wasn't something I thought about much.

But Chris? Chris? Father, husband, professor. And now Chris, who liked my mother. My mother was fragile, hurt. She didn't need the attention of a man who had affairs with students.

Beth picked at a cut on her hand. 'My mom took it badly. She made my dad move out for a while, and then she just sat around our apartment all day, and when I was in bed she used to drink bottles of wine.' She sighed.

Sarah appeared again. The light from the kitchen behind her threw a yellow glow on her back. She had her dressing gown on, a light flowery wrap that stopped just above her ankles.

'Megan, in you come.'

I got to my feet. 'I'll see you tomorrow.'

'What about later?'

'I don't know.'

'Oh come on, Megan. Don't be a baby. It's fun.'

'I'll see,' I said and ran to where my grandmother waited.

Truth was, I didn't want to get into trouble, and I most especially didn't want to worry Sarah. Night swimming would have to wait for another time.

✿✿✿

Inside, Gemma was reading in the front room. The radio played in the corner, something soft and jazzy. She looked up when I came in, folded a bookmark between the pages and put her book aside. The fireplace, empty and swept out for summer, had a candle where firewood would be in winter. The fireplaces were in almost every room, even the bedrooms, identical black cast iron. The candle Gemma had lit was almost burnt down to a stub.

'Off to bed?' She held her arms out. I squeezed onto her lap. 'You won't be able to do this for much longer!' She smoothed my hair off my face, ran her fingers over my ponytail. Her eyes were dark green in the half light. I touched her cheek. I knew I should tell her about Chris and the student, warn her. But what words did I have then to speak adequately about revelations of such enormity?

My mother kissed my forehead, my cheeks. 'You're very serious. Is everything okay?'

I wound my fingers through her hair, rested my face against her. Her skin was cool to the touch. 'Everything's fine. I'm just a bit tired.'

Gemma rested her cheek against the top of my head. Her breath was warm, comforting.

I needed to protect my mother. Her ghosts weren't enough.

I had to be strong. And good.

My mother needed me.

16

I heard voices, just like the first time, the night of the garden party. Nights were so quiet then that the slightest disturbance to the hush, the merest trembling of the silence, travelled through the darkness and reached me, light sleeper that I was. My flung-open window admitted the low whispers, the stifled laughter.

I crept down the stairs. The kitchen doors were open onto the deck and I stepped outside, careful not to make a sound. Just as they were the last time, my mother and Chris were night swimming. The record player was back outside, Pink Floyd spilling into the darkness. Gemma's hair was in a plait, falling over one shoulder. She and Chris were sitting in deckchairs, in the same spot where Judith had sat only a few hours before. Gemma, I wanted to whisper. Don't do this. Don't try and be Judith, or replace her. It won't work. Chris had sex with his student and everyone knew. He was sent away because of it, and now he likes you.

But I couldn't say a word.

I hid on the wooden steps, the feathery bougainvillea obscuring me in the darkness. Wine glugging in a glass. The faint chink of the bottle being set down quietly on the flagstones. The wooden scrape of a deckchair being moved. I poked a hole in the bougainvillea, just enough to see through.

Chris was splayed in his chair, which he had pulled into position beside my mother's. They both faced the garden, the flowers and fruit bushes just abstract shapes in the non-light. A glass in his hand was almost empty and he soon reached for the bottle again. A string of fairy lights rigged above the French doors was the only source of illumination, apart from the candle in a jam jar set on the patio between my mother and Beth's father. The lights were new. Who had hung them? The moon was silver in the night sky, the barest hint of light in the navy expanse. Orion's Belt, its three studs visible, glittered off to the right. Gemma had told me when I was small that it was believed the pyramids at Giza had been built so that their points aligned perfectly with Orion. They weren't aligned any more, so either the world had tilted, or the theory had been wrong. I liked to think of it, though, all those thousands of years ago and the Egyptians building tombs for their dead, placing them so the stars would watch over them, guide them to the next world. Gemma had sat with me in her lap, a large book of photographs on the table in front of us. I remembered those moments, and I still loved to be close to my mother, keep her in sight and out of harm.

'If this was the South,' Chris was saying, gesturing with his glass, 'we wouldn't be able to talk with all the noise from the yard. Crickets, mosquitoes, frogs. Cicadas. They make a noise at night that you wouldn't believe.' I thought of Daniel and how much he would love that.

Gemma murmured something I didn't catch. Chris laughed, a hearty man-laugh, head thrown back, a slap to his thigh.

Where was Judith while her husband was sitting with my mother? Was she sleeping? Or reading one of her cookery books from the great pile stacked in the tiny kitchen?

Judith was nice. She was kind. She knew what a quetzal was. She knew all about food. Green chilli cheeseburgers, tortillas, beef jerky. None of these things had ever entered my lexicon before meeting Judith. I'd overheard her telling Sarah that she had asked her sister to send her a box of green chillies.

'Isn't Chile a country?' I had asked.

'Oh Megan, you're just the cutest,' Judith had said, her hand cupping my chin. 'Chilli is also a vegetable. Well, technically it's a fruit, but you know what I mean. Chilli is a dish. So, a chilli can become chilli, but chilli can never become a chilli. Get it?' Judith laughed at her own joke. I didn't get it and neither did Sarah, by the blank look on her face, but we both smiled and made pleasing sounds in agreement. Beth had rolled her eyes.

Judith had told me about New Mexico too. It was landlocked, but it had lots of white sand. White sand but no beaches. The capital was Santa Fe, which meant holy faith but sounded much nicer. The state flower was the yucca flower, white and bell-shaped. Best of all, New Mexico was where Georgia O'Keeffe did a lot of her painting and I loved Georgia O'Keeffe. So did Gemma. She had a book of her pictures in the attic, and sometimes I liked to leaf through it. The paintings were unlike most of the art that Gemma liked, all pale colours and skulls, barren landscapes and white skies. Judith brought newness and I liked her for it.

Chris shifted his deckchair again, angling it so that he was facing my mother slightly more. Gemma sat with one hand in her lap, the other holding her glass. Occasionally, her fingers played with the end of her braid.

'You have beautiful hair,' Chris said.

Gemma smiled, looked down.

'You have. I mean it.' He laughed. 'You're very different to what I'd expected Irish girls to look like.'

'Hardly a girl,' Gemma replied.

'You know what I mean. Girl, young woman.' He shrugged. How like him Beth was, with that one gesture.

'I'm not far off thirty. Not exactly what you'd call a young one.' Gemma laughed softly. 'I also have a child.'

'And she's a lovely kid.' Chris reached to fill Gemma's wine glass, but the bottle was empty. 'I'll get another one of these.'

Gemma covered her glass with the palm of her hand. 'No, not for me. I have to get up in the morning.'

'You sure?'

'Very.'

'Okay, I won't have any more either.' A pause. 'You're very insistent about going to bed, aren't you?' But his tone was light and there was no meanness in the words.

Pink Floyd petered out and the night sounds rushed to fill the gap in the music's wake. A distant dog barking. The snuffle of sleeping pigs over the back wall. A single car out on the main road, swishing through the darkness. A sleepy chirrup from a blackbird, hidden deep in a tree.

'When I was a kid, back home, we used to go out at night in the summers. Too hot to sleep, mostly, so we'd meet, just my brothers and our neighbours, and we'd go swimming.' Chris stretched his legs out, settled himself further into his chair. The creak of wood and canvas. 'Nothing like it. Swimming in the cold creek on those nights when you think you're going to just melt if you stay in bed.'

I knew all this. Night swimming. Just what Gemma and Chris were doing now, except there was no river to jump into, just the back garden, the darkness and their sleeping families who couldn't disturb them.

My eyelids drooped from tiredness. Pins and needles jabbed my left foot. I moved it and the step I was sitting on squeaked. It wasn't much, but in the hush of the night garden it was like a gunshot. I froze. Gemma put her glass down slowly.

'Megan?'

Her voice was soft, but I was taking no chances. I eased myself onto my hands and feet, still hidden by the bougainvillea. Scrambling, I made it to the kitchen and bolted back to my room. Breathing hard, I leaned out of my window, the sash open far enough to allow me to hang out. Gemma hadn't followed me up. She was still below, but I heard her say goodnight to Chris, heard the distant chink of her glass being put down on the patio. Chris's voice was a rumble and then there was silence.

17

Beth laughed at something I said, sat up and shook her hair free of its band. The three-quarter moon was spectral that night and Beth's hair was the colour of raw linen in the inky darkness. It was spread over her shoulders, like pale silk scarves. Her pyjamas were white and loose, embroidered with flowers on the small square pockets, and she looked impossibly sophisticated. Chris had brought her the pyjamas from Thailand. Some lecture he gave, she shrugged. Although who wants to listen to him talk about books in Thailand is beyond me, she added. He's so boring at times. Even my mom says so. She relit the cigarette she was holding, inhaled, and blew the smoke from her nose.

Beth had thrown stones at my window an hour or so earlier, waking me with a start. Outside, she had stood in her white pyjamas, like a ghost or an angel. Come out, she'd whispered. Come on. It's wonderful.

'You look like a dragon,' I said as she blew another stream of smoke through her nose.

She reached the lit cigarette towards me, but I shook my head.

'Go on. How can you know if you won't try it?'

'I don't want to. It's horrible.'

I thought of the man who was caretaker in my school, his fingers permanently stained yellow. He walked around the school grounds, a cigarette clamped between his second and third fingers, an inch of ash wobbling at the end. My teacher in Infants smoked. She used to get us to put our heads down, then we could hear the flare of a match, the hiss of the first pull on the cigarette.

'Suit yourself,' Beth said as she lit another cigarette from the glowing stub of the one I had refused. It was a pinprick of light and it moved as Beth gestured.

We were night swimming. It wasn't planned, because I hadn't wanted to do it, to night swim. Beth said that she knew that if she'd asked me earlier I would have refused. 'I don't know why you're so against going outside at night, Megan,' she'd said. 'It's not like anything's going to happen. It's just fun to do something that the grown-ups know nothing about.'

Lying in bed earlier, I'd wondered about my reluctance to go outside at night. Ever mindful of not upsetting Sarah or Gemma, I preferred to do as I was told. And yet. They wouldn't know. Even if they did, what really would they do? Stevie's face had floated into view, his mocking smile, the taunt of his words. I wasn't afraid of getting into trouble, but I didn't want to be the cause of any worry. That was really what it amounted to. I needed to protect my mother, not cause her anguish. She only had me. How could I ease things for her if she knew I was out and about when everyone else was asleep?

And yet when the first of Beth's pebbles clinked off my window, and the second one skittered across the floor, I sat up, clasped my hands around my knees. Shadows cloaked the room, the light falling through the open window just enough to highlight the shapes. Wardrobe. Beside table. Bookshelf. Beth's voice whispering my name, barely audible.

What was I afraid of, really? The night was another world, unknown, but not unknowable. My curiosity, dormant until now, had been piqued. What could go wrong?

The floor had been cool under my bare feet. I took care on the stairs, the carpet absorbing my footfall. Outside, the night air was balmy, the fierce heat abated.

'Tell me about your father,' Beth said now. She lit a match and let it burn to the end, then did the same with another. She avoided my face, made her voice sound casual, but I knew she was curious, madly curious.

I rolled over onto my stomach, the grass dry and itchy under my skin. The reservoirs were low, the water levels dropping further each day; they would be completely dry if it didn't rain soon. Even the canal levels had plunged, I'd heard, though we hadn't been down to the canal since that day we'd watched the boys diving in.

Beth nudged me. 'What are you thinking about?'

'Nothing.' I shifted position. Tiredness weighed my limbs down, but it was a pleasant, dreamy kind of tiredness, cushioned by the knowledge that my bed was within easy reach. 'The canal. Sarah said it's got low. Because of no rain.'

'We need to go down there again. Go swimming.' She sat up straight. 'Hey! Why don't we go some night? Wouldn't that be cool? Wouldn't it?'

Night swimming in the garden was one thing, but actual swimming at night, in the canal, far from home, would be impossible. But I didn't want Beth to say I was a baby, so I said nothing.

Beth prodded me with her toe. 'So anyway, tell me about your father.' Her nails were painted red. 'You never say anything about him.'

It was my job to protect Gemma. Discussing my father, discussing Felipe, was not something I did. Imagining him was one thing. In my head, I could do whatever I wanted, including compiling a list of things I knew about him. For example: his name was Felipe. He was twenty-one when he met my mother, who had only been eighteen at the time. He was born in Sucre, but moved to La Paz when he was fifteen because his father – my grandfather – got a job in the university, lecturing in politics. Felipe was political, but mostly he was artistic, and photography was what he wanted to do. After two years in an art school in La Paz, he came to Dublin for a year, and that's when he'd met Gemma.

People say that the unrest over the tin mines was confined to a small number of people, disrupters, but it was more than that. My grandfather published an article criticising the military in a national newspaper, right after the *Noche De San Juan*, when miners and their families were shot by the president's soldiers.

Felipe's parents were dragged from their house during dinner one evening and never seen again. Felipe went back to Bolivia as soon as he could. He was alive for a while at least, because he took photos and somehow got them to the newspapers. But the photography stopped, and with it the correspondence.

Gemma never heard from him again.

Felipe was Bolivian and he was disappeared. And he was my father.

'I don't know anything.'

'But how?'

I was growing tired of her questions. 'I don't know anything because I don't know anything. All right? Now stop asking me. I don't know him.'

'So ask your mother,' Beth demanded, challenging me.

I sat up. 'Why? Why do you care?'

Beth dragged a clump of dry, faded grass from the ground. 'I'm just interested.'

Too many mountains needed to be climbed in order to uncover everything about him and I didn't have the words to approach Gemma, to ask her straight out. *What about my father?* It would never happen.

'It's easy for you,' I told Beth, who had lain down beside me on the hard ground. Our shoulders touched, our faces tilted towards the carbon paper sky. 'You have your father. He's with you, in your house. You see him and you know him.'

Felipe, wherever he was, was a stranger. A mystery. His face was shrouded by secrets and time, his features visible only in the line drawings Gemma had done of him. I looked like Gemma, so I couldn't say I resembled him. I had her eyes, her skin. Our mouths were the same. Only our hair differed.

'My father's cool,' Beth said. 'We thought at one point, my mom and I, that he'd leave for good, and that pretty much sucked. Then he stayed and it's fine, but it's different too.'

'Why's it different?'

'Oh, you know. It's like I suppose we think that he might leave anyway. My mom doesn't want to talk about it. She just acts like nothing ever happened and everything's fine. Then she drinks a lot of wine and I know it's not all fine. But I don't know what to say to her, so I just leave it.' Beth reached for the pack of cigarettes again, took one out, but she didn't light it. She just toyed with it, twirling it between her fingers.

Her eyes lifted and latched onto mine. 'You'd never steal cigarettes, would you, Megan? You're such a good girl and you do everything you're told to do. Don't you? Megan?' She tugged at my pyjamas.

I pulled away from her and she flopped down on the grass again.

For a few moments, we were silent. Around us, the night was alive with muted garden sounds. A rustle in leaves. The whine of an insect. Somewhere nearby, a door swung on a rusty hinge, back and forth, back and forth.

'I wish I had a sister. Don't you?'

Sometimes I did. It would be nice to have someone else around, someone else to share things with, to talk to. But mostly I didn't think about it. What you don't have, you don't miss, Sarah liked to say.

'We can be sort-of sisters, can't we?' Beth turned to face me. The skin on her nose was beginning to peel. Her eyes were green, the same colour as Chris's. They were alike, Beth and Chris. The hair, the eyes, the shrugs.

'I suppose.'

'We could do that blood brothers thing, except it'd be blood sisters. You know, you prick your fingers and rub your blood together. We could do that.'

I was flattered, to be honest, that this tall American girl wanted to be my blood sister. Taking my lack of a no for agreement, Beth disappeared indoors, then returned almost immediately. 'Look!' A pin, tiny and sharp, was pinched between her forefinger and thumb. 'We can do it now.'

'It's too dark,' I said, stalling for time because I really didn't want anyone pricking my finger.

Beth retrieved the jam jar from the patio, lit the candle inside. It sputtered momentarily, then garnered strength. 'Hold up your finger.'

Reluctantly, I did as I was told. The prick was infinitesimal, nothing, and the resulting molecule of blood was a tiny bead on my skin. Beth did her finger too, and we touched the pads of our forefingers together.

'Blood sisters,' Beth whispered.

'Blood sisters,' I repeated, then burst out laughing.

It seemed so ridiculous, pledging ourselves on the withered grass, on that hot night, the moon waxing above us. Maybe it was the heatwave that was making us crazy. Or maybe it was something more, a need for friendship, someone to talk to.

The white candle stub guttered in the jar between us. Our families slept behind the red-bricked walls of the house, encased in their own private slumbers, and we, blood sisters now, lay on our backs and contemplated the vastness of the black sky above us.

18

The canal water was murky, peaty. Pond weed floated on the surface. The levels had fallen, but not much. It was still deep enough to swim in, and there were boys jumping in, whooping like gibbons as they flew through the air. Their shouts carried along the still, silent canal as it snaked its way down towards the Grand Canal Dock. A wooden barge was moored further up, its red and green paint flaking. A man sat on deck on a fold-out chair, a book in his hand. He paid the boys no heed, seemed not to hear their shouts as they dived off the lock and into the brackish water.

'I want to swim,' said Beth, removing her sandals and slipping her feet into the water. 'It's so hot.'

Stevie pulled his T-shirt over his head and dived into the water.

'Wait for me,' Beth laughed, pushing her shorts down. We both wore our swimsuits under our clothes, to make things easier.

Daniel and I stood up to our shoulders in the water, watching as Beth and Stevie swam to the wooden lock and hauled themselves onto the chipped wood. Water ran off their skin and they glistened in the midday sunlight that pooled everywhere, near-blinding. I shaded my eyes with my hand. Stevie hollered as he jumped into the water, sending glittering drops in every direction. Beth followed quickly and swam over to where Stevie was treading water.

'Come on!' he shouted to Daniel and me. 'Or are you too scared?'

Beth laughed and it infuriated me. I touched the point on my forefinger that she had pricked with the pin. Blood sisters. Except when Stevie was around and then no one else mattered. Beth's hair was fanned out on the water around her, long and streamer-like. She flipped onto her back and used her hands like paddles to keep herself afloat.

'Will we go over to them?' Daniel asked.

So it was back to Daniel and me again, with Daniel looking to me for guidance and allowing me to take the lead.

'I don't care.'

He frowned at me. 'Sorry. I won't bother asking you anything again.' He turned away, his attention grabbed by an insect that had landed near us on the water's surface.

He was right. I shouldn't have taken out my annoyance with Beth on him. He hadn't done anything wrong. I touched his arm with my fingertips. 'Sorry, Daniel. I didn't mean it.'

'Doesn't matter.'

But it did matter. I knew it did. I could see it in the way his face had fallen at my harsh tone, the hurt that passed across his eyes. Our bare shoulders rubbed, brown from weeks of sunshine. 'Daniel.'

'I said it doesn't matter.' He turned to me, his hand outstretched. 'Here. Look at this.'

An insect I hadn't seen before crawled slowly up Daniel's wet, suntanned arm. Its wings were translucent, outspread as though it might take flight at any moment. Its body was iridescent, its eyes bulging. It buzzed gently, nothing more than a barely audible vibration.

'What is it?'

Daniel shook his head. 'I don't know. I've never seen one before. Maybe it's one of those foreign insects that've arrived here because of the heatwave.'

The heatwave was changing our lives in so many different ways, and now I couldn't imagine what life had been like before the sun didn't shine every day, before we had to stay in the shade and make sure to drink plenty of water, yet not too much for fear of running out. It was hard to remember green grass and making sure to always have a cardigan when leaving the house, and checking the forecast to see when the rain would be due. Because before the heatwave there had always been rain, lots of rain, and it had been the yardstick by which we measured our lives. Not any more, though. Now, it was the sun and the heat and threat of a water shortage that kept our attention. Mrs Brennan ran out of ice pops every day. Tar melted darkly on the roads, and when we dug our nails into it, half-moon crescents were left behind. Last week, a dog left in someone's car all day had died. Gemma told me that morning that cities were hotter during a heatwave because the buildings and roads absorbed the sun's energy. 'I don't miss the rain, do you?' Gemma had said.

I didn't. Not a bit. My mother thought that maybe we all needed the madness that only a heatwave could bring, a change from our usual routines. It was good for people to worry less about what everyone thought, to have less to fear than usual. Irish people were great with fear, Gemma said. There was always something to be afraid of. The Church, hell, each other. Gemma thought that the heatwave was a bit like being stranded in a strange land, where new customs and routines had to be learned, got used to. It did everyone good to break out of their comfort zone. I liked that phrase, *comfort zone*. Gemma explained that it just meant the things that we kept doing because we liked doing them and they felt safe, even if they weren't the best things for us to do. I could use comfort zone next time I played Scrabble. Or would Beth allow two words?

The canal's surface nearby was corrugated from Beth and Stevie's splashing. Stevie turned to us and ran his arm over the water, sending a wave in our direction.

'Hey!' Daniel shouted, as his insect took off. 'Look what you did. I'd never seen one of those before.'

Stevie stuck his lower lip out. 'Oh poor little baby's lost his precious fly. Are you going to run and tell your mummy?'

'Leave him alone, Stevie. Go and pick on someone else.'

Stevie laughed. 'Like who? You? And have your granny run after me?' He laughed again, but it wasn't a proper laugh. Mean-edged, his laughter was anything but funny. 'I'd like to see her try.'

Anger was a sudden, pulsing rush. No one was allowed laugh at my family. Sarah was unfailingly nice to Stevie and it stung me to hear her dismissed so contemptuously by him. Sarah said Stevie had suffered the most when his father forgot to come home. He's the eldest, Sarah had said. It's always hardest on the eldest because they have to take responsibility, be the man of the house. I wanted to say that if Stevie had been my son I too might have forgotten to come home, forgotten on purpose.

'Just watch yourself, Stevie.'

Stevie laughed again, a mocking shout that disturbed the hush of the day. I turned instead towards a family of swans that floated nearby, four cygnets scrambling to keep up with their graceful parents.

'Just swim, you guys,' Beth said. 'It's so nice.'

I was treading water. My hands were ivory under the water, my movements slow, ponderous. My body looked like a phantom. Dark specks in the water swirled around me. Daniel ducked under, not surfacing until he reached the far bank. Then he set off for the barge. I remained where I was and observed as he spoke to the man on the deck. He put his book down as Daniel spoke to him, Daniel's hands clutching the tow rope that kept the boat in place. The man pointed to something on the barge, then to something else. Eventually, Daniel hauled himself onto the deck. Water rushed off him. I imagined it splashing on the sun-bleached wood under his feet, then quickly evaporating as the hot air inhaled it. The heatwave claimed all moisture for itself, making it disappear as quickly as it had materialised.

✿✿✿

'Megan!' Daniel waved. 'Come over here. Come on!' His voice was impatient, echoing on the water's surface. Behind me, Beth and

Stevie had started jumping off the wooden lock into the narrow part of the canal, the part where the boats passed through when the lock was open, right before the bridge. It was the most dangerous part, the spot where those boys had been jumping the first time I was there with Beth. Stevie was doing it to impress Beth, and Beth was following his lead to prove she could keep up with him. I wanted to warn them, to say something, but they were too busy shrieking, their bodies smacking off the dark water that lay on the other side of the lock. There was an old sign nailed to a wooden post, warning of the dangers of swimming in that section, but it was faded and peeled, and no one took any notice of it. Certainly not Beth and Stevie, anyway, in their eagerness to show off to each other.

'Megan!'

I turned my attention back to Daniel and swam towards him. The man helped me onto the deck of the barge. His hands were large and he pulled me easily on board. I stood beside Daniel, water streaming off me. It was so hot that I didn't miss having a towel or something to wrap around me. The sun warmed me, heating the skin on my shoulders, the backs of my legs.

'Megan, look!' Daniel held out a book. 'Look what he has.'

It was just an ordinary book, nothing remarkable at all. The red cover was dog-eared and creased, the spine beginning to peel at the edges.

'It's the insect book I was telling you about.' Daniel began leafing through the pages, pointing out the ink drawings of bugs, their bodies sectioned for labelling. Daniel had told me, when his love of creatures began to take hold, that an insect was an animal with a notched or divided body. It came from the Latin *insectare*, meaning to cut up. According to Daniel. He was full of facts. Useless facts, Stevie said, but I liked hearing about things that I wouldn't normally have come across.

'This is Stan,' Daniel said. 'He studies insects.'

The man stood near us. He wore a straw hat and his checked shirt was short-sleeved. He had shorts on and his feet were bare. His chair was further down the deck of the ancient barge, another book face down like a tent on the seat.

'How did you know Daniel liked insects?' I asked.

Stan shook his head. 'I didn't, but a dragonfly landed on those reeds over there and I wanted someone else to see it.' He pointed with his thumb over his shoulder. 'My wife has no interest in any creatures at all and this was such a beauty that I didn't want to be the only person to see it.'

As if on cue, a woman came up the steps to the deck, squinting in the dazzle of sunlight. She was about Sarah's age, her hair caught up in a bun at the back of her head. 'Good Lord, the heat down there is a killer!' she said, fanning herself with a magazine. 'I don't know how much longer I can do this, Stan.' She stopped when she saw Daniel and me. Her smile was sudden and warm. 'Well, hello there! Who are you?'

'These fine people are future entomologists,' Stan announced proudly.

'I'm not,' I interrupted. 'Just Daniel.'

'Good for you, lovey,' the woman said. 'One insect person in the family is more than enough, thank you very much.'

'Barbara's just saying that,' Stan said, laughing. 'She loves the little creatures underneath it all.'

'I'm Barbara,' she said, offering me her hand.

'I'm Megan, and this is Daniel. We live nearby.'

'Well, aren't you lucky? What a lovely place to live.' Barbara gestured with her hand. 'To have all this around you! Very lucky indeed.'

'Where do you live?' I asked.

'Oh, we're from Kildare. We come up here most summers so Stan can look at insects.'

'Do you come on this?' Daniel asked, indicating the barge.

'Oh yes. We take the canal all the way. But we're usually not as lucky with the weather as we've been this year. Now, can I get you children something to drink? Some water? Orange, maybe?'

'Well, I know I'd love some orange,' said Stan.

'Me too!' Daniel and I said at the same time.

Barbara disappeared down the narrow steps and when she emerged she was carrying a tray with four glasses and a bottle of orange.

I shaded my eyes with my hand and watched as Beth and Stevie pushed each other off the lock and into the water.

'Do you know those children?' Barbara asked, pointing. 'What they're doing is terribly dangerous.'

'That's my brother,' Daniel said. 'And Beth lives downstairs in Megan's house. They're just swimming.'

Beth's shrieks ricocheted off the flat surface of the water. Her laughter stirred up something within me. I wanted her to laugh like that with me, to think that things I said and did were equally as funny and exciting as whatever Stevie was saying and doing.

Barbara put the tray down on the deck. 'You need to tell them to stop. A boy drowned doing that in Kildare last summer. He fell and the water levels were too low and he died. It was dreadful.' She waved both her arms in the direction of Beth and Stevie. 'Yoo-hoo! Hello there! Would you like a glass of orange?'

Daniel looked at me and a giggle bubbled deep in my throat. Please God, don't let me laugh, I prayed. It would be like those times in school when laughing was totally forbidden, which only just made it even more impossible to avoid. I looked away, but Daniel's bare foot soon found mine and he pressed down on my toes.

'Yoo-hoo! Orange!' Barbara called. Beth and Stevie must have been deliberately ignoring her, because everyone who passed by could hear her and we weren't that far away from the lock. I hoped no one I knew was passing at that moment, as Barbara called out. *Yoo-hoo. Yoo-hoo!* It was embarrassing, but funny too. I somehow suppressed the laughter that threatened to rise out of me. Daniel's foot pressed harder, squashing my bare toes against the flaking surface of the deck.

Just as I was about to surrender to the laughter, something caught my eye. Beyond the weeping willows that grew along the bank near where Stan's barge was moored, a flash of red fabric appeared and disappeared, weaving among the green leaves and the pale-brown branches that curved towards the water. I knew that skirt, that particular shade of red. I had seen my mother make it. Magenta, she said the colour was. Named after the Battle of Magenta, in Italy, where they had waved flags dyed red. I had watched Gemma cut the fabric, tack stitches along the hem, then sew it all together on Sarah's sewing machine. I would have known that colour anywhere. Squinting, I shaded my face with my arm. A glance of pale-blue blouse, a brown arm. Suntanned foot in an espadrille.

The appearance of my mother distracted me, stemmed my urge to laugh, and I turned towards the trees, ready to call out to her when she came into sight again. I opened my mouth, but closed it again when I saw that she wasn't alone. Along the narrow path that ran parallel to the canal, my mother was walking with someone.

With a man. With Chris.

Daniel hadn't seen them weaving in and out of the weeping willows, sunlight catching them and shadows hiding them. No one had picked up on the fact that my mother was with a man who liked her, who night swam with her. Barbara still yoo-hooed to Beth and Stevie, who had finally responded to her and were swimming over to the shabby barge. Daniel had turned to Stan, who was pointing out a pair of circling dragonflies in the reeds. I was the only one who had noticed my mother. By the time Beth and Stevie had hauled themselves on board, canal water rivering down their bodies and splashing onto the bone-dry deck, Gemma and Chris had disappeared, over the bridge at Portobello and into the bustle of the late-morning crowds.

I could see all the people, even from here. Unwrapping sandwiches on canalside benches, sitting on the grassy banks, crossing the bridge. Cyclists chained bicycles to lamp posts, office workers drank tea from flasks. Further up again, boys were jumping into the water. Their cries looped back to where I stood, a glass of orange undrunk in my hand.

I was aware that something was stirring, or had already begun, but try as I might to imagine it, I was unable. I had wanted to call out to my mother, to shout her name. *Gemma!* But something had prevented me. Even though it was midday, even though I was with my friends, I knew I'd seen something I shouldn't have, something adult, secret. Forbidden.

Barbara cut across my thoughts with an offer of more orange. I shook my head. No, thank you. In the others' glasses, ice jangled and pale liquid splashed. I felt the sun on my shoulders and my skin tighten in protest. My T-shirt was discarded with the rest of my things in a small pile on the canal bank, and there was no shade in which I could shelter. I was irritated with the sun, with the heatwave, with all the red skin I saw around me. I was tired of having to save water, watch what we used, worry about running out. The grass was like hay. The flowers were dying. And now my mother was out walking with Chris. I had to protect her, keep her safe, but she was like mercury, slipping out of my grasp every time I tried to hold on to her.

Beth fished an ice cube out of her glass and, holding it between unsteady fingers, ran it across Stevie's shoulders, right where the sun was doing most of its damage, turning his skin red and freckled. Stevie let out a shout, but Beth shushed him.

'Quiet. This feels great on hot skin.'

Stevie wriggled a little, but he quietened down, closed his eyes, allowed Beth to run the ice over and back across his skin. He opened one eye to watch her, then closed it again, his face free of expression.

As quickly as she had started, Beth stopped and flung the melting ice into the canal. It disappeared with barely a ripple raised on the water's still surface.

And all I could think of was Chris doing that to my mother, crossing boundaries I hadn't even known existed.

'I'll be back in a sec,' I said, setting my glass down, the orange barely touched.

'Where are you going?' Daniel asked. He rubbed his nose, sunburn making it peel. Mine too was beginning to shed its skin, a delicate unfolding of burnt flakes. Despite the peeling, we both had a scatter of tiny freckles across the bridge of our noses.

'Nowhere, just saw someone from school.'

'Who?'

But I was gone, slipping off the barge and onto the canal bank, the heat-deadened leaves dry and prickly under my bare soles.

✿✿✿

I found them quickly. Gemma's laughter was distinctive, and with no mother or daughter to cause her to smother it, it rang out, loud and pure. They sat on the grass under a tree, not far from Portobello Bridge. Gemma and Chris must have heard the chat and the laughter from the boat, but if they did, they clearly didn't bother looking around to see.

Using a weeping willow to shield me, I watched my mother and Chris Jackson without being seen. Gemma had taken her espadrilles off. Her toenails were painted red, the same deep shade as her skirt, which circled the ground around her. Chris sat beside her, leaning back on his elbows as they talked. He pointed something out to my mother. As Gemma followed his index finger, Chris took a strand of her hair in his other hand and tucked it behind her ear. She turned to him, smiling, and repeated his gesture, curving her finger around a lock of his dark blond hair and hooking it behind his ear. Chris grabbed her wrist and Gemma laughed.

Scrambling backwards, I slipped on a discarded ice-cream wrapper and fell. Not giving myself time to dust off, I scuttled back to the barge, under the cover of the weeping willows. The light through the leaves threw dappled shade on my skin. The canal glinted in the sunlight.

19

That evening, at dinner, I pushed my food around my plate. It was too hot to eat much and my appetite had dwindled. My shoulders were sunburnt and my skin felt stretched, sore. The omelettes Sarah had made were light and fluffy, and bright yellow from the eggs she bought from a woman around the corner who kept hens in her garden. Omelettes were one of my favourite things to eat, but now they somehow didn't seem that interesting.

From downstairs, new smells drifted, something sweet and warm and yeasty, like cakes or bread. Judith was cooking again, probably something else new and different. The previous day it had been stacked enchiladas, with fried eggs on top. Judith had offered me one, but I was afraid to try it, scared of not liking it and not wanting to appear rude. Beth had urged me to sample it, but I made an excuse about my own dinner being ready upstairs.

Upstairs, downstairs. How quickly and easily our house had been divided into two separate worlds, two entities that could not have been more different. Upstairs, life was regulated by punctual mealtimes, good behaviour, consideration for others, hard work. Downstairs was altogether more fluid, with meals taken when and if necessary, sulking was tolerated as something verging on whimsy, permission was rarely sought but assumed, and nothing was thought of the martini glasses that often littered the kitchen table, or of the other, stranger-sounding drinks that were consumed. Daiquiri. Sloe gin fizz. Harvey Wallbanger. Tequila sunrise. I shaped their strangeness with my mouth, dredging my mind for something, anything, that would give me a clue as to what exactly they contained, but absolutely nothing came forth. I was as in the dark as if the Americans had been speaking another, unknown language. Which in so many ways they were.

July

I felt my extreme youth, my childishness, like it was a blanket surrounding me. It had never bothered me before, but it chafed now, kept me on the edge of things. Being around Daniel was such a relief, when I no longer had to pretend to know what the Americans were talking about when Judith and Chris offered to make each other a Singapore sling or a pink lady. Daniel had shepherd's pie for dinner, not panocha with extra sugar, or smothered burritos. It was almost too much at times. I thought that when people arrived in a new place it was they who had to learn to fit in, who endured the feeling of otherness for an indeterminate period of time, and not the other way around. It was a strange thing indeed. The surroundings were the same: the house, its red bricks on fire in the July sunshine, the garden with its familiar borders of herbs, the raspberries on their canes. Our books and our art supplies were in the same places, on the same shelves, yet everything was out of sync. It was culture shock without even leaving the house.

'What did you do today?' I asked my mother, who was also toying with her food. Did I imagine a tiny smile ghosting the edges of her mouth? The top she wore looked new, a short-sleeved shirt with pale blue and white checking. 'Is that new?' I rubbed my fingers on the sleeve.

'This? No.'

'I've never seen it before.'

'I've had it for a while. I just haven't worn it.'

'Why haven't you worn it? It's nice.'

'Megan, stop. I bought it a while ago and forgot where I'd put it.'

'But how could you forget?' I was baffled. My mother had one wardrobe and one chest of drawers. All her clothes were there.

'When are the lessons starting?' Sarah asked her, cutting across.

Gemma was going to be teaching art two evenings a week for the rest of the summer, in a small gallery in town. She was excited about it, thrilled to have been asked.

'Thursday.'

'Who knows, maybe they'll keep you on after the summer.'

'With a bit of luck. God, that'd be great, it really would.'

'Well, you never know. Keep your head down and work hard.'

Gemma fixed her mother with a stare. 'I always do.'

Sarah shook salt over her plate. 'I know you do. That's why you're so good.'

Gemma and Sarah slid in and out of conversation while I, alert as a spaniel, kept watch. From the garden, Chris's voice rose above the drone of lawnmowers and the shouts of Daniel and Stevie next door. Something about dinner, a walk, Beth. I swiped my forehead with the back of my wrist. The heat was dragging on me, making me tired.

Later, when I was pouring the water Sarah had collected during the day over the plants, Chris appeared again. He smiled and raised his second and third fingers to his forehead in a mock salute.

'How are you, honey?'

I said I was fine. Mistrust caught me unawares. Like the heat-wave, it hovered in the air between us. Chris had been out in the garden a lot recently. In this case, he wasn't gardening, although he had taken over grass-cutting duties from Sarah. He wasn't reading either, although a book was face down on the striped deckchair he preferred. It seemed as though he was busy waiting to see if my mother would appear. It was all so difficult. Chris was an adult, and I was brought up to respect my elders, not suspect them. Chris was a nice man, a kind man. He was full of smiles and good humour. He asked questions that he enjoyed hearing answered, he sought out details of our days and what we did. He had been our downstairs neighbour for only a short while, but he had slotted in and seemed to genuinely care about what went on. Beth was used to having a father, used to being the centre of his attention, but it was new for me and I liked it. I had little experience of men as fathers. Mine was disappeared. Gemma's was dead. Daniel's was lost. The other fathers I had encountered were usually preoccupied with work, with golf, with sports. Children were an irritation, an intrusion. Yet here was Chris, who engaged us, suggested books to read, slipped loose change into our hands if we went to the park or to the canal, which we had been doing with greater frequency lately, something Sarah had yet to worry about. Chris, who had promised Sarah he would find a television for us. The Americans' surprise when we said we didn't have one had made us laugh. Chris said he'd sort it out. He knew someone who had a black and white set they didn't use any more.

Maybe Chris was being kind so he could look good in my mother's eyes. Kind men were thin on the ground, I'd heard Gemma say to her friend once. Yet here was a kind man, living downstairs, always being nice. But a married man all the same, with a wife who drank wine from a bottle and a daughter who had become my friend. And there was, behind it all, the fact that Chris had already strayed with a student. What was there to stop it all happening again? His hand on her hair. Her hand on his. My mother didn't need anything that would make her unhappy, anything that would cause more gossip about our family. And yet. And yet, really, my suspicions were just that: suspicions. A hand on hair could mean nothing. My mother did it to me all the time, to keep my hair off my face. It didn't have to mean anything.

A family of spiders was disturbed by the spray of water from my bucket. Like crabs, they disappeared into dark corners, behind stones, up walls. I shivered. Years of being Daniel's friend had thwarted in me the desire to squash creepy-crawlies, but I still didn't like spiders.

If Chris had noticed my reticence, he was gentleman enough not to comment on it. I watched him part the voiles and go inside. Music started up on the record player, and over it, his voice called to Judith. A pizza, he was saying. Let's go out and get a pizza. A reply, something muffled, then Chris's voice again. No, just a pizza. I'm not in the mood for anything else. Something else inaudible, then Chris's voice again, louder this time. Jesus, all right. Don't bother. Then his voice, raised. *Bethy!* Beth's head materialised from over the wall in Daniel's garden.

'Yes, Daddy? Oh, hi, Megan,' she said, giving me a little wave when she saw me, standing there, bucket in hand, my bare feet wet and dusted with clay.

'Why are you in there?' I asked.

'Just hanging with Stevie. What do you want, Daddy?'

Chris reappeared on the patio. 'I'm going out to get a pizza. Want to come?'

Beth hoisted herself up on the wall, swinging her long brown legs deftly over and dropping like a dancer onto the grass. 'Sure!' She put her hand on her father's arm. 'What's Mom doing?'

'Oh, she's making bagels.'

'Bagels? But it's evening time, Daddy! Why's she making bagels now?'

'I have no clue, honey bee. But she wants to, and what Mommy wants, Mommy can do. Megan, would you like to come too?' Chris had his hands in the pockets of his jeans. His shirt sleeves were rolled up, the shirt itself crumpled, his bare feet tanned in his flip-flops. He looked like a father from the television.

I touched my shoulder, hot and pink under my fingers. I'd been hoping Beth would ask me in to watch some television. She would never guess how desperately I wanted to watch something. Anything, really – but the Olympics in particular. The games were underway and they were showing highlights of the gymnastics after the news.

I shook my head. 'No, thank you. We've already eaten.'

I had seen Beth and Judith sit outside, plates on their laps, glasses of water on the ground beside them. Sometimes Beth didn't eat breakfast, if she didn't feel like it, and Judith never seemed to worry that she would starve to death. Starving to death was a preoccupation for Sarah, and our meals were eaten with military precision, always at the table, always at the same time. Deciding to *go for a pizza* was something that would never enter Sarah's consciousness. She wouldn't even know where to go. It simply wasn't done. Even in a heatwave. Thinking about it, Sarah was the one person who seemed least affected by the heatwave.

'Next time, okay?' Chris winked at me, slung his arm around Beth's shoulders. 'Ready, baby girl?'

They vanished and I returned to my watering. Even though it was only old water, clouded by washed dishes and rinsed clothing, the plants soaked it up, the arid earth crackling as the water disappeared. Despite the weight of the heat on the garden, the flowers seemed perkier after being watered, their scent more defined. A butterfly, its wings tattered, flitted from flower to bush and back again. Daniel called to his sisters. The watermelon sky stretched above me, not a hint of cloud to disturb its perfect canvas. Downstairs, Judith baked bagels, whatever they were, and upstairs my mother wore a shirt that she claimed to have bought a while ago and magically forgotten about. It was definitely a new shirt.

It was exhausting, wondering about Gemma. To distract myself, I decided I would paint. There were too many colours swirling above and around me that evening, and the only way to make sense of them was to paint them. That's what Gemma did. I retrieved my watercolours from a basket I'd left on the mantelpiece in the front room, decanted an inch of water into the bottom of a jar, settled myself on the deck and watched the thick paper suck up the water wash, pulling colours in all directions across its surface.

The evening emptied itself onto the watercolour block on my lap. The only sounds were the brush rinsing in the jar, the quiet slosh of paint, the sweep of bristles across wet paper. As I painted, an understanding about art came to me. It doesn't have to be anything specific in order for you to enjoy it, and you don't have to talk about it unless you want to. I liked that. It was like hiding.

20

Sarah made curtains. Proper curtains with lining and intricate hemming. She kept her sewing machine in the dining room, which we only ever used for dining in at Christmas, or if there were people over. It was an old machine, a Singer, and she kept it under a dust cover when it wasn't in use. The folding doors that divided the front room from the dining room had been opened when the weather got warm and hadn't been closed since. It kept the flow of air moving, especially when the windows were open.

Now, Sarah had an order for six pairs of curtains. A woman from Rathmines had asked her to make them for her, so Sarah had taken over the dining room. Great swathes of fabric surrounded her. Tiny boxes of pins and foil sheets of needles were always within arm's reach. She used the collar of her blouse as a holding place for needles and pins, their razor-fine sharpness winking in the sunlight like some kind of modernist brooch. As though Picasso had designed it, Gemma remarked, laughing.

My mother was laughing a lot. Sarah was happy for her. 'A bit of sunshine does everyone a world of good,' she said, as I stood beside her, holding out a length of heavy velvet while she measured it, wrote feet and inches down in her notebook, moved the measuring tape further along the fabric.

I wasn't so sure it was the sunshine, though it was good to see Gemma happy. She used to be like that all the time, when she was young, Sarah said. Full of life. She was still full of life, Sarah had added, possibly discerning something in my face. It's just different being a mother, that's all. The responsibility makes you more serious, more aware of all that can go wrong. 'You'll see that when you have your own children,' she added, taking the velvet from my outstretched hands and folding it carefully.

The thought of having my own children at that time was as foreign to me as space travel. Some girls in my class already spoke of being mothers, but I couldn't imagine it. I wanted to do lots of things first. What, exactly, I had no idea, but I knew there were many things I would experience. Mostly, they took on the unfocused shape of dreams, these ideas of mine, but I would do them. Being someone's mother wasn't top of my list, wasn't even on my list. Few mothers I knew gave me the impression that motherhood was anything but drudgery and sacrifice. Children weren't important, not really. There were too many of them, of us, too many mouths always open for food, talking too much, making demands, fighting. Mothers seemed to prefer the company of other mothers, talking over garden walls, outside supermarkets, in groups at the school gates. Often, they smoked cigarettes, laughed and said things like *I wish* or *if only* or *chance would be a fine thing*. I had no inkling of what it was they longed for, these mothers, their heads covered by scarves knotted under their chins, shopping bags in their hands, coats buttoned hastily over house dresses in a vain attempt to conceal their true roles. In school-friends' houses, it was the same. Mothers sending their numerous offspring out to play, shooing them out to the garden as though they were cats.

Men were more important, it seemed to me then. Men who came home, took off coats, read newspapers, were asked about their day by their combed, lipsticked wives. Because I didn't have that, it made me all the more curious, so I watched these fathers, gods in their domains, rulers of the domestic roost. They shed suits like onion skins, wrestled with sons, chucked daughters under their chins, then removed themselves again, away to home offices, fireside seats, the black and white sanctuary of broadsheet newspapers. My friends' fathers decided where their families went on holidays, what programmes would be watched on the television, accepted cups of tea without having to ask for them. They absented themselves from the family home for the greater part of the week, but made themselves known the minute they returned, lest anyone should forget the pecking order.

Even though Gemma was different to every mother of my limited acquaintance, I knew she wanted me and loved me. It was something I accepted, like an extra layer of clothing in cold weather, something that was always there and that I didn't have to question. Those other mothers, with multiple children and husbands who sat like military commanders in their favourite armchairs, probably didn't lie with their children at night like my mother did, reassuring me of how special I was, what a joy I was to have in her life.

'Penny for them,' Sarah said, through pins she had held between her teeth. She gestured to me to pick up a bolt of lining, which I did, unrolling it across the table. 'You're very far away.'

'Just thinking about the gymnastics.'

Beth and I had watched Nadia Comaneci the previous night, on our new television. Chris had arrived at our front door two days earlier, an old television set in the back of Brad Zimmer's car. Not sure if you need this, he had said, but you might get some use out of it. Sarah hadn't wanted it, not really. Reservation displayed itself in the set of her mouth, the smile that was bright but not real. However, good manners and a wish to not hurt Chris's feelings had allowed her to clear a space in the corner of the room for Chris to carefully place the set on a small table that had been liberated from its weight of newspapers and back issues of magazines.

Gemma and I were delighted with the new television. Of course we were. Even Sarah, for all her hesitation, was late with dinner two days in a row because she'd been watching a man called Charles read the evening news. Another shooting in Belfast and two buses hijacked. Violence and rioting in the townships of South Africa. Idi Amin in Uganda. A new government for Spain. Gemma watched with Sarah, heedless of me, her daughter, lurking in the doorway, eavesdropping on this man, this Charles, with his BBC voice and all the bad news falling effortlessly from his well-trained tongue. Sarah eventually shooed me away, asked me to check on the lamb chops under the grill, which I knew was just a ruse, a ploy to keep me from knowing about the darkness engulfing the world. Leave her, my mother said. She'll find out sooner or later. The news on the telly was just the same as the news on the radio, but now it had pictures. Smoke, flames, the shells of cars. Crowded streets. People crying.

As we watched the Olympics, Beth had kept up a relentless stream of chatter throughout Nadia's routine, starting with her disbelief that anyone could have a black and white set, and how difficult it was to know what colours the gymnasts were wearing when everything just looked grey. Back in New York, as in Dublin, Beth had a colour set, and the New York one was huge. You should see it, Megan, she said, demonstrating with her hands just how enormous this television was. It's like being at the cinema, almost. I felt defensive about our new, humble set, compelled to stand up for it. Later, Beth had shushed me as Nadia won the first round. We watched in silence as she bent her head towards her coach, her tracksuit hiding her muscled legs, her ballerina's body. Her hair was neat and shiny, and she smiled and waved. 'She's only two years older than me,' Beth announced. 'That could be me in four years.'

'What could be you?'

She nodded at the television. 'There. In the Olympics. That could be me at the next ones.'

'But you don't do gymnastics.'

'I could do them. I'm going to start.' Beth had folded her arms and stared at me, a sign I had come to understand as the end of a discussion.

Sarah removed the pins from between her teeth and hooked

them through the hem of the piece she was working on. 'I'll have to watch them with you the next time. What did I miss?'

I wrapped a piece of fabric around my hand. It was fraying at the edges. 'Nadia Comaneci got the highest score in the first round.'

'Isn't she a great little thing?'

'Beth says you can't see properly with only black and white.'

Sarah rummaged in her work basket for her scissors. A fabric measuring tape fell out and unspooled as it hit the floor. 'Don't mind Beth. Of course you can see properly. That child has too much, and it's not a good thing.'

Sarah started cutting through the velvet. Her scissors made sawing sounds in the quiet room. Beyond the open sash window, the heat had settled down for the day, the air heavy with pollen and the sullen yellow dust of the summer gardens. A bee trapped in a spider's web droned in a corner of the window. The frightened sound of the captured insect vibrated on the quiet air. For some reason, I thought of Judith. I turned to Sarah. 'I'm roasting. Can I go outside now?'

Sarah kept her eyes on the straight line she was cutting through the dense fabric. 'Of course you can, but put your hat on.'

I slipped outside through the kitchen, deliberately forgetting the campero. There had been a piece on the news the previous evening about sunstroke and it had provoked Sarah into insisting again that I wear something on my head. No way, José.

21

Beth was doing a handstand on the grass. She wasn't very good. Beth was usually good at everything she attempted, so it was strange to see her struggle with something so easy. Over and over she tried.

'You're doing it wrong,' I said, walking over to her.

'What?' She flopped down on the grass. 'It's impossible.'

'It's easy,' I said, and I showed her.

'How did you do that?' Beth asked as I brought my legs down. 'I can't get my legs up and they won't stay straight.'

I caught her ankles as she tried again, and held her up, like one of the older girls at school had done for me when I was learning handstands.

'Okay, put me down.' Her face was reddened from exertion. 'God. That's so hard.'

'If you're going to be in the Olympics you need to be able to do it properly.'

'How did you learn? I didn't know you could do gymnastics.'

We tried again. Beth's legs were heavy and she swung them into my hands with such force that I staggered under the weight. We lay on the grass, laughing, allowing our breathing to calm.

Then Daniel stood over us, his head blocking the sun. 'What are you doing?'

I squinted up at him, his face darkened with shadow. A jar in his hand.

'Handstands,' I said.

'Did you see the gymnastics last night?' Beth asked. She sat up, shook her ponytail free and retied it. Daniel's eyes travelled the length of Beth's hair. Jealousy flashed inside me.

Daniel shook his head. 'Stevie was watching the swimming.'

Daniel's television was even older than the one Chris had given us. It only worked if you banged your fist on the top of it every five minutes. That settled the screen, stopped all the wavy lines from jumping across. His mother kept a tight surveillance around it, discouraging her children from watching it too much. The work of the devil, she sometimes called what was on it. Daniel and I had tested this theory out once when Mrs Sullivan was at a Pioneers' meeting and we knew we had at least a couple of hours before she returned to the house. But with only one channel to look at, there wasn't any evidence of the devil. Just a gardening programme, all close-up shots of dahlias and compost, slug pellets and tulips, followed by the news. There had been a report on the new king of Spain. Maybe he was actually the devil in disguise, we reasoned, but we never got the chance to find out because Daniel's sister had caught us and said she was going to tell.

'Nadia lives behind the Iron Curtain,' Beth announced. This was new. The only thing I knew about Nadia was her age, fourteen, and her ability on the bars and the beam, not to mention her floor exercises.

'What's that?' I asked.

'It's a big curtain made of iron, which runs all along the side of Russia. If you live behind it you can't get out.'

'Nadia Comaneci is out,' Daniel said.

'That's different,' Beth said, impatience colouring her voice. 'She's in the Olympics. When they're over, she'll go back behind the curtain again.'

'There was a boy Mummy knew who had an iron lung.'

Beth snorted. 'That's totally different. This is an actual curtain, and only the government can pull it back if you need to get out.'

'What happens if you try to get out on your own?'

Beth shook her head. 'Terrible things. They beat you and they starve you and they take all your stuff.'

All of this was new to me. Sarah went to great lengths to

conceal much of the workings of the world from me. The Troubles in Northern Ireland, the Vietnam War, even though it was over. Now there was something else terrible – a curtain you couldn't part, with punishment for trying to open it.

'Who does that to you?' Daniel wanted to know.

'The people who live there. They're called communists. America hates them.'

'Why?' I asked.

Beth pulled a face. 'I don't really know. My mom says it's because communists hate America and freedom, but my dad tells her not to be so stupid. He likes communists, but he's not allowed say that out loud. My mom's afraid he'll say it at his university and then he'll lose his job.'

'What else does he say about them?'

'My dad says that the communists are the only ones with any real ideas, and if they were in charge the way they should be, then America wouldn't be the world's biggest war machine.'

'How can America be a war machine?'

A languid shake of her head. 'No clue. But it is.'

'Is that why you're here?' Daniel asked. 'Because of the communists and the war machine?'

Beth laughed. 'No, we're here because my dad is on a transfer.'

'What's a transfer?'

'It's when your university sends you somewhere else, and another professor comes and takes your place while you're gone.'

'Why?'

'I don't know. So you can try out other places, I suppose. He's really clever. He's always working and writing.' Beth's pride in her father was evident. 'But hey, you guys.' She leaned towards us, conspiratorial in her whispers. 'We have to fill the pool.'

Daniel shook his head. 'We can't. We tried before. It's too far away and anyway, there's a ban on hoses.'

'Beth found a tap in the lane,' I explained. 'It's right there behind the house.'

'Plus, me and Stevie can open the door in the wall. All we need to do is borrow the hose, use the lane tap and hey presto. A swimming pool.' Beth touched Daniel's shoulder. 'Come on, Dan. It'll be fun.'

Daniel wasn't ever called Dan. That was his father's name and Daniel's mother was determined that there would be no other Dan in her house ever again.

He shook his head. 'I couldn't. I'd never get out the door without Mummy hearing me.'

'We'll just wait till it's really late, when everyone's asleep. Come on, it'll be fun. No one will know. Stevie will come too.'

Daniel's conflict was obvious. He was so transparent, his emotions swarming on his face. I poked him in the ribs. He squealed, squirming away. 'Come on, just give it a try. You never know.' Convincing Daniel to come made me feel braver than I'd felt about night swimming up to that.

'But I'd be killed.'

'No, you won't. And you can always just blame Stevie.'

He smiled. 'That's true. Okay, maybe I will.'

Beth leaned towards us. 'Maybe we should go to the canal tonight. We need to sort out the hose and have all that ready before we start filling the pool. And …' she nodded significantly towards the French doors, 'we can't do too much while they're around.'

Daniel looked from Beth to me. 'That's okay with me.'

I nudged Daniel, thrilled that he would join us on our adventure. Then I gave a sideways glance at Beth, but she had moved on to other things, was already attempting some kind of flip. She failed and fell on her back, where she remained, still, for a moment. Daniel shook the Mason jar.

'Look.'

I couldn't see anything. He shook it again, gently. A leaf dislodged itself, revealing a dragonfly.

'I found it this morning. I came downstairs early to put out water for the birds and this was on the wall.'

We admired the creature, its bulging eyes, its threadlike legs. I felt sorry for it, trapped in a glass jar, even though I knew Daniel would never mean it any harm. The dragonfly swivelled its unblinking stare towards us. Daniel trailed his finger over the glass. Behind us, Beth gave up trying to do a flip and dropped to the ground. The dragonfly disappeared once more beneath the green protection of the sheltering leaf.

I stretched out on the grass and thought of rain. Beyond my reach, on the patio, was a bottle of lemonade and three glasses, left by Judith just after Daniel arrived. Thirst was suddenly greater than tiredness, and I got up and went to retrieve the bottle and the glasses. The house was quiet, nursing its cool interior. I could hear Sarah upstairs, her sewing machine running like muted gunfire. The French doors were open, the voile curtains a film concealing the inside.

'I could have been a chef. Why wasn't I a fucking chef? Tell me. *Tell me!*'

I froze, lemonade bottle in one hand, glass in the other. Invisible behind the screen of curtains, Judith and Chris argued.

'You could've been a chef if you'd wanted. I didn't stop you.'

'Oh no, you've been so supportive. Just the perfect husband, really.'

'It's a bit early for a martini, isn't it?'

'Don't do this to me. Don't fucking do this to me.' Rage and resentment gathered like thunderstorms in Judith's voice. 'You always do this.'

'I'm not the one doing anything, honey girl. You're doing it all to yourself.'

'Fuck you.'

They couldn't see me, couldn't have known I was there, but the bottle of lemonade was too heavy and too wet with its own perspiration and the sweat of my hot hand, and before I could put it down and slide back to where Beth and Daniel lay on the grass, the bottle slipped from my grasp and smashed on the paving. The sound was an explosion, and instantly it quelled Judith and Chris's argument. In a flash, they were both at the door. I looked at them, beyond them, to the inside.

I held my hands out. 'I'm so sorry. The bottle just fell.' The wet patch bloomed, picking up speed as the spilt lemonade spread. A sticky residue was drying around me on the paving.

Judith was quickly beside me with a broom. 'Don't worry, sweetheart, it's only a bottle. Don't move your feet. You don't want to get bits of glass in them.' Chris stepped over the sweeping brush and lifted me under my arms and swung me over to the grass. He poured water over my feet, then wiped them with a piece of paper towel.

'That'll wash away any rogue pieces of glass, sweet pea.' He smiled, chucked me under the chin. Did he know that I had overheard him, them, fighting? His voice didn't even sound tired any more, not the way it had when he was still indoors. He looked over my shoulder, raised his voice a notch. 'So who's coming out with me to get an ice cream?'

Beth and Daniel whooped. Chris peered at me. 'Coming?'

I nodded and pulled on my sandals. Judith was still sweeping the patio as we left through the Americans' kitchen.

'Chocolate or strawberry?' Chris asked her.

Judith waved her hand. 'Nothing.'

'Suit yourself.'

On the small kitchen table there was a jug of water and two glasses, but no martinis. I looked, but I definitely didn't see one. No olive on a cocktail stick, no telltale triangular glass.

22

That night was marginally cooler. Beth threw a pebble at my window, waking me. Outside, the light was indigo, spilling over the gardens and walls, filling up every crevice with its ink. I had no idea what time it was, but both Sarah and Gemma were long asleep, so I crept down the stairs, avoiding the squeaky steps that always sounded like a cannonade in the hush of night.

Stars were splashed like glitter across the blackened sky. To the left the full moon flouted the darkness, huge and luminous. On the patio outside the French doors, a minuscule light danced. A firefly, I thought, immediately looking around for Daniel. We had never caught a firefly, had hardly been lucky enough to even see one. But it was only Beth, a lit cigarette travelling the space between her mouth and her knee where her hand rested. She was in the deckchair.

'Any sign of the boys?' I asked.

She blew smoke from pursed lips, shook her head. How much older than I she seemed. 'We'll give them another few minutes,' she said, dropping the cigarette on the ground. A small shower of sparks flared briefly before she brought her sandalled foot down firmly on it.

'Sarah will go mad if she sees that.'

Beth clicked her tongue. 'God, Megan, you really are a goody two shoes, aren't you?'

'I am not! If Sarah finds it, she'll think it's your mum or dad, and then she'll say it to them, and then they'll know it was you and you'll get into trouble.'

'My mother wouldn't say a word to me if she thought I was smoking. She's not like that.'

What was Judith like, then, I wondered. Mostly, she seemed

to hover around her husband and daughter, cooking for them, smoothing their way. Until earlier that day, she hadn't seemed to have as much presence as either of them. But then I remembered her anger, a ball of fire in the scorched afternoon. *I could have been a fucking chef.* She was kind and she was gentle, but Beth treated her with a brusqueness that would not have been tolerated by either Gemma or Sarah. I liked her, even if most of what she cooked sounded crazy. Atole and tomatillos, chalupa and beef jerky.

Beth had tried to explain jerky to me, but it was lost on me. I knew nothing about food, not in the way the Americans knew food. Before them, I hadn't ever seen people swooning over recipes, or discussing ways to tweak dishes so they turned out just so. Never had I been urged to try something proffered on a spoon with the assurance that I would die, just die, from how good it tasted. Now I knew that jerky had something to do with spices and buying it on the side of the road, but all I could think of was the dusty, traffic-poisoned sides of Dublin roads and how they would be the last place I would ever buy food. With most meals, Judith insisted on serving flat things she made herself: tortillas, or something else I had tried called *sopaipillas*, which she liked to stuff with eggs and eat for breakfast. Judith got excited about food the way the rest of us got excited about sports or holidays.

Food was just food, when I was nine, and there was nothing about it that was worth discussing. Most food was just a slightly altered version of itself. Meat with gravy, meat without gravy. Vegetables of some sort, boiled and slightly mushy, and rarely appealing. Potatoes in every form imaginable. Soup for lunch, if we were at home. Otherwise, sandwiches. That was it, mostly. I didn't dislike food, but neither did I think about it unless I was hungry. Judith had a box of cookbooks, and she even got a special magazine in the post about cooking. At least, she had until they moved to Dublin. Now she had to content herself with back issues and cuttings she had taken from the magazines she bought here, all bundled into a folder with special stickers and notes all over them.

I didn't understand it at all.

Beth nudged me with her foot. 'Here they are.'

Daniel and Stevie had clambered over the wall and were walking towards us. Daniel was still in his pyjama top, his shorts crumpled, probably from being on the floor. Stevie had that swagger that he brought out any time Beth was to be seen.

'I've no idea what we're going to do,' Daniel said. 'If Mummy wakes up and we're not there, she'll go mad.'

Stevie elbowed him. 'Just shut up. She never wakes up, so she's not going to know we're out. If you're that worried, just go back inside.'

But Daniel stayed where he was. 'I've brought a jar, just in case,' he said.

'In case of what, Dr Doolittle?' Stevie laughed.

Beth put her finger on his lips. 'Sshh. We can't wake anyone.' She kept her finger there, smirking at Stevie's widened eyes, the flush that marked his cheeks.

For once, Stevie was shocked into silence.

✧✧✧

The door into the lane creaked as I pushed it open. We stopped, waited. We crept out when we were sure that no one had heard us. The main road was quiet. A lone taxi swished by, a couple of drunks wished us a goodnight as they passed on unsteady feet, and a tomcat knocked the metal lid off a bin. It clanged as it hit the ground, then rolled away, the sound fading before it fell into the gutter. Only the streetlights were lit, all the lights in shop windows and bedrooms long extinguished. In the butcher's window, a black and white clock silently ticked the hour. One o'clock. I had never been outside so late in my life. I didn't think I had even been awake so late, unless it was to get a drink of water, which didn't really count. The darkness blunted everything. The orange sodium lights flickered, too high above us to be of much use.

The silence of the street dwarfed us, reduced our chatter to whispers. Beth and Stevie walked ahead of us, Beth's hair a beacon in the quarter light. Daniel and I followed their lead, neither of us sure what we were supposed to be doing, or where this foray would lead us.

'Mummy got a letter from Father Bob this morning,' Daniel murmured.

I wondered who we were afraid of disturbing with our talk. Everyone was tucked away in bed, sleeping off the heat of day before it all started up again in a few hours – the unending cycle of heat, sunshine, heat.

'What did he say?'

I liked hearing about Father Bob. I especially liked seeing the photos he occasionally enclosed with his letters to Mrs Sullivan. His last missive had included a picture of him, surrounded by small children. They hadn't looked anything like the starving babies we were told about in school, the ones who would suffer and starve further if we, thousands of miles away, didn't finish all our food and thank God for it. Our teachers were very fond of reminding us of the poor starving creatures with bellies swollen from hunger, flies buzzing around their heads, red dust coating their skin and hair. The children in Father Bob's photo were dressed, smiling, with beautiful white teeth. His priestly arms were around them, his face wrinkled against the desert sun.

'Just boring things,' Daniel said.

'Any photos?'

'None this time.'

'Pity.'

'I know.'

I thought about Mrs Sullivan, asleep while her two boys wandered through the velvet darkness. She definitely wore her headscarf in bed, I imagined, and kept her fingers closed tightly around the heavy silver cross of the crucified Jesus that she wore around her neck. I was sure she also muttered prayers in her sleep, asking for deliverance and a safe night.

'Mummy was happy to hear from him. He said thanks for the money she sent him.'

'Was it much?'

'Don't know. Probably.' Daniel stopped to examine a moth that crawled along the glass window of the hardware store. 'She's doing a novena for him.'

'Which one?'

Mrs Sullivan had a list of prayers that she kept on the wall of her kitchen. Anyone who needed prayers or intervention was on it, written in her neat, orderly hand. Over the list hung a photo of the Pope and one of the Sacred Heart. The picture of the Pope I didn't mind much – he just looked like any old man. But the Sacred Heart was spooky; the thorny crown and the bleeding heart – or was it the soul? – made me avert my eyes any time I was in Daniel's kitchen.

'The nine day rosary one.'

'Oh.'

Mrs Sullivan was prone to extended periods of prayer, often inviting others to join her. Sometimes these groups said their prayers outdoors, their chanting rising and falling in waves of monotony. Sarah didn't like Gemma's smart remarks about the prayer groups next door. Live and let live, she reminded my mother, whenever Gemma's eyes rolled. Mrs Sullivan had loaned Gemma baby clothes, had helped her with breastfeeding when I was finding it difficult to latch on. She had minded me when both Sarah and Gemma were busy. There had been no words of judgement from her, Sarah said, at a time when all that Gemma was getting from most people was judgement. Remember the kindness, Sarah always said, and return it. It's the best thing we can offer someone.

'She wants me to join her at the novena.' Daniel's voice was gloomy now. 'In practice for being a priest.' He stuck his lower lip out and examined the jar in his hands.

Ahead of us, Stevie and Beth had reached the canal.

✿ ✿ ✿

The streetlight reflected imperfectly in the unmoving black water. The outline of Barbara and Stan's barge was up to the left, its occupants stowed safely for the night. The lock had been opened earlier and the water levels had risen. In the stillness of the night, the gush of canal water was thunderous. The weeping willows were carved into the darkness, trailing their branches in silence. A duck quacked. We leaned against the metal of the bridge, our reflections lost in the darkness and depth of the water.

Beth produced a crushed packet of cigarettes from the pocket of her shorts. Without offering one to Daniel or to me, she handed one to Stevie, flicked a lighter at his cigarette and then lit her own. She exhaled a long thin stream of smoke, tapped the ash into the canal. When had she become such an expert smoker, I wondered. Standing there beside Stevie in the weak light, she looked years older. Stevie puffed on his cigarette, but I could tell by the speed of his inhaling and exhaling that he wasn't enjoying it. Inhale, exhale, inhale, exhale. He'd make himself dizzy if he didn't stop. Too quickly, he flicked the half-smoked stub into the water.

'Want another one?' Beth offered.

'Later.'

I nudged Daniel. Stevie was out of his depth with Beth. Whenever she was around, he seemed mired in a perpetual game of catch up, forever trying to emulate her, impress her. Was Stevie in love with Beth? I dismissed the thought. Stevie wasn't capable of love.

'What will we do now?' I asked.

Night swimming wasn't very interesting or exciting, if all we were going to do was hang around the canal.

Beth shrugged. 'Who cares? We're outside, aren't we?'

Suddenly, night swimming was in danger of losing some of its gloss. Beth and Stevie leaned side by side against the bridge, murmuring. Daniel and I, excluded from their shared whispers, stood idly by. It wasn't cold, but I shivered. Then I yawned. The tiredness that had kept itself at bay since Beth woke me collapsed on me, and all I craved was my bed, with its single cotton sheet and the coolness of the night air slipping through the opened sash window. I thought of Sarah and Gemma asleep in their beds, each of them ensconced in dreams, neither of them having the slightest idea that I was anywhere but in my own room.

'I want to go.'

Beth looked at me, another cigarette dying between her fingers. The smell of the smoke had stagnated on the still night air. It tickled the lining of my nose and made me want to sneeze.

Beth pointed her cigarette at me. 'You want to leave? We've only just got here.'

'It's boring. All we're doing is standing around.'

Stevie made a sneering noise, but he didn't intimidate me. 'What?' I asked him. He dug his fists into the pocket of his shorts and looked away.

'I want to go too,' Daniel said. 'There's nothing happening. We're not doing anything.'

Beth flicked her cigarette butt into the air. It landed on the road where it was quickly obliterated by a passing car. A snatch of music blared from the car's open windows and a slurred voice shouted at us to go home.

'We need music,' Beth announced. 'Next time we come, we'll bring a radio.'

I thought of the radio, huge and cumbersome, in the front room, and Sarah's small transistor that she kept by her bed when she wasn't downstairs or in the garden. Neither would be an option.

'I'll take my mom's little radio, her portable one,' Beth said. 'Then we can listen to music while we're here and no one will hear us.'

Daniel pointed to Stan's barge. 'Stan and Barbara will.'

'Then don't come with us,' Stevie said. 'It'd be better without you anyway.'

'Leave him alone.'

It was something I seemed to say to Stevie with increased regularity. Leave Daniel alone. Stop picking on him. I turned to Daniel, who was examining the low stone wall that ran along the side of the canal to the lock. Lock six, it was called. The lock-keeper's cottage, abandoned now, was across the road from where we stood, its red bricks black in the night. In the old days, only the keeper could open the lock for passing boats, and he lived with his family in the tiny cottage that came with the job. Daniel started chasing something along the wall. An insect, no doubt.

'I'm going,' I said to him. 'Coming?'

Beth, despite her reluctance to leave, turned to Stevie. 'Come on, we'll all go.'

Stevie didn't argue with her, but he made his displeasure known in the filthy look he threw at me. I turned away. What Stevie thought didn't interest me.

Beth tried to justify her early leave-taking. 'If we don't all go together, then we run the risk of waking my parents when we get back. If we wake them, there'll be no more going out at night. If they don't know what we're doing, they can't stop us.'

✿ ✿ ✿

We whispered goodnight to the boys as they slipped soundlessly up the granite steps to their front door. Stevie had a key on a piece of string around his neck. I had wanted to return by the lane, but Beth had insisted on using the front door and I was too tired to argue. The door to the garden flat squeaked briefly as Beth pushed it open. She put a finger to her lips as she let me pass her by. The small wad of paper she had wedged into the door to keep it from closing fully was still in place. She picked it up and stuffed it in her pocket, alongside the defeated cigarette box. Behind a closed bedroom door, Judith and Chris slept. Not a sound disturbed the silence of the lightless flat, not a murmur or a snore. Beth accompanied me to the French doors, one of which was still open. She retreated back into the house as I slipped out into the garden. The two deckchairs were on the patio. Chris's record player sat, squat, between them.

It was more a sense of something than any actual proof. A change in the air, an inkling of a presence. The deckchairs. A candle dying in a glass jar. The record player. Sure, they had been there when we had met in the garden an hour or more before, but now they seemed different. The angle had changed. A record sleeve that hadn't been there before now leaned against the opened lid of the player. Two more candles in jars placed at intervals on the stairs.

A squeak on the wooden steps warned me and quickly I hid. The strap of my sandal caught on stray shoots of bougainvillea that crowded the ground at the foot of the stairs, but I managed to stop myself from falling. I ducked behind the steps, darkness and a cloud of blooms obscuring me.

I didn't need to peep to know that it was my mother and Chris on the stairs. More creaks told me that they were sitting down. I held my breath, afraid of discovery. What could be the worst thing? Confessing to being out night swimming, or my mother knowing that I had seen her doing some night swimming of her own? Like a tiger I crouched, my breathing shallow and rapid. Staying quiet seemed the best option.

23

The conversation on the steps above me wasn't enough to keep exhaustion from buzzing, persistent and demanding as a mosquito, in my brain. Sarah's night-scented stocks, in their terracotta tubs, filled the air around me with their fragrance. Normally, I inhaled them. Now, I tried to keep from sneezing.

Gemma's skirt ends trailed between the green wooden steps. She was wearing the magenta skirt again. I could see her bare heels, the glint of her silver ankle chain in the candlelight. The stem of a wine glass where she laid it down. I imagined her hair, piled in a knot on top of her head, like a pagoda, a pencil stuck into it to keep it from slipping.

Above me, the conversation unfurled like a flag, the dipping and swelling of their voices, murmurs of assent, whispered laughter. Their words fell around me, mist-like. Gemma told Chris of her painting, her night classes in the gallery. She told him of a scholarship she had been forced to turn down, years before, but she didn't tell him why. I didn't know anything about a scholarship, hadn't known Gemma had said no to an offer of study. Hispanic studies and art history. It would have meant a year in a Spanish-speaking country and Gemma hadn't wanted to leave me.

'You can always go back to it,' Chris offered, as he poured wine into my mother's glass, before filling his own. 'That's the great thing about education. It's always there, waiting for you.' A dull clunk as he put the bottle down.

Gemma sipped from her glass. 'You sound like my mother.' But I could hear the smile in her voice.

'Then your mother is a wise lady. Learning is there for the taking. Your time will come around again.'

'The most important thing, for me anyway, is not to regret anything.' Gemma paused. 'And I don't, you know? Not a thing. Not in my life, anyway. I couldn't change anything, because then I wouldn't have Megan.'

I held my breath at the mention of my name.

'She's a sweet kid. She could teach my lady a few manners.'

'Beth's a nice girl.' I heard hesitation in Gemma's voice, a hint of a lie.

'She is, when it suits her. Me? She's fine with me, but she gives her mother a hard time. And she always has done. This is nothing new, no pre-teen hormones or whatever you want to call it. She senses something in Judith, call it weakness, whatever, but she's on it and she never lets up. Then Judith overcompensates for it, instead of calling Beth on her tricks.' He drank his wine. 'Makes the whole thing worse.'

'Why don't you step in?'

Chris laughs and Gemma shushes him. 'Me step in? What can I do? I just leave them to it; let them sort it out themselves. I'd only make everything worse.'

'How did you meet her?'

'Judith? Oh, through friends. She was sous chef in a restaurant. Someone I knew had been there, got her number, then decided that she was more my type than his. The usual.' I couldn't see his shrug, but I sensed it, that fluid roll of the shoulders that Beth had inherited. Dismissal. 'I don't need to tell you, things aren't great.' Another laugh, but this time the warmth had drained from his voice. Chris shifted on the steps. They creaked above me and I worried that they would collapse on top of me. 'This posting was supposed to be a good thing, but really we're just killing time till we kill each other.' Again, that laugh.

'But isn't she lonely here? I mean, away from home and everyone she knows?'

'It was her idea. A clean start.' Chris stood up abruptly. The noise disturbed a spider. It scuttled over my foot. I suppressed the urge to shriek. 'Anyway. I'll get you that record I was telling you about. I hardly ever play it now. Reminds me of that whole time we were at war in Vietnam. America's shame.'

Gemma didn't say anything. She held out her hands and allowed Chris to pull her to her feet. Standing, they were more visible. I saw Gemma smile up at him, and he didn't let her hands go until she said he should get the record before the sun rose and all the neighbours saw them. But she laughed as she said it, and Chris laughed too, even as he dropped her hands. Then, quietly, so carefully that I almost missed it, Chris put his hand to my mother's head, pulled out the pencil from her topknot and let her hair fall in a heavy sheet over her shoulders and down her back.

'That's better. I've been wanting to do that since the first moment I saw you.'

Gemma said nothing and the silence tipped itself over them and held them apart from me. The only light was candlelight, and the adults' outlines were barely visible from where I crouched, intruder-like, behind the wooden staircase. Chris put his thumb to my mother's lips, his other hand on her hair, and I watched him drag his fingers, slowly, through its darkness, again and again. Then it was over and, as though nothing had happened, they went over to the record player.

'Come inside for a second and I'll get another record that I think you'll like. But quietly, mind.' Chris put his finger to my mother's lips, and she held it there with her hand.

I seized my chance to go upstairs while they were indoors. The steps squeaked as I took them two at a time, but I didn't care. In my room, I pushed the window up and I could hear Gemma and Chris still talking, their voices a slow murmur now, honeyed in the darkness and the lingering heat. Out over the gardens to the east, the sky was already lightening, silver streaks disrupting the cover of night. Soon, it would be morning.

The sheets were cool on my hot skin. I tried to replay what I had just seen and heard, but it was impossible. Sleep swooped out of what was left of the night, gathering me up in its embrace. I imagined Chris putting his record on the turntable, the scratch of his chair on the patio flagstones as he settled himself to watch the dawn break. I imagined Gemma climbing the stairs to her room, a glass of water in her hand. I wanted to think about the ways in which life was suddenly changing direction, but I could barely comprehend them myself. Sleep was a relief for my crowded brain. It emptied me.

24

The hose was old, and dusty from lack of use. Beth and I lifted it off the patio and carried it down to the door in the wall. Stevie jiggled a wire coat hanger in the lock, and the door swung silently out into the lane. The smell of pig was strong. There was just enough moonlight to allow us to see, and we dragged the hose to the tap in the lane and attached it.

Stevie was already opening the lock on the door in the empty garden as we lugged the heavy rubber over. 'Come on,' he hissed, holding the door open. It was half rotted and one of its hinges had fallen off with a clang.

'We're going as quickly as we can,' I whispered.

'Well, you need to be faster. I can't hold this thing up forever. It's going to fall off.'

It was only a short distance from the tap to the garden, and the hose slithered like a python behind us as we hurried along the poorly surfaced lane.

The pool was black in the moonlight. Its coating of leaves and clay lay thick on the bottom. We let ourselves down by the rickety ladder and scooped up as much of the debris as we could with the plastic spades we'd brought, flinging it up onto the ground around the pool. It took much longer than we'd thought it would. Stevie eventually clambered out of the pool and went into the lane to turn on the tap. Water hissed from the hose onto the grass, the flow jerky and uneven.

Stevie gestured impatiently at the hose. 'Come on, it doesn't matter about leaves. Let's just get it filled before someone comes along.' Somehow, he managed to prop the door up on a brick so it wouldn't fall off the remaining hinge. Picking up the nozzle, he dropped it into the pool. Water splashed over our feet, our pyjamas, soaking us. I yelped. Daniel squealed.

'Sshh,' Beth whispered. 'Someone'll hear us.'

Laughing, we scrambled up the ladder. Part of it had come away from the pool, and it moved every time our feet met the rungs.

✿✿✿

'What do we do now?' Daniel asked. Some time had passed and we were still sitting on the dry ground. I peered over the edge of the pool to look at the water's progress. It looked as though hardly any had accumulated, the remaining leaves floating on a few inches.

We tensed when muffled voices materialised from the Dohertys' garden next door, a man's and a woman's. Laughter ensued, more noise. Then we heard a man grunting. Beth's eyes widened. 'Who's that?' she whispered, pointing. More grunts.

'Is it the pigs?' Daniel asked, to which Beth and Stevie started laughing.

'What?' asked Daniel.

'Nothing, Dan,' Beth said, laughing again.

'Must be all the sandwiches she's feeding him,' Stevie said, and he and Beth exploded again. Maybe they were too loud, because the noise stopped and the night fell silent again. The water gurgled and spluttered. 'This is going to take all night,' I said. 'We can't just sit here for hours, waiting for it to fill.'

'Then go home,' Stevie said.

Beth glanced at Stevie, and I caught something in her look, something I couldn't quite understand. My mind was suddenly far down the road, in the park, behind the thick trunk of the chestnut tree. I could see small, pig-like eyes, a T-shirt concertinaed by insistent hands. I heard a tennis racquet on bone.

'Come on,' I said to Beth, getting to my feet. Stevie wasn't anything like those boys at the park, but Beth seemed to need his attention. When Stevie was around, I was superfluous.

She shook her head. 'I'll stay with Stevie. You two can go home. That way you can cover for us if anyone notices we're missing.' I noticed Stevie's knuckles pressing into Beth's thigh, her short pyjamas barely covering the tops of her legs. She returned the gesture. Her giggles were soft, edged with excitement.

What power did I have to divert Beth's parents from noticing their daughter's absence from the tiny white bedroom in the garden flat? What could I say to make them believe that she was safe? With Stevie, it was different. He slept late every morning, so it would never occur to Mrs Sullivan that her firstborn would be anywhere but in his bed. She never checked on him in the mornings, so he was safe. But with Beth, it was different. Judith's hovering, anxious presence constantly sought reassurance that all was well with her daughter.

Daniel and I crept back up the lane, made our way through the door that we'd left propped open. Already, the sky was lightening, the glitter of stars fading to nothing. Our whispered goodnights were the only sound. At the top of the steps, just outside the kitchen door, I paused. The trees were outlined in the blossoming dawn, the light silvering. I fancied I heard the glug of water through cracked rubber, but maybe it was just my own anxiety. I didn't want to leave Beth alone with Stevie, wide open to the possibility of being caught with contraband water, two open garden doors and an abandoned swimming pool stealthily filling.

As it turned out, I needn't have worried. The next morning, early, I crept outside. The door was closed, the strands of the clematis rearranged to make it look as though the door had never been noticed, let alone opened. The hose had been returned to its original position on the patio, coiled around its holder. Only a telltale smudge of leaked water hinted at anything remiss.

25

Gemma's dress was definitely new. Sarah noticed it too.

'When did you get that? I didn't know you were going shopping.'

Gemma's irritation was a brief spark in the hot kitchen. 'Mother, I don't have to tell you everything.'

Beyond the opened doors, another yellow morning was settling under the unmoving carpet of heat that had already compressed all the air out of the day. A blackbird trilled, but it was half-hearted, defeated. The heat was winning.

Sarah put toast on the table, her calmness unruffled. 'I wasn't aware of ever saying that you did. It's a very nice dress.'

'Thank you.' Gemma smoothed the dress over her legs, like a child. Unsure.

'Where'd you get it?' I asked.

My mother poured coffee in her cup. This was something new too. Coffee for breakfast. Gemma only ever drank coffee when we were out. She was a tea drinker, always had been. I observed her stirring a half teaspoon of sugar into the dark liquid. Milk was added. More stirring.

A new dress and coffee at breakfast. The heatwave was finally getting to my mother. Everyone does funny things in the heat. Patterns were broken, new ones begun. And now my mother was wearing a pale blue denim dress, as she sipped coffee.

'Where did you get it?' I repeated.

'The Dandelion.'

'Was that when you met Ruth?'

Gemma finished her coffee and poured more. I didn't recognise the pot she was using.

'Is that a coffee pot?' I asked.

'Yes.'

'Is that new too?'

'It is, Megan.'

'Why did you buy it?'

My mother put her cup down and looked at me. 'Why all the questions?' But she wasn't annoyed with me. I could tell.

I picked up a piece of toast. 'Just wondering, that's all.'

'I was in town with Ruth and we went to the Dandelion. She bought one of these dresses in another colour and she got a teapot. I bought a coffee pot. It's called a cafetière.'

'Is that Spanish?'

'It's French. You put coffee in it, then water, and that's it. Very simple.'

'I thought you liked tea.'

'I do. But I like coffee sometimes too, and I thought I'd buy this.'

Gemma wasn't one for buying things. She made her own clothes, and she was so good at it that people often asked her where she got them.

Something else crawled into my head. Like a wasp, I tried to swat it away, but it stayed there.

Chris drank coffee.

I was being ridiculous.

But he did. Chris drank coffee. I had seen a pot, not unlike Gemma's new one, the cafetière. I had seen a smaller one in the kitchen downstairs.

'Can I go with you the next time you meet Ruth?'

Gemma smiled at me, pushed my hair off my face. 'Of course you can.'

Sarah was looking at my mother. She did that sometimes, watched her. I thought it was maybe to check that everything was all right with Gemma, that she was happy. I knew that Sarah worried about Gemma. I'm happy with how things are, Gemma insisted any time Sarah said anything to her.

But was she? If my mother was happy, would she have a secret friendship with Chris? If she was happy, why would she go night swimming with him?

But there was no doubting that Gemma was happy. She didn't sigh as much as she used to, and she was painting more than ever. She'd abandoned her portrait of me because she was too busy to work on it, something she seemed to regret. I didn't mind. Even though I loved her attic and was still curious about the ghosts, it was too hot to spend more than a few minutes up there. Gemma kept the skylights open and an ancient fan on the floor, whirring the air around the room, but still it was too much for me. Even the ghosts were losing some of their hold on me. It was as though I'd moved on from that, somewhat. Other things were occupying me, others things to be done and experienced. The portrait would be finished during the winter, if the winter was ever actually going to come. I had a feeling that all we were ever going to have now was heat. I imagined Christmas in the sunshine, eating turkey and ham out in the garden, pulling crackers under a hot December sun.

Gemma touched her fingers to the ends of her hair, which she had braided into a long plait. Two silver bracelets jangled as they slid down her arm. They were new too. I opened my mouth to say so, but closed it again. Gemma got very self-conscious if too many things were said about her, particularly in front of Sarah. She was very sensitive. I think it was because of all that had been said about her after she'd had me. She tried not to care about what other people said, and mostly she didn't, but I could see now, in her new dress, her hair shiny and her face relaxed, that it probably wasn't the right thing to say at that moment. I could ask her about the bracelets later. One of them had a tiny fish that dangled on a link. Its scales caught the light as Gemma touched her hair again.

'More toast, anyone?' Sarah asked, getting up to slice some bread.

Outside, I heard Stevie kicking a ball against the wall. He called to Daniel to go in goal. Daniel said he would, in a bit. Music filtered through the heat.

'Good Lord, not that bloody record player again,' Sarah said, working the bread knife through the loaf.

'What's wrong with it?' I asked.

'Nothing, nothing's wrong with it. I just don't want to have to listen to Blue Floyd, or whatever they are, all day. Beth does whatever she likes, whenever. No regard for anyone but herself.' Then Sarah closed her mouth, having broken one of her cardinal rules of not criticising others in front of me.

Gemma and I burst out laughing. '*Pink* Floyd, Mother. Pink. Not blue.' Gemma shook her head and winked at me.

'Pink, blue, purple. What difference does it make? A ridiculous name is a ridiculous name, regardless of the colour.'

'I like Pink Floyd,' Gemma said, picking up her new coffee pot.

'You would.'

'What's that supposed to mean?'

Sarah sighed. 'Gemma, it doesn't mean anything.'

'I like them too.' I felt I should side with my mother, and besides, I *did* like Pink Floyd. Their music was dreamy, like balloons and streamers drifting on a hot summer day. Like today. It was appropriate heatwave music, though it could also be night swimming music, all quiet and secretive. At home in the darkness.

26

The tiny kitchenette downstairs was stifling. Judith fanned herself as she stood by the cooker, a pan of something spicy spitting on the stovetop. Gemma and I had just returned from town, and I had come down to the garden flat to show Beth the new skates I had got. They were a most unexpected gift, their extravagance matched only by my mother's enthusiasm in buying them.

'These are awesome!' Beth held the skates by their straps. 'Mom, I need skates.'

Judith shook the pan, wincing as something hot shot out and burned her hand. 'Darn it!'

'Mom!'

Judith turned to Beth. 'Yes, dear?'

'Mom, I need skates.'

'Talk to Daddy, sweetie.'

Beth exhaled sharply. 'He's not here, is he?'

But Judith had turned her attention back to the stovetop. A cookbook, propped against the radio, was spattered with spots of grease.

I would never have been allowed speak to either Gemma or Sarah the way Beth spoke to Judith. The unconcealed irritation, the demanding tone, the impatience. It simply wouldn't have been tolerated.

'Except I'd need mine with boots. Mom!'

'Yes, Beth?'

'I said I'd need skates with boots.'

'Yes, sweetheart.'

Beth rolled her eyes.

'Why do you need boots?' I took my skates back from her.

'Oh, you know. I'm way bigger than you and these would fall off my feet.'

I showed her how the skates could be made bigger, by sliding the metal plates further apart. The toe holds could be laced more loosely, to accommodate a bigger foot. But Beth's attention was elsewhere, caught by noise from outside.

'Megan, honey, would you like to try some?' Judith was holding a spoon towards me.

I hesitated. A lot of what Judith cooked looked scary. I looked for Beth, but she was nowhere to be seen.

Judith smiled. 'Go on, it won't hurt you!'

I felt sorry for Judith, cooking in here in the heat, with no one to taste for her. *I could have been a fucking chef.*

'It's a chilli paste. I'm trying something new. Beth loves chillies.'

I remembered what Judith had told me about chilli and chillies, how one could become the other but not the other way around. Cooking chillies is an art, she explained.

'They need to be done in such a way that they are the base of the flavour, but not the whole flavour.'

I nodded, not understanding a word.

Chris strode into the room, preventing me from having to sample more of the tongue-melting chilli paste. 'Well, hey there, Megan! How are you, honey pie?' He turned to Judith. 'What's this? Cooking in the homesick restaurant?' He squeezed her waist and she yelped, but in a delighted way. Chris looked at me. 'We always know when Judy here is missing New Mexico more than a little bit, because out come the chillies and the spices, and Beth and I are subjected to long discussions about beef jerky and the best way to cook an enchilada.' Chris laughed. 'You know you're with a New Mexican when they get all jumpy at the smell of a roasted pepper.'

Judith swatted Chris with a dish towel, but she was laughing.

Chris turned to his wife. 'Well now, I have some plans for the weekend, honeybunch, so you can just put that thing down before you hurt someone.'

Judith's mirth subsided. 'Chris, I can't do anything this weekend. It's the spouses' picnic, remember?' She gestured towards the pan. 'That's why I'm trying this out.'

Chris groaned. Beth cartwheeled outside, and I grabbed my chance to escape the steaming heat of the kitchen and the adults' banter before I was asked to try anything else.

Outside, the garden grass was turning khaki. Despite Gemma's illicit night-time watering, the heat was shrivelling everything green, reducing the plants to droopy versions of themselves, their colours bleached by the endless sunshine. Beth did a handstand, then flopped down beside me.

'What were they saying?'

I shook my head. 'Nothing. Your dad wants to go somewhere for the weekend.'

Beth pulled her hair free from its ponytail. It fell around her shoulders, the colour of sand. Not the sand on Irish beaches, all dark and damp and brown, but the sand I'd seen on postcards, island sand, whitened by the sun. 'He's doing that on purpose.'

I frowned at her. She began to braid her hair, draping the plait over one shoulder. 'Doing what on purpose?'

'Getting the car this weekend. He knows my mom has that American picnic and that she won't be able to come with us. He knows. But he'd prefer if she didn't come, and now he has the perfect excuse.'

She spoke so like an adult at times that it was hard to believe she was only twelve. There was no anger in her voice, no irritation. Just stating the facts.

'But why wouldn't he want her to come?'

Beth snapped the elastic on the end of her plait, then flipped the braid over her shoulder. She closed her eyes and turned her face to the sun. 'It's just easier for him. He can say and do what he likes and he won't have my mom sighing and being all disapproving. You know.'

I didn't. I had no idea what it was like. I only had Sarah and Gemma, and they didn't behave like that.

'My dad likes to roll the windows down, play the radio up loud, keep one arm out the window as he drives. My mom's always telling him that it's dangerous, or it's too cold, or the music's too loud. That sort of thing. Then they argue and she won't speak to him, and I just can't be bothered.' Beth kept her eyes shut and slid back onto the grass. 'So you'll come with us, right?'

The grass prickled my bare legs. A ladybird landed on the back of my hand and I watched as it tracked its way over my skin.

Beth nudged me. 'Won't you? We'll get Stevie and Daniel to come too. It'll be fun!'

The ladybird took off when I blew on it. A day in a car with loud music and the breeze on our faces sounded like perfection.

'Okay.'

✿✿✿

The car was huge, a station wagon with wooden panels along the doors and a sunroof that was propped open. Chris had backed it onto the driveway of the front garden, gravel popping like corn under its fat tyres. Because of the heat, he had rolled all the windows down and opened the boot so that some air could get in. In truth, there was no air, at least none that wasn't already stagnant, yellowed with the sultriness of the early morning. Above us, the sun was silent, watchful. Our shadows were squat at our feet.

Chris wiped his forehead with his wrist. He was wearing a red T-shirt. Damp circles widened at his armpits as he carried things to the car, things I hadn't encountered before. A cooler. A separate box, filled just with ice. The biggest flask I had ever seen, with a spout for pouring. I carried two blankets that Sarah had given me, enormous woollen ones. They were heavy in my arms and they irritated my skin.

Daniel had a bag hanging from his hands, his fishing net like a flag from where it was wedged among his belongings. Chris had only told him to bring his swimsuit and water, but I knew that Daniel also had his insect book, a jar with a lid and a pair of binoculars that Stan had loaned him the last time he had been down at the canal. Daniel confided that he had gone alone to visit Stan, twice. They had sat on the deck of the barge, watching insects and talking about creatures of all kinds. Daniel hadn't told his mother because she would worry. He asked me to come with him the next time. Stan had told Daniel that when he was older he could go to the university where Stan worked, to study animals. It was outside Dublin and the science department was still small, but by the time Daniel got there it would be much bigger, Stan promised, with more labs and opportunities. Daniel's cheeks were pink with the wonder of it all. 'Imagine, Megan,' he said. 'Studying animals. Working with insects.'

Already, our paths were making tiny inroads at diverging, our futures forking in different directions. My future was still a blur to me then – vague ideas of art or English or music sometimes hovering in my mind – but nothing definite had taken shape yet. There'd just been Gemma's and Sarah's suggestions of things that I might possibly like.

Mrs Sullivan appeared at their front door, calling Daniel's name and waving something blue and white. 'Daniel, bring an extra T-shirt.'

Daniel flushed. 'No thanks, Mummy. I won't need one.'

Mrs Sullivan was insistent. 'I know what you're like. One splash of water and you'll be soaked.' She shook the shirt. 'Come on now, put it in your bag.'

Reluctantly, Daniel ran over to his mother and stuffed the offending garment in his bag. 'Thanks, Mummy.'

I wondered if Mrs Sullivan was going to shake her bottle of holy water over us, or light a candle for the journey.

Sarah had made sandwiches and these were packed in an extra-large Tupperware box that Judith had provided and were then stowed in Sarah's ancient picnic basket. Everything with the Americans was extra-large, Sarah had remarked, as she cut the sandwiches into triangles.

'You'd swear you were going away for a week.'

It was true. The Americans were only here for a limited time and yet they still managed to have more, better and bigger things in their temporary cupboards than we had in our entire house. We used biscuit tins for transporting picnic food. Judith produced, as though by a wave of a wand, special food boxes with labels and matching beakers.

We were only going away for the day. Chris had been loaned the car by one of the men who had been at the Fourth of July party. I couldn't recall which one. Maybe it was the bearded man who had been keen to talk about a film about a killer shark. Whoever it was, anyway, had given Chris his car for the weekend, after Chris had confessed to not owning one. It didn't seem like much to us – not having a car. Sarah didn't drive. We lived practically in the city centre. All the buses we needed passed by our front door. I walked to school. My piano teacher lived down the road. Gemma took the bus or cycled to wherever she needed to go. A car would have been pointless, a waste of garden space. Americans loved their cars, Beth had said, even though her family didn't own a car either. You didn't need a car in New York, she said. The subway was enough.

As expected, Judith couldn't come because of her American wives' gathering, which she insisted Chris had known about, while he, equally adamant, denied all knowledge of any such gathering.

Beth and I had heard their voices, raised and frustrated, as we listened to Queen outside, the previous evening. I'd eaten dinner in the flat with Beth, a margherita pizza made by Judith, quite possibly the most delicious thing I'd ever eaten up to that point. Beth had rolled her eyes at her parents' bickering.

'They're always like this,' she had said, reaching for her glass of lemonade. Judith seemed to have an unending supply of lemonade in the small fridge, rising early each morning to squeeze lemons and boil sugar.

Gemma was coming as the other adult. It had been Beth's idea. Chris wanted to go to Wicklow for the day, bring a picnic, go for a hike, find a river to splash in. Breathe some cooler air.

Sarah had been enthusiastic. 'What a great idea! What can I make?'

Beth had been vague. 'I'll ask my mom.'

And so Sarah had spent half an hour making sandwiches, assembling all the fruit she could find in the kitchen and putting it in a brown paper bag, and slicing a cake she had made the day before.

'Is your mother looking forward to it?' she asked Beth.

'Oh, my mom can't go. She's got this thing on, something with other American women who live here. A picnic of some sort.'

'So who's going to go as well?' Sarah didn't say *what woman*, but it hung there, unvoiced in the hot kitchen. Sarah didn't trust men to keep as close an eye on children as a woman would. Men didn't notice things like wet shoes and clothes, tended not to take note of who ate what and how much. They usually failed to do a full sweep of belongings when things were being packed up, and they more than likely fed too many treats to children and not enough proper food.

Beth shook her head, pulled a grape off the bunch on the table. 'No clue. Gemma?'

Sarah hesitated. It was a fraction of a second's wavering, but I caught it. Sarah's eyes darted to the kitchen doors, beyond which Chris was calling over the wall to Daniel's mother, asking if he and Stevie would like to go too.

Gemma came into the kitchen in that moment, her painting shirt on, her hair caught up with a pencil. 'Gemma what?' She poured two jam jars of paint-cloudy water down the sink, rinsed them and refilled them, as Sarah murmured a caution about wasting water. 'Mother,' Gemma chided Sarah, 'I'm not pouring painty water on the bloody flowers. The world won't dry out because I'm rinsing a bit of glass.'

Sarah said nothing.

Beth jammed her hands into the pockets of her shorts. 'My dad's taking us out for the day, but my mom can't go and I said that maybe you could come instead.'

Gemma brushed at a clot of dried paint. 'Oh, I don't know.' She too looked out at the garden, to where Chris was charming Mrs Sullivan over the garden wall. *Sure, we'll take care of him! He'll be a big help when we're looking at creatures that crawl.* Mrs Sullivan's laugh, restrained, self-conscious. I could almost imagine her blessing herself.

'You're busy, Gemma,' Sarah said briskly. 'I'll go.'

'But you have those curtains to finish, don't you?'

Sarah waved away the suggestion. 'I'll finish them this evening. We'll be back early.'

Chris stepped up to the kitchen door, tapped the glass with his fingers. 'Morning, ladies.' He touched his forehead with two fingers, a mock salute I had seen him do several times now.

Gemma's hand flew to her hair, to the pencil that was stuck like a chopstick in her bun. Sarah's eyes swivelled in her daughter's direction and Gemma's hand went back to join the other one. She pulled at the fish charm on her silver bracelet, kept her face neutral.

July

'Good morning, Chris,' Sarah said, tearing paper towels off a roll and folding them.

Sarah didn't much care for Chris. Unfailingly polite, Sarah would never let Chris know, but I knew. I could tell. Her usual warmth had dissipated, her smile faded.

'I'm sure baby girl here has told you ladies that I'm taking her on a day trip. Wicklow. The garden of Ireland.' He laughed. 'I know Megan is joining us, but we're a mom short. Maybe one of you wouldn't mind chaperoning? I have no problem bringing a car load of kids anywhere, but sometimes mothers like to know that their babies are going to be fed, that they won't be forgotten some place by a careless man.' Chris laughed again, a manly, heaving sound, the like of which we were unused to hearing in this small, hot kitchen. He may have been speaking to both Sarah and Gemma, but his gaze was on my mother only. Gemma tucked a strand of hair behind her ear.

Sarah turned away, occupied herself with putting things into our big picnic basket. Annoyance radiated from her, in the rigid set of her shoulders, her lips clamped shut. She did not look up when Gemma said that she would go.

'I wouldn't want to interrupt the artistic flow,' Chris said, leaning against the door frame, his arms folded, a smile widening his mouth.

'You won't,' my mother replied, arching an eyebrow. 'When do you want to leave?'

'As soon as.'

Beyond the door, the morning had brightened and the heat palpitated. The smell from the piggery intensified. It was a good day to go exploring.

27

'Say it again.'

Gemma laughed. 'Why? They're just words.'

'I like how they sound.'

'Ath na Sceire.'

'And it means?'

'The ford of the rocky place.'

'Very cool indeed.'

We were passing through Enniskerry. Gemma had been reading the signposts in Irish, sounding out the words and translating them. This was something new. I'd never thought of my mother as an Irish speaker. I told her so.

'I'm not, Megan. Knowing a few place names doesn't make me fluent.'

Chris smiled. 'It's pretty impressive, though.'

Gemma shook her head. Her hair, caught by the warm breeze that came in through the open car windows, lifted off her shoulders. 'It's not. After fourteen years of learning it at school, being able to say a few place names isn't that remarkable.'

'They're great names, though, when you think of it. All that poetry in every word. And then the English forced the beauty out, with their ridiculous phonetics.'

A discussion on the Troubles followed, which I didn't bother listening to. A car bomb had exploded in Belfast early that morning. I'd heard it on the news on the kitchen radio, before Sarah had reached over and switched the radio off. Seven people dead. Buildings evacuated. The army on the streets. The newspaper photos of Belfast were familiar now, the rubble piled to the sides of the roads, the smoke suspended in the air, the children, unsmiling, staring at the cameras. Chris asked Gemma about the Troubles. You have to look at history, Gemma said. It's never as simple as it seems.

Beside me, Beth leaned her head against the door, her hair blowing in long sheets about her face. Her mouth was set in a single line of bad temper. Stevie hadn't come with us. He'd been at a daytime summer camp for the week and this was his last day. Stevie had already left by the time Chris asked Mrs Sullivan if the boys could come with us. Daniel and I ignored Beth's sulking. I was wedged between the two of them on the back seat, the leatherette covers sticking to my bare legs.

Chris nudged Gemma and pointed to another black and white signpost. 'This one?'

'Kilmacanoge. *Cill Mocheanóg.* The church of Mocheanog.'

'Who the hell is Mocheanog? What a name!'

'No idea. Some local saint, probably.'

'He was Saint Patrick's friend,' Daniel piped up. 'He baptised the Children of Lir.'

We all turned to stare at Daniel, who had turned his face once again to the window. I nudged him. 'How did you know that?'

'*Lives of the Saints.*'

Gemma reached around and patted his knee. 'Well done, Daniel! That's brilliant.'

Chris eyed Daniel through the rear-view mirror. 'My man. Amazing.'

Daniel remained quiet, but his cheeks were flushed. He looked very happy with himself.

Even Beth looked impressed, her sulk momentarily discarded.

'Well, it looks like I'm travelling in a car filled with geniuses,' Chris said.

We were all quiet after that, for a few moments. Chris let his arm dangle out the window as he drove through the winding rural roads. His fingers on the steering wheel kept rhythm with the music on the radio.

Gemma leaned forward and turned the radio up. 'I love this song.' She turned her face to the window, mouthing the words quietly to herself. Chris glanced at her, a smile hovering at his lips. Maybe this is what it would be like to have a father. Another adult, someone else who cared. And someone who had his own private world with my mother, a quiet place that they could slip in and out of almost without being noticed. I'd never missed having a father and it wasn't something that crossed my mind much, but here, now, in this big car filled with people from different families, I wondered what it would be like. There would be other days to remember like this one, other car trips with the windows down, music on the radio and squabbling in the back seat.

Immediately, I felt guilty for imagining such scenes, felt as though I was betraying Gemma and Sarah after all they had done to provide me with everything I needed for a happy childhood. I was frequently reminded by them of the many children who had less than I, who had nothing. Children born in famine, in war. Abandoned babies, children doing their growing up in homes that weren't theirs, without their mothers. Children in the laundries and industrial schools, their lives shrouded behind high stone walls that kept them in and, more importantly, kept the rest of the world out. It was only later, as an adult, that I would come to know more about these particular children, would read with horror of the lost lives and wonder how I had never known.

I had never doubted how much I was loved, how wanted I was. And yet still I'd allowed that other life, the one I hadn't lived, to seep into my thoughts – even if just for a few moments.

My mother leaned back against the headrest, her lips forming the shape of the song lyrics, and her happiness evident. I loved her. I snaked my hand through the front seats and touched her cheek. She patted my hand with hers and we stayed like that for a long time.

We wound our way over narrow roads that spiralled through

the countryside. Other signposts flashed by: Djouce. The Fortified Height. Roundwood. *An Tóchar.* The Causeway. Glendalough. *Gleann Da Loch.* The Valley of Two Lakes. Laragh. *An Láithreach.* The Ruins.

Finally, when Beth began to complain of feeling carsick, and the three of us in the back seat were tired of being flung around at every twist in the road, Chris pulled the car into a lay-by and switched off the engine. The silence that rushed in to fill the gap left in the wake was as sudden as it was complete. Then the engine ticked. The keys jangled on their chain. The road map crackled on Gemma's lap as she unfolded it. Seat leather sucked at our skin as we shifted. The door creaked open and Daniel's feet hit the grass.

'Where are we?' I asked, unsticking my thighs from the hot seat. Tiny hexagons had imprinted themselves in my skin, bumpy to the touch.

'Not far from the Wicklow Gap,' Gemma said, consulting the map.

Chris opened his door and got out. 'This is gorgeous,' he said, shading his eyes against the sun. 'Come on, everyone out. Look at this view!'

28

The immense silence stretched infinitely, it seemed, in every direction, further than we could see. We disturbed the stillness with our very presence. Around us, our voices echoed. The slam of the car boot bounced back to us, our footsteps on the dry earth scratchy and loud. We were intruders where we did not belong.

The sea, a single line of blue on the horizon, provided no breeze to cool the landscape. A sheep bleated in a nearby field, scratching itself against the wooden gate. I felt sorry for the poor thing in its woolly coat. A cow lowed out of sight.

We were infinitesimal beneath a sky so bright we could not see it, the sun burning out of sight. Thirst made my tongue stick to the roof of my mouth.

'Well, folks,' Chris said, rubbing his hands together. 'This seems as good as place as any to start our expedition.'

Gemma shaded her eyes with her hand. 'Are you sure you can just leave the car here?'

'I can't see why there'd be a problem. It's hardly populated around here.'

'I know, but still.'

'Gemma, honey, it's fine.' Chris gestured at the car, quiet now, the engine cooled and no longer ticking. 'Who's going to come along? This looks like a legit place to leave it. We're in off the road, not blocking anyone. It's fine.' He pointed towards a narrow pathway. 'Let's check that trail out.'

'Do we have to?' Beth dropped her bag on the ground. A small cloud of dust rose in protest. 'It's too hot to go walking.'

Chris consulted the map again. 'Look. This trail leads down that hill there. There's a creek you can swim in. We can eat there, take another hike. Come on, Bethy. We're in Ireland. Time to explore!'

He set off, his sandals kicking up dust as he strode. Obediently, we followed him in single file along the tapered path. On either side were fields, their boundaries marked by low, scruffy bushes. The grass was dry and yellowed. The animals were tired, lethargic-looking. In the distance, a red tractor hummed.

The blankets were heavy to carry and too warm on my skin. Beth straggled further behind, kicking her bag every so often. Gemma caught up with Chris, and I watched them side by side, her hair lifting off her shoulders in rhythm with her striding. Gemma held Sarah's picnic basket. Her camera, I now noticed, hung on its wide strap around her neck. Chris gripped the cooler in one hand and a bag in the other. Bits of conversation floated back to me, but nothing that I could draw much meaning from. Beside me, Daniel kept stopping to look at things on the ground: insects, plants, anything at all that caught his attention. Each time he moved, his fishing net, tucked in his bag, was like a flag, the red net swishing around on the long pole.

Chris looked back over his shoulder. 'Dan! Come on, little dude, we're never going to get anywhere if you keep stopping.' Chris and Gemma were quite a bit ahead of us now and I didn't want to lose sight of them.

Beth, who'd caught up with us, gestured vaguely at the ground. 'Daniel, I'll never figure out what you find so interesting about all that.'

I again encouraged him to hurry up. Chris and Gemma were nearly out of sight.

'Go on ahead and leave me alone.' Daniel was on his knees, picking up a tiny insect. He slipped it in his jar and tightened the lid. Air holes he had punched in it previously meant that the insect wouldn't suffocate before Daniel got a chance to examine it.

'It's like being in a lab,' Beth said, 'every time I'm around you.'

'Then don't be around me,' Daniel said, stowing his jar carefully back into his bag. 'I didn't ask you to walk with me.'

Up ahead, Gemma had stopped. 'Come on, you stragglers! We don't want to lose you.' Her voice carried clearly across the hush. We walked a bit quicker. Gemma waited. 'My God, we'll never get a swim at this rate!' But she wasn't being serious, and her mouth on the top of my head when I reached her was full of its usual tenderness. My mother kept her arm around my shoulder as we walked. I kept pace with her, matching my footsteps to hers. Our feet were identical in our sandals, same-shaped toes, same small mole on our right feet. Gemma's toenails were painted bright pink.

I pointed at her toes. 'When did you do those?'

'A day or two ago.'

'Will you do mine?'

'When we get home.'

Daniel touched my shoulder as he ran past, his bag bouncing, the fishing net in danger of falling. 'Come on, Megan. I'll race you down.' He pointed to where the trail we were walking dipped into a sloping path through a huge field and towards the river.

I looked up at Gemma. 'Do you mind?'

She laughed, tugged on my ponytail. 'You do what you want. Off you go.'

The path was difficult to manoeuvre with my burden of tartan blankets. I couldn't see my feet properly as I ran, picking up speed as the path slanted downward. I ran as fast as I could, knowing I wouldn't win, but not wishing to give in. Long grass whipped at my legs, the ground uneven and bumpy in parts. Daniel got further ahead when I had to stop to reorganise the blankets, which were slipping out of my grasp. It didn't bother me when Daniel reached the river first. He was always a gracious winner. I stopped running when he got to the river. He unhooked his net and immediately plunged it into the water. Chris put a hand out from where he was unpacking, having made it to the riverside well ahead of the rest of us.

'Careful there, son. We don't need any accidents.'

Daniel smiled at him. Chris could have been his father, the way he went over to him, made sure Daniel didn't fall in. His hand on Daniel's shoulder was kind, assured. I glanced back at Gemma. She was making her way down the slope, holding on carefully to the wicker basket. She didn't look up to see Chris being kind to Daniel, and I didn't say a word.

The river was wider than I'd imagined and dark, its water peaty and brown. Until we stood in it and it flowed clean and clear over our feet. The cold made us gasp.

'This isn't a proper river,' Beth said. 'Not like the Hudson, or the ones upstate. Or even the ones in Georgia. This is a stream.'

It was clear that her mood hadn't improved much since we'd left the house.

'Baby girl, I'm going to ask you to sit further downstream if you don't park that bad attitude.' Chris didn't look at Beth as he spoke. Instead, he peeled off his jeans to reveal a pair of red swimming shorts. 'I'm sorry Stevie is at his summer camp, but that's not anyone's fault and you're not going to make everyone else's day miserable.' Chris pulled his T-shirt over his head and stepped into the water. 'Man, that's cold.' He looked at the rest of us, standing there. 'Aren't you getting in? We've come all this way, might as well cool off.'

It wasn't too deep, but where we were the river was wide enough to attempt to swim. Chris stood in the middle, the water stopping at his chest. Then he disappeared and popped his head up a bit further upstream.

He whooped and shook his head so his hair swung. 'Hell, it's freezing. Now, who else is coming in?'

Daniel surprised us by being next. He threw his fishing net onto the bank and worked his T-shirt over his head, flinging it after the net. It missed and fell into the water, so he had to run over and scoop it, soaking, out of the water. Once the T-shirt was safely on the bank again, Daniel leapt in and shrieked as the river enclosed his body. He kept his head above water and bobbed like a small dog. The ends of his hair dipped in the water and darkened. Chris called to him and Daniel paddled over to where he stood.

'Are you coming in?' Chris called to Gemma, who was helping me lay the blankets flat.

'Give me a minute.' Gemma rooted in her bag, pulling out towels for the two of us, plus our swimming things. 'You can change over there if you like.' She nodded towards a straggle of bushes set further back. 'I'll come with you.' Carefully, she laid her camera on the blanket.

✿ ✿ ✿

The water was much icier than the canal, where we had done most of our swimming that summer so far. I looked down at my feet, white and bloated-looking from the rushing water, flecked with peat and river weeds. Stones were smooth under my soles as something else soft and squashy worked its way between my toes and I wondered how on earth I was ever going to manage to submerge myself. Gemma squeezed my hand, then let me go as she waded into the centre and allowed herself to plunge with grace into the enveloping cold.

I stood where I was, the water nudging at my waist. Daniel splashed with Chris, their voices echoing off the surface of the brackish water. Daniel called to me for his net and I waded back to the bank to retrieve it. By the time I handed it to him the water was up to my chest. My mother floated on her back, her hair fanned on the water about her head. Even Beth was making headway, lowering herself gingerly into the water.

She caught me watching her and waved. 'This water! How can you stand it? It's the coldest river I've ever been in.'

I trailed my fingers in loops by my sides, watched as the ripples diminished. 'It's okay.'

She laughed, for the first time since we'd left the house. 'No, it's not! You're not even getting in. It's freezing! Hey Dad! This is insane, right?'

Chris looked up from where he was examining something Daniel was showing him in the bottom of his fishing net. His finger and thumb pinched the net, something tiny and silver flashing in the red mesh. 'What's that, baby girl?'

'I said, this water is insane. Cold.'

'Oh, it's fine once you're down. Just get yourself in and you're set. Remember what we always say?'

Beth rolled her eyes. 'Swimming teaches you endurance.'

'Good girl. Come on, now!'

I wondered if this was what being part of a larger family would be like, with a father around to offer another, different view. Women coddled each other and their girls. We wore our protection like an invisible cloak, not noticing it until we needed it. Men were more bracing, less inclined to indulge the thousand minuscule pieces that made up a child's daily world.

For the first time I thought it mightn't be so bad after all to have a father around.

29

Later, after our picnic and another swim, Chris got to his feet. 'I propose a bit of exploring. Who's on?'

Daniel jumped to his feet. 'Me!'

Beth lay on her back, her hands shading her eyes. 'Count me out.'

Chris clicked his tongue. 'No you don't, honey bunch. Come on.'

Gemma nudged me. 'Up you get.'

I protested slightly, but rooted around for my sandals, pulled them on and stood up. My mother held her hands out and I dragged her to her feet. She found her sunglasses and put them on. They were the big ones, the ones that made her look like a film star. She had plaited her hair and it fell in a loose braid down her back.

'Things are safe here, right?' Chris asked.

'They're fine.' Gemma indicated our surroundings. 'There's no one around to take anything.'

'Everyone set? Off we go.' Chris flexed a long, thin stick in his hands.

Daniel held his jam jar in one hand, his net in the other. Beth walked beside me, her thumbs hooked in the belt loops of her shorts. Up ahead, Gemma walked beside Chris. I strained to hear their conversation, but only snatches drifted back to me. I wasn't sure what exactly I was hoping to hear. Some things were clear: Chris liked my mother. My mother responded to him. I had spotted them out walking, had witnessed them night swimming. Gemma had a new dress, new silver bangles, new shirts. Painted nails and different perfume. But even from my nine-year-old perspective, there wasn't a whole lot to go on. Maybe they just wanted to be friends. Gemma didn't have too many friends any more. Some were married, some had left Ireland. Life gets in the way, Gemma said once, when I'd asked her why she didn't see as much of her friends as she used to. By *life*, I knew she meant me, but that was okay. She was busy with me and I did take up a lot of her time. That's what being a mother is about, she told me, and I wouldn't change that.

But still the possibilities crowded my head. I wasn't stupid. I'd seen how Chris looked at her, had seen how much Gemma smiled when he was around. She had sat on the canal bank with him, had allowed him to tuck her hair behind her ear. Really, though, what did any of it prove?

'Megan, look!' Daniel beckoned, cupping his hands. 'It's a Painted Lady.'

Inside his hands, a pair of wings fluttered. I could just make out the orange and black, the white dots on the edges.

'Beth, you have to see this.'

Slowly, Daniel opened his hands. The butterfly was motionless for a moment, then, with a beat of its wings, it was gone.

'Why didn't you put it in your jar?' Beth asked.

'Because I can't feed it, silly.' Daniel pointed to the thistles that grew along the path. 'That's what they eat.'

'Your mom should paint it,' Beth said. 'I'm going to say it to her.'

Up ahead, Gemma and Chris had walked on, unaware of our stoppage.

The grass was long and it caught at our feet. The river wound its way alongside us. A family of ducks floated past. My mother's laughter drifted back to us.

'Where exactly are we going?' Beth's mood had improved only slightly by the time we had caught up with the adults. 'Why are we walking so far?'

'We're exploring, baby girl.' Chris didn't turn around to answer her. He used the stick to point out things to my mother. They kept pace up ahead, but there was no hurry in their steps, no sense of urgency. Gemma stopped every so often to photograph something. We trailed behind again, Daniel stopping to examine various insects.

'I wish he'd stop calling me that,' Beth muttered.

'Why?' Daniel held his hand aloft, a fat green caterpillar inching its way across his outstretched palm. The bones of Daniel's shoulders were visible under the tight stretch of his skin. His back was beginning to redden under the white heat of the sun.

'Because I'm going to be thirteen.'

'But not for ages,' Daniel pointed out.

'It doesn't matter. I'm not a baby.'

'I don't think he means that you're actually a baby,' I offered.

'So what? It's just stupid. He doesn't listen to me and I'm always telling him.'

Daniel blew on the caterpillar, but it didn't budge. 'You're lucky to have a father. And he's nice.'

'Whatever.'

Daniel plucked a leaf from an overhanging tree and placed it beside the caterpillar. 'But he is. He's always in a good mood and he's nice to all of us.' Daniel didn't look at Beth once the whole time he spoke to her, his eyes only on the fat green grub on his palm.

Beth's hands pulled at the long grass that grew alongside where we walked. She was barefoot. Like my mother, Beth had painted toenails.

'Where's your father?' she asked Daniel.

I looked at my best friend, absorbed by his latest creature. Daniel's father was a closed book. He was not spoken about or referred to. When he forgot to come home, Mrs Sullivan had given him lots of chances to remember, but slowly, over time, he had been erased from their family. They didn't speak of him or wonder any more where he was. It was as though he no longer existed, and I supposed, for his family, he no longer did. Birthdays came and went, Christmases too, and Mr Sullivan missed them all. He had missed school concerts, holidays, Communions, all the things that go into the fabric of family life. My own father had missed everything too, but he had never been around to begin with, so his absence had made no difference to my life. But I knew that Daniel missed having a father, and his fierce loyalty to his mother made it even more difficult for him. I know he had forgotten to come home one day after work, but I had heard other things too, whispered conversations that spoke of another family, of England. Another child. A brother or a sister that Daniel would never meet. But Daniel never breathed a word about it and I didn't have the words to ask him.

'Gone,' he said and flicked the caterpillar off his hand.

'Gone where?'

I cut across Beth and her questions. 'Let's catch up with the adults again. They're going to leave us completely behind.'

She silenced me with a raised finger. 'Where'd he go, Daniel?'

'It's none of your business,' I warned.

Beth placed her hands on her hips. 'Why isn't it? I'm his friend too. I just want to know.'

'He went to work one day and he forgot to come home. That's all.' Daniel started to walk on. But Beth followed him, ignoring all the signs that were in evidence that Daniel didn't want to talk about his father.

'That's stupid. You can't just forget to come home. Who forgets to come home? He's an adult, isn't he?'

'I don't want to talk about it.'

'Why not? It's the only way you'll find out what happened.'

Daniel stopped. He turned to face Beth. The sun shone down directly over us. The silence poured itself into all the spaces around us as Daniel glared at Beth. The family of ducks quacked on the river, a dragonfly alighted on a branch beside us, but Daniel didn't pay any of these the slightest bit of notice.

'Why do you want to know? What difference will it make to you?'

It was the first time I saw Beth falter. 'I just thought that –'

'That you'd be nosy? That you'd ask me about something I don't want to talk about? What's wrong with you, Beth?'

'There's nothing wrong with me.'

'Then lay off me.'

Beth stomped her foot on the dusty trail. 'You people! You're so silent about everything. No one says anything about anything. Look at the two of you. No fathers, and you don't know anything about them. What's wrong with asking? How else will you find out? What are you afraid of?'

Maybe fear had something to do with it. We weren't a silent family, but maybe Beth was right. The one thing we didn't talk about was my father. It wasn't that he was banned as a topic of conversation; we just didn't discuss him. There wasn't really anything to say. But what if I was afraid? And if I was, what form did my fear take?

We walked on in silence. I wanted to say something, to break up the lines of tension that had wound themselves around us. I wished the Americans had never come to live with us. There would be no worrying about my mother. I could be on my own with Daniel without anyone else crowding us. Then I remembered how much I liked having Beth around too, how nice it was to have a girl that I could see every day. Then I felt guilty again about Daniel. I should have defended him more ardently, told Beth to stay quiet, but underneath it all there had been my own curiosity, all the questions I wanted to ask Daniel but never felt I could.

Up ahead, Gemma and Chris had stopped. They weren't looking at us and instead faced the river, where Gemma was pointing something out to Chris. She had uncapped the lens on her camera again, was aiming at something on the water. Possibly the light.

Gemma loved light and always reminded me how important it was, how much it affected us in ways we couldn't begin to understand. Gemma had two lenses, a close-up one for portraits and a wide-angle lens for scenery. She carried them in a special bag, along with rolls of film in canisters. She kept her pictures in albums in the attic, along with the photos Felipe had taken. The ghosts kept watch over them.

When we were almost beside them, Gemma held up her hand. 'Hold it there, the three of you. Now smile!' The click was audible in the summer hush. Two kingfishers flew by at great speed. Daniel immediately broke free of our grouping and ran to the river's edge. Gemma turned her lens on Chris. 'Your turn!' Another click, then the whirring of the camera as it wound the film on.

❖❖❖

'Why the long faces?' Gemma whispered to me, as Beth and Chris followed Daniel.

I shook my head. 'Nothing much. Beth asked Daniel about his dad, that's all.'

'Oh God. What did he say?'

'Nothing. Told her to lay off.'

Gemma sighed. 'She shouldn't ask him. It's not fair.'

I looked up at my mother, but she had put her camera to her eye again, was training the lens on the trio on the riverbank. Daniel and Chris stood in the river, up to their ankles. Daniel swished his net around the water, Chris pointed things out to him. Beth sat on the grassy bank, plaiting daisies into a chain.

'Why isn't it fair?'

'Because there's nothing Daniel can say about it, is there?'

'What about my father?'

The question fell into the space between us.

Gemma kept the camera in her hands, her gaze on the river, but I knew she wasn't thinking about the scene in front of us. Seconds ticked by. Birdsong blended with the vague babble of water. Off somewhere in the distance, an engine chugged. A tractor, maybe, or a country bus.

Gemma blinked, but she didn't move. Then she looked down at me, smiled, turned her attention to the lens cap.

'Well?' I sounded braver than I felt.

Gemma cupped my cheek with her hand. 'I suppose I've been waiting for this, but you've taken me by surprise, I have to say.'

'It doesn't matter. Really.'

'No, of course it matters. You have a right to know.'

'Beth asked me about him before. She thought Jim was him.'

'Jim?' Gemma laughed so hard that I thought she was going to choke. 'God, no.'

'He's really nice.' I felt compelled to defend him against my mother's mirth.

'Jim is lovely, but he's not your father.' Gemma touched her fingers to the corners of her eyes. 'He's definitely not your father.'

'Who is?'

Gemma quietened, her laughter subsided. 'I'll tell you properly another time.' Something in my face must have caught her, because she put her arm around me and drew me in to her side. 'I will, my love. I promise you. I'll tell you all about him, but not now. It's not the time and it's definitely not the place.' She kissed the top of my head, then knelt down in front of me. I was taller than her when she did that. 'Look how big you're getting! I forget sometimes that you're not a baby any more.'

'Beth hates when Chris calls her a baby girl.'

'Does she? I think it's nice. It doesn't mean she's a baby, it means she's his baby.'

'That's what Daniel said.'

'And he's right. It's just an expression. Beth's not in a good mood today, is she?'

We looked at Beth, sitting apart from Chris and Daniel, picking and shredding wildflowers, her daisy chain on her head like a crown.

'No, she's not.'

'Is all this over Stevie?' Gemma laughed. 'I hope I don't have the same problems with you when you're twelve!'

I was appalled. 'That's disgusting. Stevie's disgusting.'

My mother shushed me. 'No, he's not. He's just a boy. He's annoying, but he's not disgusting.'

I didn't like to hear my mother defend Stevie. 'He is.'

'He's Daniel's brother. You wouldn't like to hear anyone saying Daniel is disgusting, would you?'

A thread had escaped the embroidery on the front of Gemma's blouse. I pulled on it. 'I'd hate it.'

'There you go. See? He's a little dote. A good boy.'

'You know he's not really that holy, don't you?'

'I know. It's his mum. And that's fine too. She's a good person.'

'Even with all the prayers?'

'Even with them. She's had a difficult time.' Gemma shook her head. 'All those kids and your man gone. I'd kill him.'

'Did he really forget to come home?'

My mother smoothed my hair with her hand. 'They never do. Sometimes men just leave.'

'Why?'

'Because they can.'

More questions bubbled on my tongue, curiosity driving them on, but Chris called to us and we were compelled to go to him, to look at the tiny frog Daniel had found. I needed to ask Gemma about my father again, about the line of tango dancers and the photographs from old newspapers. The poster of Che. The tin miners and *los saleros*. *Los Desaparecidos*. But the moment was gone, replaced by something else.

A small frog sat squat on the back of Daniel's hand. Chris called us again, pointing at the tiny creature. Even Beth was interested, and we were drawn back into the weave of conversation. Chris winked at my mother over our heads. She smiled, looked away, distracted herself with the camera around her neck. Her smile was secret, meant to be hidden, but I saw it. Don't smile for him, I wanted to say. Don't be anything but his friend. But I couldn't say a word because saying such things out loud would be to make them true and then it would all be my fault. Better to keep them unsaid, unspoken. That way, there is always the possibility that nothing will happen. Despite how Beth scorned us for keeping things out of view, I understood why it had to be done. If we all started talking about Mr Sullivan, then it would be true that he had abandoned his family and his home for other people, another place. If he was simply the victim of memory loss, on the other hand, there was always the possibility that he would come back.

Secrets had their place. Lies, less so, but secrets kept the world at bay, helped us to navigate the dangerous path of life, and if we were less informed because of them, then was that really such a bad thing? At nine, I had felt that I knew enough to keep going. There would be time to decipher Gemma's secrets, unfold my father's mysteries, but now wasn't the time for doing it. First of all I needed to admire Daniel's miniature frog before it found its mother and leaped away.

I needed to keep an eye on my mother, make sure she didn't wander any further down this road of painted nails and white wine, televisions and station wagons, a world of record players in the garden and night swimming when everyone who cared about her was fast asleep in their own beds and not there by her side to warn her not to make any dreadful mistakes that couldn't ever be undone.

30

It was late by the time we got home. Darkness had edged its way across the sky as we drove back in the borrowed station wagon. Songs still unravelled on the radio, but more quietly, filling in the background instead of being all that there was to hear. Dinner had been eaten in a restaurant, Chez Jules, a treat of enormous magnitude. Chris had spotted it that morning, and swerved into a parking space outside when we passed it on the way home, much to everyone's delight. It was huge, with one wall made entirely of glass. It was also busy, and Gemma and Chris had a drink at the bar while we waited for a table. We had Coke in bottles, with straws, and we fought happily over the dish of peanuts the barman set down in front of us. Our table was in a corner, by the window. There was a huge potted fern behind my chair and it tickled the back of my neck each time I leaned back. The three of us ordered the same things: steak, chips, more Coke, desserts in tall glasses eaten with long spoons. Gemma ordered chocolate cake off a trolley that was wheeled to our table by a white-bloused waitress whose name was Molly. Chris declined the offer of dessert, but somehow managed to eat at least half of Gemma's, without one word of complaint from her. Again, I'd had that sense of belonging to a larger family unit, when the waiter asked Chris if his wife would like wine too. Gemma had gone to phone Sarah to tell her we were eating out, and Chris, in her absence, failed to correct the waiter. Tiredness had settled itself along my limbs and my skin tingled from a day under the sun as we'd sat around the restaurant table. Hunger compelled me to finish everything on my plate and allowed me to pick at Daniel's uneaten chips after he had finally pushed his plate away. We were not dressed for eating in a restaurant, with our T-shirts and shorts, but no one minded. Gemma and Chris were less untidy and hot looking, and Chris commanded such authority with the staff that no one could have objected to the trio of tangled, field-dusty children.

I was impressed with how Chris ordered, asking about the wine and tasting it before accepting the bottle. He enquired about the length of time the meat had hung, something I'd never even heard of before. His American accent allowed him to get away with it, and the waiter addressed him as *sir* with each answer. Chris paid for everything, with a plastic card, and he waved away Gemma's offer of splitting the bill with a swift *don't even ask*.

Sarah was asleep when we got home and the lights in the garden flat were also extinguished. We said goodnight to Daniel on the steps up to the front door and he hopped over the railing that separated our houses. A whisper of a tap on the front door and his mother in her nightdress opened it at once. She called out hushed thanks to Chris and Gemma as she shepherded her son indoors, then disappeared inside her dark house. The door closed with a click behind them.

'I don't have my key,' Chris said, patting the pockets of his jeans. 'Can we come inside with you and go out through your kitchen?'

'Sure.' Gemma shrugged.

I could have sworn I'd seen Chris pocket his key as he walked to the car that morning.

'The garden doors will be open,' Beth said when I asked her how they would get in. 'We never close them.' I wondered what Sarah would have to say about that.

✿✿✿

I was in bed, almost asleep, when I realised that my mother hadn't come upstairs. There had been no telltale creak on the steps, no roar from our ancient plumbing as she brushed her teeth. Of course, she could have been watching the late news, or reading downstairs, but then I heard the record player starting up and music, faint but definite, reached me through the darkness, and I knew where she was and what she was doing.

Curiosity stretched itself within me, cat-like, but sleep's pull was stronger. I thought I heard a cork pop as it was eased out of its bottle, the faint chink of glass, the hush of muted conversation. But maybe I imagined it all. Maybe my mother wasn't night swimming, sipping wine in the midnight garden, with records spinning on Chris's record player. Maybe candles hadn't been lit in jars and the warm night air wasn't heavy with scented stocks, roses, the herbs in the pots on the deck. The bougainvillea still wound its way up the banister, its blooms papery, leaves feathery, but possibly Gemma didn't notice them because she wasn't there. As I fell into sleep, I thought, yes, the murmured wisps of conversation that reached my open bedroom window were likely coming from next door, or further away, the muted laughter someone else's mirth.

31

Sarah had to leave us for a little while, to go and visit her sister. My great-aunt lived in Galway and Sarah spent a week with her each year. Usually, I went too, but this year Hannah was recovering from a broken leg and so Sarah wanted to go alone.

'You don't mind, do you?' Sarah asked, anxious. Her small suitcase was open on her bed, as she put the final items of clothing in. She came over to me and put her hand on my face. 'I hate not bringing you, and Hannah will be so disappointed not to see you, but it'd be too much for her, with her leg in a cast.' She tucked a piece of my hair behind my ear. 'I don't want you not to have a holiday.'

'It's okay. Really.'

Truth be told, I didn't mind. Gemma and I would be fine by ourselves, and sometimes it was nice to have my mother to myself.

'We'll have a few day trips when I come home, and we can go down to Hannah after Christmas, if you like. She'd love that.'

I nodded. Hannah was a year older than Sarah, but like Sarah, she was active and brimming with vigour. It would take much more than a plaster cast to dampen her spirit for long.

As Sarah fanned herself with a magazine – the sash windows were pushed open, but no air stirred in the room – I ran my fingers over the bedspread. Tufts of candlewick were fashioned into a pattern of flowers and leaves. The fabric was faded around the edges, almost threadbare in patches.

'Will it be hot in Galway?' I asked.

'Oh God, I hope it's not as hot as here. But at least we can walk along the promenade.'

Hannah lived in Salthill, right along the seafront. Most of her neighbours ran bed and breakfasts, but Hannah had been a teacher until she took early retirement. Her three grandchildren lived nearby, and I always loved seeing them.

'Hannah's leg is broken,' I pointed out.

Sarah laughed. 'True, but at least I'll be able to go.'

I touched my fingers to my grandmother's hand. 'I'll miss you.'

Sarah kissed the top of my head. 'And I'll miss you, sweetheart. But it'll be good for you and Gemma to have the house to yourselves for a while. You don't need me around all the time, getting in the way.'

'You don't get in the way!'

'I know, but it's good to be on your own, just you and your mother. And it's only for a week.'

Before Sarah left for the train station, she gave Gemma a list of instructions. Water plants each morning and evening. Put rent money from Judith in post office (account book in drawer in kitchen). Settle account in greengrocer's (money in small envelope beside post office book). Defrost lamb for dinner tomorrow. Curtains ready for collection were folded in piles on the dining room table, each neatly labelled with their owners' names.

'Make sure they pay you before taking the curtains, will you?'

'There's no worry there,' Gemma said. And there wasn't. Last year, when Sarah and I went to Galway, a woman had collected six pairs of curtains that Sarah had made, with the promise of dropping the money in the following day, but we had never seen the woman again. Sarah was furious, not with Gemma, but with herself for being too trusting. Now the rule was payment on collection, or no curtains.

'Thanks, love. You can lodge that money too.'

'I will. Just have a good time, and give Hannah our love.'

Hannah was Gemma's godmother and Gemma liked to spend time with her too. Usually when I was back at school, Gemma went to visit her on her own, as she would later that year as well. When

Gemma had been expecting me, she went to stay with Hannah for a while, till she decided what she was going to do. Gemma didn't tell me much about that time, those months she spent in the old house along the seafront, but I knew that it was to give her a chance to decide whether she was going to keep me or give me away. Sarah wouldn't like me to know that, because she was fierce in her conviction that babies should stay with their mothers, but I knew that my mother had had to make that decision herself. And it didn't bother me because she had kept me. She'd always known that I would be hers. That's what she said, and I believed her.

✧ ✧ ✧

It was strange at first, not having Sarah around. We were in such a routine, the three of us, that losing Sarah for a week knocked everything off tilt.

'We'll be fine on our own,' Gemma said, her arm around my shoulder as we went back inside after waving her off. The hall was dark, not quite taking in the white light of morning. The fanlight threw shattered reflections on the polished floorboards, highlighting the imperfections of the wood.

'Sarah said it'd be good for us,' I said, looking at my mother. Something silver caught my eye. I reached up and touched her ears. 'Are these new?'

Gemma put her fingertips to her earrings. 'I just haven't worn them before.'

'But I've never seen them in your jewellery box. They're new.'

She shook her head. 'They're not.' In a brighter voice she carried on. 'Anyway, let's see what's on the cards for today.'

'I don't mind what we do.'

'We could go to the sea, or into town. Then again, it's too hot to be in the city.'

'When's the heatwave going to end?'

My mother started towards the kitchen. 'Oh don't even think about it! We'll be shivering with the cold all winter long and wishing we still had a bit of warmth.'

I couldn't quite remember what it was like to be cold. I had a memory of it, but conjuring the precise sensation of that icy winter chill was impossible. Just as it would doubtless be impossible to recall this fierce blast of heat once summer was over.

We spent that morning, my mother and I, in close proximity, but not exactly together. Gemma moved her paints downstairs and set up her studio in the dining room for the week, so as to be close to me as I played in the garden or read my books in the slightly cooler environs of indoors. All the windows were thrown open to the hot morning, the kitchen door wedged open with a chair. It made little difference. Inside, as out, the day sweltered, the pollen-tinted air unmoving.

Beth and Judith had taken the bus into town. They were going to the shops, to lunch with an American family they knew, and to have a wander around the city centre. Daniel and I took our bikes out and went for a cycle. It had been so long since I'd used my bicycle that it was coated with dust and cobwebs when I dragged it out from under the wooden staircase. I gave it a hasty swipe with a rag. Mrs Sullivan gave us a sandwich each and a bottle of water.

We cycled side by side down the main road, through Ranelagh. We took the road that ran alongside the canal as far as Portobello, up through Rathmines, and zigzagged our way back towards home through quiet streets with rows of red-bricked houses, small squares of gardens enclosed by railings, children playing outdoors. Instead of going straight home, though, we made our way to the park, but I didn't want to go anywhere near the tennis courts or playground, for fear that the boys would be there. Instead, we went and sat in the old bandstand by the duck pond across the road and ate our ham sandwiches. The bread mills behind the high wall that surrounded the park released their warm, yeasty scent.

Daniel finished his sandwich, stuffing the crusts into his mouth. 'Will we shout up?' he asked, pointing to the grey bakery building behind us. Sometimes, if we were very lucky, and we shouted loudly enough, someone inside would throw a fresh loaf out of a window at us, and we would then go and feed the ducks.

I drained the last of the water from the bottle. 'Okay.'

We stood at the right spot for bread begging and jumped up and down, waving our arms and shouting, laughing at each other. Daniel paused at one point to examine a caterpillar that inched its way up the high wall, but I carried on.

We were not lucky: the windows remained closed, despite the heat. Bored of shouting into the void, we picked our bikes up from where we had abandoned them by the bandstand. We circled the pond, cycled over the grass and wound our way home.

By the time we got home, it was already mid afternoon. There was no sign of Beth. I leaned my bike against the outside staircase and took the steps two at a time up to the kitchen. Chris was sitting with my mother at the kitchen table. Her arms jangled with silver bangles, her hair piled on top of her head, pagoda-like, skewered with a red pencil. Chris poured water from a jug. Mint leaves floated on the surface, obscuring thin slices of cucumber that Gemma had cut earlier. The coffee pot was drained, but the smell of coffee lingered. Two mugs had been pushed away. They were empty.

❖ ❖ ❖

Later, Beth came home from town while I was watching the gymnastics, and she came upstairs to watch with me. We waited for the final scores. Nadia was looking like a dead cert for the All Around and we wanted to see her claim the gold.

Nadia was on the television in her white tracksuit, smiling and waving to the crowds. Both her arms were in the air, both hands as synchronised as her floor routine. Around her neck, the big gold medal flashed when it caught the light. She wasn't overwhelmed, just happy. As though she had expected to win. Her face had none of the teary gratitude I had noticed in other winning athletes. She was simply happy. A job well done. A medal earned. Her fringe moved as she turned to the crowd, her ponytail with its ribboned bow bobbing. Would she disappear after the Olympics, back behind the Iron Curtain again? Would Checkpoint Charlie stamp her passport, let her through? Then I remembered Beth had said Checkpoint Charlie was somewhere else. Germany, maybe. I needed to ask Gemma.

It was then that Beth turned towards me and broke my spell.

'I think my father is in love with your mother.'

32

Of course it was all nonsense. I knew it was, but that didn't stop Beth telling me again, as matter-of-factly as if she'd been talking about Nadia winning gold. *My father is in love with your mother.* I shook my head. It wasn't true because Chris was married to Judith and my mother had me.

'You're very naïve, Megan,' Beth said, crushing one of the biscuits Gemma had given us, the crumbs falling on the plate. She sat cross-legged on the floor. I lay on my stomach beside her. She drew shapes with her forefinger in the crumbs, before licking her finger clean.

'I don't even know what that means,' I admitted.

I kept my gaze on the television, even though Nadia was gone and the men were beginning their rounds. Men's gymnastics had failed to enthral me. The men lacked the lightness and grace of the girls, and while normally I would have switched it off by now, it gave me something to look at besides Beth.

'Are you even listening to me? Megan?' She poked my shoulder.

I jerked away from her. 'Stop. I don't want to hear any more.'

'But it's not bad. It's just what I think. And I know I'm right.'

I turned over onto my side to look at her. 'You have to stop saying these things. My mother isn't like that.'

She smirked. 'Isn't like what? She had you, didn't she?'

The slap came out of nowhere. I hadn't meant for it to happen, but I was overtaken with a rage that was as instant as it was fierce, and my hand stung, the palm rapidly reddening.

No one spoke about my mother like that. Beth's smirk said it all, spoke more loudly than any words she could have uttered. She was a phoney and I knew it. Really she just wanted something to gossip about. She thought she was better than us. Better because her mother had been safely married before Beth had arrived, better because people didn't point and turn away and whisper about her.

But she wasn't better than us and I knew that. If you think you're better than someone, that is proof enough that you're not.

Beth sat, her hand to her face. Shock had paralysed her features, silenced her tongue. The only sound was the commentator from the men's gymnastics, praising someone's prowess on the parallel bars. Upper body strength. Six days' training a week. The pinnacle of his career. The possibility that he would be beaten by the Russians. Although the commentator didn't say so, it was implied that to be beaten by the Russians would be a mark of shame. The gymnast must have been American. I allowed the sound to wash over me, blurred and disjointed in the aftermath of the slap. Beth's face a still life in astonishment.

Cradling her cheek, she got to her feet. Her sandals had been tossed aside and she didn't bother putting them on. Without a word, Beth left the room, barefoot. From the kitchen, I heard Gemma ask her something, but only silence lingered in the wake of her departure.

✿✿✿

The next morning, Daniel and I made an extension to the hideout. We dragged a huge discarded cardboard box over the wall from the lane, and somehow managed to add it on to the corrugated roof. It wasn't perfect and we knew it wouldn't last past the first rain, but it worked for now and it made the den bigger. I had lost interest in the hideout, to be honest, but it suited me to be there because I didn't want to see Beth. Besides, I liked being with Daniel. There was no pressure to be anything other than myself, and he didn't think about such things as my mother and Chris, or even notice that maybe something was up.

Daniel had his jars of insects placed beside him while he read.

Mrs Sullivan had brought him to the library earlier that day. Daniel had got a book out for me, a mystery story, and this now occupied me. I tried my best to keep Beth's words out of my head, but every so often they slithered back in, unbidden.

So much was happening, and my mother was not herself. Possibly it was the weather, which was affecting everyone in different ways. Mrs Doherty next door must have read most of the bookshops and libraries in Dublin dry by now. The milkman had taken to wearing nothing but shorts and a T-shirt under his white milkman's coat, something Mrs Sullivan said was a disgrace. She said to Sarah that she had a good mind to report him to the dairy, but Sarah said to leave him alone, he wasn't doing any harm. The owner of the pigs had started watering the pigs, even though it was illegal to use water like that, but he said, when we asked, that if he didn't then they'd overheat, burn their skin and die. And no one wanted that to happen. 'There'd be no sausages or bacon if the pigs died, would there?' The man laughed at his own words, but Daniel went pale. He hated eating meat because it was cruel to the animals. Daniel was determined to be a proper vegetarian when he grew up, as well as an entomologist and a pilot. He'd have been one already, only his mother said it was nonsense and that he'd starve if he didn't eat any meat. Daniel didn't really think he'd starve, but Mrs Sullivan always took it personally whenever he said he didn't want to eat meat any more. Her face took on a look, all tightened lips and furrowed brow, her arms folded in disapproval. She and Daniel reluctantly came to an arrangement: no pork, no beef, just chicken and fish. Daniel told me that he'd work on getting out of eating both of those eventually. The big problem was what else could he have instead? Beth offered Judith as a guide. Judith knew everything there was to know about food, and eliminating meat from the diet was a minor problem as far as she was concerned. Judith had even started to provide Mrs Sullivan with recipes that cut out meat, while remaining delicious. Mrs Sullivan had been hesitant at first, circumspect about this new departure in family meals. She gave in eventually, though, because Daniel was her favourite. Her good boy. He made sure to give his mother extra hugs for the effort she was making.

It wasn't just the food served in the Sullivan household that was changing. Gemma was different now, and I wanted to believe it was the heat, but it was more than that. I could see things for myself. Chris Jackson, with his blond hair to his shoulders, his sandals and jeans, his records and his Southern drawl had somehow bewitched my mother.

I'd always hoped that I was enough for Gemma. Even though I was young, I wasn't stupid, and I knew she was lonely. She shouldn't have been; Gemma was beautiful, young, talented. But she was a mother without a husband, and for some reason that made a big difference back then. She told me once that a girl she'd been in school with, who had grown up down the road, had stopped being friends with her after I was born. The girl's mother had said Gemma was a bad influence and didn't want her around. That made me sad. Anyone could see how nice my mother was, how good and kind she was. Sarah said we mustn't judge others, that we should always look inside ourselves first and see what we lack that makes us fear other people. It was good advice, but not always easy to follow. Chris saw Gemma for who she was, and that made it difficult for me to be annoyed with him and impossible for me to dislike him. He saw her beauty, yes, but he also saw her intelligence, her talent, her fierceness. But love, the love that Beth had mentioned, was another thing entirely, and it worried me. If Chris was in love with Gemma, it changed everything. I tried to blot it out. Maybe if I didn't think about things, they would go back to the way they were. If I could forget about the silver bracelets, the fish charm, the tiny stud earrings, they would cease to exist. Perhaps.

Daniel looked up from his own book, a mystery that was similar to mine. 'Do you like the book?'

The pages were cool beneath my fingertips. 'It's good.'

'We can swap when we're finished.'

'Okay.'

It was so easy being his friend. I never felt I had to watch out for what he was going to say, didn't worry about his misinterpreting or misreading signals.

The water I had brought in a milk bottle had warmed slightly. Through a gap in the cardboard, the sky was visible, a clear pure blue, the blue of paintings and photographs. In those moments the hideout felt like exactly that: a sanctuary, an escape.

Then Beth had to ruin it all by finding us.

✿ ✿ ✿

'This is cool!' She didn't ask if she could come in, just pulled aside the makeshift door and flopped down beside me. 'Your mom's wondering where you are.'

'What did you tell her?'

'Nothing. I didn't know where you were.'

Beth didn't say a word about what I'd done. It was shaded in the hideout and her face was shadowed, but I could still make out the dark bloom of a bruise on her skin, right above her cheekbone. I fancied I could see the marks of my fingers, my imprint, but maybe I was just imagining it.

'How did you find me?'

Her laugh was short. 'Where else would you be? If you're not at home, you're with Dan.'

'It's Daniel.'

'Same difference.'

'It's not. No one calls him Dan. You're not allowed to.'

Daniel was never called anything but his full name, which means

God is my judge. In the Bible, Daniel is famous for his wisdom and his righteousness. He was well named, Gemma remarked to Sarah when I delivered the history behind my best friend's name. Not sure about the father, though, referring to Daniel senior. Sarah replied that it was just as well they shortened it in his case, because Daniel's father had been short on wisdom and righteousness, and then they both laughed. Possibly, that was why he forgot to come home. If he had been wiser, he wouldn't have got lost.

Daniel's mother called him and he scrambled to get to her, almost bringing the cardboard extension down in the process.

In the quiet that followed his departure, I resumed reading. If Beth wanted to apologise, she could do so; there was no way that I was going to say sorry.

She reached over and touched Daniel's insect jar. It rolled on its side, rocking the ladybirds on their leaves. 'What does he see in all these bugs?'

I kept on reading.

'Megan.'

I ignored her.

'Megan.'

The page flicked between my fingers.

Beth put her hand on my book and pushed it to the ground. 'Stop ignoring me.'

'I'm not ignoring you. I just don't want to talk to you ever again.'

'I'm sorry. For what I said about your mom. About Gemma.' She sighed. 'I shouldn't have said that. I didn't even mean it. I was just angry.' She touched her fingers to her face. 'And you won anyway. Look at this.'

'I don't care. You deserved it.'

'I didn't.'

'Yes, you did.'

'I was just angry with your mom.'

'Why? She hasn't done anything to you.'

Beth looked surprised. 'But she has.'

Anger suffused me, but I held onto it, didn't allow it to surface. Kept my hands to myself. I was surprised at myself, at the way rage broke through me so easily. It was new to me, that feeling of being angry enough to smack someone. I felt responsible for my mother, had a primitive need to defend her. If I couldn't take her side, who could? Sarah was away. Besides, Gemma was my mother. It was because of me that people felt they had a right to make careless, throwaway comments about her.

'I'm sorry, Megan, I really am.'

I remained quiet. From somewhere nearby I heard the hiss of a hose, furtive and muffled.

She jostled my arm. 'Megan. I'm talking to you.'

I wondered what it would be like if we were in a real hideout, somewhere in a jungle, hidden by a double canopy of leaves. It wouldn't be any hotter than it was here.

Beth blew air from between pursed lips. 'Boy, you don't make it easy, do you? It was wrong to say that about your mom and I'm sorry.'

I regarded her squarely. Her eyes were darkened in the dim light. 'Why did you say it?'

'Because I'm pissed off right now. With her, with my dad, with my mother. If we hadn't come here, none of this would be happening. Your mom has done something to my father and it's not fair.'

'Gemma hasn't done anything.'

'Maybe she hasn't done any actual thing, but my dad is obsessed with her.'

Slamming the covers of my book shut, I leaned towards Beth. 'Don't be so stupid.'

'But he is! The first thing he does when he comes home from his classes is go out into the garden. And I know it's because he wants to see if she's there. My dad is forty-five. Forty-five! He's practically old. It's so embarrassing.'

Forty-five was old, I agreed with Beth on that. But it wasn't Gemma's fault if Chris liked her.

'Do you think they're doing it?'

She confused me. 'Doing what?'

'*It*. You know, having sex. Doing it.'

The thought repelled me. Gemma wasn't doing anything with Chris. No way.

'She isn't. They're not. Not a chance.'

'Well, I think you're wrong.'

'Want a bet?'

'Sure. Fifty pence says I'm right.'

We shook on it. I had no idea where I'd get fifty pence if I was proved wrong, but there was simply no way Beth could be right. It was impossible.

'Want to come out tonight? We need to use the pool.'

It was true. We'd gone to all that trouble, three hours to fill it, and so far we hadn't used it. We had checked on it the day after filling it, and after we'd scooped out the remaining leaves and twigs from the surface, it looked like any other swimming pool. Cool, blue, inviting.

Daniel parted the cardboard flaps and crawled back inside. He had a bottle of lemonade. There was a hiss as he twisted the cap. Suddenly, I was very thirsty. He held the bottle out to Beth and me. 'Want some?'

Beth took a swig. 'We're going to swim tonight. Proper night swimming.'

Daniel looked at both of us. 'Okay. I don't mind. What happened your face, Beth?'

'Megan hit me.'

Daniel laughed. 'No, she didn't! She never hits anyone.'

Beth fingered the swelling on her face. 'Well, she hit me.'

Daniel turned to me, still laughing. 'Did you really?'

I shrugged.

Beth nudged me. 'But we're friends again.'

I shook her off. I wasn't ready yet to be fully friendly towards her, not after what she'd said about my mother.

'Are you coming, Megan?'

'Don't know yet.'

'Oh come *on*. I'll throw stones at your window.'

'Maybe. I'll see.' I took the lemonade bottle from her and drank too much. The liquid fizzed in my nostrils and my throat, and I coughed. 'Gemma and I are on our own, and I don't want to leave her.'

Beth laughed. 'Why? She's a grown-up. And she won't even notice if you're gone.'

'But what if she did notice?'

'How could she?'

'All she has to do is look in on me.'

Beth shrugged. 'Suit yourself. I'm going anyway, so if you want to come, I'll be out. I'm going to ask Stevie too. It's not like we'll be far away. If your mother calls you, at least you'll hear her. And what's the point in having a pool if we don't use it?'

I nudged Daniel with my foot. 'Will you definitely go?'

Daniel held up his insect jar, tapped very gently on the glass with his index finger. 'Maybe. I don't want to worry Mummy. It's my dad's birthday today and she's feeling a bit sad.'

I wanted to say something to him, but the words would not allow themselves to roll off my tongue. Daniel didn't talk about his father, for the same reason. Things that are too huge for words can be like that: easy to think about, but impossible to put into a conversation with others. Often it can be easier to say nothing.

My reticence seeped into the stifling heat of the hideout. Despite the cardboard's shade, it was too hot, and the three of us had almost no room to move. I stretched out my legs, knocking the bottle over, spilling the contents. Beth jumped up, her head hitting the cardboard roof, sending its tentative structure into disarray. The rush of fresher air when the taped joints split apart was welcome, though, and the three of us laughed.

'Come out tonight, Megan,' Beth said, shaking my arm. 'We can have fun. Come on. Don't be a baby.'

That irked me. 'I'm not a baby.'

'Then come out with us. I'll throw a stone at your window when I get up.'

The prospect of the cooler night air and the freedom of being out and about was tempting. The lure of the pool, so welcoming, so cold, so near, was more than I could withstand. And Beth was right: what was the point in all that work filling it, if we weren't going to use it?

33

At first, it was the sound of splashing water. Then a whisper, followed by another. Next came laughter, muffled.

I wondered if I'd been dreaming. My single sheet was too much for me and I pushed it away. My pyjamas were flimsy cotton, but still I was too hot. The curtains covered the open windows, and I got out of bed and pushed them to the sides. It made little difference to the heat in the room. Back in bed, it was impossible to sleep.

Then I heard it again. It was only a faint splashing sound, but it was definitely water.

The creaky step yielded to my weight. My bedroom, eight steps up from the bathroom, was close enough for me to hear the plumbing, which was ancient, emphysematic. The door was open, the mottled glass of the panels shining with tiny imperfect lights. Candles. Gemma had lit candles.

Again, the sound of water, the barest splash. Gemma was having a bath. Sarah, the gatekeeper of water usage, would be horrified by such extravagance. So as not to give my mother a fright, I hesitated before I called her name. Then a voice that was not my mother's said something, laughed softly and was shushed. By Gemma.

I suppose I had been waiting for that moment of clarity. In hindsight, it was obvious. Like a reel of old film, patchy and shaky, the other times ran through my head. Gemma at the canal, her magenta skirt like a bright flag among the weeping willows. Gemma walking along the trail by the river in Wicklow, her camera around her neck. Gemma's new earrings, tiny shining studs of silver. The new bracelets, the new dresses.

Maybe I should have been angry with her, annoyed that someone else was getting her attention. Probably it would have been better to be angry, but all I felt was sadness. My mother, my beautiful, young, talented mother was lonely.

The man who was in the bath with her, however, was the opposite. He had everything: a wife, a daughter, yet still he sought out my mother, my fragile mother. In a way, I hated him for that, for seeing her loneliness and using it for himself. Who knew, possibly Chris Jackson loved my mother, but he was still greedy. He had his own family, yet still he was reaching over into ours, dipping his hand in and taking what he wanted.

The sound of water running, the squeak of the old tap as it was turned off again. The plink of rogue drops. I smelled lavender. Gemma's bath oils, an expensive gift from her friend Ruth. Gemma eked them out, made them last a long time. I imagined my mother, up to her neck in forbidden bathwater, drifts of lavender bubbles reaching to her chin. I saw her hair, piled on her head, stray strands floating on the surface of the water. I didn't want to think about Chris, either in or out of the bath. Beth's words raced into my mind before I could stop them. *I think they're doing it.*

Slowly, the whispers in the bath separated into words. They distilled themselves on the hot night air and travelled to where I was caught, on the third step, frozen. So many words that I had to put my hands to my ears to stop them from making sense. Words that should not have been spoken to my mother, not by a man who could not make good on his promises and for whom his words were just words.

Words like *beautiful girl.* Words like *sweetest Gemma.* Words like *you are incredible.*

I needed to move. To go back to my room would be to trap myself. I chose the other option and went downstairs as quietly as I could, my hand slipping easily over the polished banister. From the kitchen, I saw a sheaf of white hair in the garden. A raised hand. Beth. Moving onto the deck, I whispered her name. She lowered her hand.

'I was just about to throw the stone. Are you coming?'

My swimsuit lay over the back of a chair. Hurriedly, I pulled it on, first throwing my pyjama bottoms on the table.

The boys waited for us in the lane. The night was black, all light swallowed by the darkness. We slipped out the door in the wall. The stars were scattered like muted glitter and the waning thumbnail moon had disappeared. Out on the main road, a taxi swished by and was gone. I fancied I heard the snuffle of pigs, but they must have been asleep, worn out from the heat and waiting for the abattoir.

The pool was navy ink and we slid into it with barely a ripple. It held our four bodies and it still had plenty of room for us to move around. The cold made us all gasp at first, but quickly it enveloped us, soothing our overheated bodies, calming us. We made a concerted effort to be quiet, so there was little splashing, no diving, nothing to disturb the hush of the night. We were mermaids, we were sirens. We swam blindly underwater, we grabbed each other by the ankles, we thrashed our legs, and we did it all without making noise. No one knew we were there. The silence, the blackness of night, gave us a freedom we had never managed to procure before, and it intoxicated us and made us drunk.

34

The pool opened up the nights to us. We were proper night swimmers, the four of us. I had no Sarah to be conscious of, who would be alert to my nocturnal comings and goings. Gemma took to painting in the evenings, after I'd gone to bed, bringing her paints back up to the attic as I made my way upstairs. For those nights, I made no effort to stay up past my bedtime, did not wheedle my mother for extra time in the garden. If Gemma noticed, she said nothing.

It was funny how quickly we adjusted to the new routine: bed, stones at the window sometime after midnight, swimsuit, garden. Daniel and Stevie were usually in the pool when we arrived, and we slid into the water with an urgency that felt as though everything depended on it. Which in a way, it did. We didn't know it then, but it was a way for each of us to make a mark outside the confines of childhood, a means of reaching forward and doing what we wanted rather than what was expected of us.

We didn't spend the whole time swimming, though; we often sat with our feet dangling in the night-cool water, as the darkened garden of the empty house held us in its shadows. The trees and shrubs were all overgrown, the garden itself tatty and in need of care. For us, though, it was the perfect place to be invisible, away from the protective gaze of the adults.

'Look!' Beth said, standing at the edge of the pool, her toes curled under. 'Watch me.' She executed a perfect dive, making only the slightest sound as her body sliced through the water. She surfaced, her hair plastered to her skull. Wiping the water from her face with both hands she grinned up at us.

One by one, she instructed us in the technique of diving. Stevie, eager to be good at everything in Beth's presence, did it over and over again, Beth's praise making him smile more broadly than I'd ever seen him do.

Diving made me nervous; sometimes it still does. Conjuring all sorts of images of bashing myself off the bottom of the pool made me reluctant to let go and dive in. Daniel suffered no such worries; he sprang into the lightless water, sometimes graceful, other times clumsy as a toddler. But it was Beth and Stevie who took everything to new heights, new levels of accomplishment and competition. Up to that time I hadn't realised Stevie's prowess as a swimmer, his strength. He and Beth vied to outdo each other constantly with back flips, airborne somersaults, complicated dives. Daniel and I eventually lost interest in their struggle to come out on top. We retired to the edges, contenting ourselves with holding our breath underwater, counting to ten, fifteen, twenty, before exploding like salmon to the surface, drawing air deep into our lungs as though our very lives depended on it. We touched the bottom of the pool, first with our toes, then with our fingers, picking up pebbles that had settled there. There was never enough time, and the telltale line of dawn on the horizon each morning was a disappointment that was hard to quell. Maybe the finite nature of swimming at night made it more precious, more difficult to let go. It was with reluctance that we dragged ourselves out of the water at dawn and back to bed. Wet hair, wet swimsuits, a trail of wet footprints, glinting like silver, that dried in our wake.

35

And what of my mother? With what did she occupy those nights?

The first night, she slept. Putting my eye to the crack in her bedroom door, she was a dark huddle in her bed, her hair spread across her pillow in both directions. Gemma preferred to sleep with the shutters open in summer. Shadows thronged her room. Beyond the sash window, the sodium streetlights were orange lozenges that burned and crackled in the hush.

The second night, or rather, third morning, as we returned from our swim, I hesitated before creeping back into the garden. Peach light edged the darkness. Beth behind me, impatient with my dawdling. Hurry up, Megan, I'm getting cold. What's the matter?

There was no need to worry. Nobody occupied the striped deckchairs. The record player, its lid closed, sat squat on the patio. Leaving my wet swimsuit on the bedroom floor, I pulled my dry pyjamas on, my damp skin making the fabric stick. As I tugged, I heard a noise from upstairs. The attic? For a second I thought of ghosts, but ghosts don't talk, not even in soft voices, and they don't laugh either.

Gemma's room was empty. Carefully, quietly, I crept up the stairs to the attic. The door was closed, but there was enough of a gap under the door to let sound out. Lying down, I manoeuvred my head into a position that allowed me to look under the door. There was enough light from the dawn to allow me to make out shadows, then, as my eyes adjusted, for the shadows to take form. I saw two pairs of bare feet, side by side. Gemma and Chris were sitting on the floor, leaning against the wall. I couldn't see more of them than their feet and their legs, but I could hear Chris's voice, soft and slow. It was definitely him. Their legs were touching, all the way from their hips down. Chris's legs were longer than Gemma's, her ankles reaching a point above his. No matter what way I contorted myself, I couldn't see anything else. They weren't speaking about anything in particular, just a general swoop and fall to their voices. They were talking not to be heard. By me.

Chris was the first to move. His words not as soft. 'Christ, I have to go. The time! I've a meeting at eleven. I need to get a few hours' sleep. You do too.'

'When do you actually start teaching?'

Feet slipped into flip-flops. 'Late September. This is all just prelim stuff, summer classes, that sort of thing. No pressure.'

Like a serpent, I slid down the stairs and back to my bed. Chris and Gemma were almost silent in their descent. The door to Gemma's room closed over, a chink of new light falling through the gap.

◇◇◇

The third night was more complicated. Gemma and Chris were still sitting outside when we wanted to go swimming, trapping Beth indoors. Climbing on a chair, I took the key to the door to the basement off its hook and slotted it into the lock. It turned with an audible click. Carefully, I opened the door to the staircase that led downstairs.

Halfway down, I whispered Beth's name. No response. 'Beth!' Slightly louder this time. She heard me and crept on bare feet over the tiled hall floor to where I stood in the shadows.

'What are you doing there?' She climbed the stairs behind me. I closed the door after us. In the kitchen, she stopped. 'How did you know I couldn't get out?'

'I saw them outside.'

'Jeez, I couldn't believe it. How can we go to the pool now? They'll see us for sure.'

The deck was attached to the wall that separated our garden from Daniel's. Potentially, we could get on the wall and drop over into the Sullivans' garden. But we'd have to be extra careful because the wall was higher at that point than further down.

We tried it and, other than Beth landing awkwardly on her ankle, it worked just fine. On our return, Gemma and Chris were no longer outside and we were able to sneak back to our beds.

The following morning, though, disaster almost struck. Gemma was in the kitchen when I finally woke up.

'You're up late.' She wasn't annoyed, but she knew I'd been up to no good.

How could she have known about the night swimming? All sorts of possibilities ran through my mind: she had seen Beth and me clambering over the wall, despite the care we took not to be discovered. Someone had seen the swimming pool. We'd been heard while night swimming. All that splashing and diving had to have created some level of noise.

'What time is it?' I asked.

'Almost ten.'

It wasn't that late. The way my mother had said it, I thought it might have been lunchtime.

'Megan, have you been using those stairs?' With a thrust of her chin, she indicated the door to the basement and the staircase behind it.

I froze.

'What did Sarah say about keeping that door locked?'

I shrugged.

'Don't shrug at me, Megan. You're not Beth and I'm not Judith. I won't put up with that kind of disrespect. What were you told about using that door?'

'Not to use it.' I made no effort to keep the sullen edge out of my voice.

'Exactly. Those people are paying us to live there. They deserve their privacy and they will have it. Do you know what I saw when I got up this morning?' She didn't wait for me to answer. 'The key in the door. I can only assume you were opening the door for some reason, unless there's another explanation that I can't possibly imagine.'

A wasp buzzed behind Gemma. She swatted at it without turning around.

'Well?'

I picked at a scab on the back of my hand from where I'd grazed it climbing over the wall a few days before. 'I wasn't doing anything,' I said, not looking at my mother.

'Then what was the key doing in the lock?'

'I just wanted to see if it still fitted.' It sounded ridiculous, even to my ears, but Gemma wasn't going to let it go and there wasn't anything else I could come up with. Thinking under pressure made me nervous, particularly if what I was saying wasn't the truth.

To my surprise, my mother seemed to accept this. 'Stay away from the door. Our lodgers deserve their privacy. No, they're entitled to it. Do you understand me?'

'Yes.'

'Good. Now, what will you have for breakfast?' Gemma turned to get me a bowl and a spoon.

I should have asked her why she was always hanging around Chris if the Americans were so entitled to their privacy. But of course I didn't dare. There are things that sound great when unspoken, but the minute the words are uttered they come out wrong and end up causing far more trouble than was ever intended. Part of me wanted to shout at my mother for being such a hypocrite, but there was no one to back me up. So I let it go.

36

That night, it was just Beth and me. The boys had an aunt staying for a couple of days and they didn't want to risk waking her as well as their mother.

It was nice to swim without them because there was no competition, no need to be the best at diving or holding your breath or jumping or anything else that could have a competitive edge added. Beth floated on her back, her hair billowed on the water. I tumbled in the pool, did handstands, walked on my hands. Without Stevie telling me he could do it all better, faster, longer, I took my time.

'Not bad,' Beth said, moving her hands and feet. She was a starfish on the pool's surface. 'You're strong.'

Pride blossomed inside me.

'My dad always says swimming –'

'Teaches you endurance,' I finished for her. 'I know. You said it the day we went to the river.'

'I never really knew what he meant by that when I was little,' Beth continued. 'But then one day we got caught in a pretty strong current at the beach in Brooklyn and we had to swim really hard to get back to the shore. I had to get on his back, but he managed to get us both to safety. I remember watching the muscles in his back working, and thinking how strong he was.'

A cat ran along the garden wall and jumped silently down. We watched it pad past, ignoring us. It disappeared into the long grass, only the tip of its tail visible above the overgrown lawn.

'I want a cat,' sighed Beth. 'My mom won't let me have one in New York because she says our apartment's too hot and too cramped for an animal. Maybe we can get one while we're here.'

For a while we were quiet. The only sound came from the

water splashing against the sides of the pool as we swam haphazard lengths. It was only when dawn made its telltale appearance in the eastern sky – that almost imperceptible lightening that could be easy to ignore if we were under no pressure to get back to bed for fear of being discovered – that Beth spoke. We were sitting at the edge of the pool by then, watching our feet swish through the tepid black water, leaving mini whirlpools in their wake.

'So, you know that if my dad and your mom get married that we'll be sisters.'

It was a statement, not a question, and yet I sensed Beth required some reaction. I turned to her. Her face, in profile, was unreadable. She reached down and plucked a leaf from the water, and twirled it on its stalk between her finger and thumb.

'What do you mean?'

She flicked the leaf back into the pool and it floated on the water. 'Nothing.'

'Who said they're getting married?' It was too much of a leap, surely.

'Jesus, Megan. Wake up.' She sounded like Stevie, all impatience and superiority. 'When are you going to actually open your eyes and see what's going on?'

'What's going on?'

Beth clicked her tongue. Standing up, she made a rope of her hair and squeezed it. Water splashed around her feet. 'Your mother is making a fool of my mother. That's what's going on. She doesn't seem to mind that my father has a family. She stands there, all helpless and lonely, and he falls for it.'

Scrambling to my feet, I pushed Beth. 'My mother doesn't do anything of the sort.' My voice, louder than I'd meant it to be, was amplified by the quiet garden, by the overgrowth that sheltered our secret swimming pool.

Beth put her hands on my shoulders and pushed me back.

'Bullshit. She does. She's all *oh help me, I'm so quiet and artistic, I'm so lonely and good, I'm so cool and talented.*' Beth made her voice go high and silly. Mocking Gemma.

'Fuck off, Beth.' Fury tightened my jaw, clenched my teeth so that my speech was low, unrecognisable.

'You fuck off,' she shrieked. 'Your mom's a whore, that's what she is.'

'Go and fuck right off and leave us all alone!'

I shoved her again and she fell into the pool. There was no time to assess the risk of making noise, and the splash she made was huge, magnified in the stillness.

Beth didn't surface immediately. I hoped she had drowned. This was quickly replaced by fear that she had indeed drowned, which was assuaged when her head emerged, followed by her shoulders. She had swum underwater to the far end of the pool.

'Bitch!' she spluttered. 'You bitch!'

Satisfied that Beth was still alive, I stalked off. Back inside my own garden, I locked the door in the wall. Let Beth climb over if she had to. I didn't care.

37

For two days I ignored Beth. Without Sarah to question the reason behind our estrangement, I was able to blithely go about my business without curious glances or questions from anyone. If Gemma noticed, she said nothing, but Gemma didn't seem to notice much those days. She did all the usual duties of care – the cooking, the laundry, the chatting to me – but behind it all I sensed that my mother was merely passing time until she could be alone with Chris again.

Beth had been right, loath though I was to acknowledge it. I may have been nine years of age, nearly ten, but it was blindingly clear to me, finally, that something big was happening between my mother and Chris. Probably, I had known all along, at some level, but it is a big thing for a child to accept. I was being usurped, my place at the unquestioned centre of my mother's universe expanding to fit someone else. A man. Chris Jackson.

Without Beth, I went back to observing. I noticed Judith for the first time in days. Beth had said she'd been unwell, a cold or a sore throat. Something like that. Judith had waved up at me from the patio, where she was chopping vegetables on a small folding table. She caught me watching her from the safety of the deck.

'Hello, sweetie,' she called.

I waved down.

'How are you?'

'I'm fine, thanks.'

'Good! I've baked some bread. Would you like to take some?'

I took the stairs two at a time. Everything that was baked in Judith's oven was delicious.

The bread was warm and yeasty, crumbling in the tea towel in which it had been carefully wrapped before Judith placed it in a small basket. I checked Judith for signs of drinking wine through a straw straight from the bottle, but there was no way to tell. Responsibility weighed on me, then resentment. This was my mother's doing, not mine.

✧✧✧

Daniel and I played together. His aunt helped him put up shelves in his room and we stacked his treasures for display. Snail shells, a dried-out starfish we found on the beach in Sandycove one day in early June, myriad feathers. A snake skin he'd picked up in the reptile house at the zoo. A robin's skeleton, white and brittle. Birds' eggs, an ostrich feather, a butterfly's wing.

We went on another cycle, took the path by the canal in the opposite direction and ended up along the docks by the old mills. The stench of the river and the menace of those derelict backstreets sent us scarpering back to the relative safety of the canal banks.

Daniel and I were playing Monopoly on the deck later on that afternoon. Beth had gone somewhere with Stevie. Daniel had just landed on my most expensive street when a glass broke downstairs. Then another. Our game forgotten, we looked at each other.

Judith's voice rang out. 'You absolute bastard! I cannot believe this is happening again. Again! All this uprooting of our daughter, all this resettling into a new place, and you do it all over again. We may as well be back in Manhattan for all the difference it's made.'

'You're overreacting, honey bun.'

'Don't call me that! And I'm not overreacting to anything. I'm absolutely correct.'

'You're letting your imagination run away with you, as usual. I'm not up to anything.'

'Chris, stop. You must think I'm stupid. Or blind.'

'I don't think any such thing, Judy. I'm just saying that you're reading too much into things. A few late nights, a glass or two of wine, and suddenly you're throwing plates at me.'

'It's not a few late nights. It's much more than that, and you know it. I'm right about this.'

Some honeyed words from Chris. Then another smash.

'Don't do this! She lives upstairs. She's got a child.' Judith's voice reached a new pitch, swooping at the end. I remembered *I could have been a chef*. The anger poured into her words, the unrestrained ire. 'You're ruining everything, again!'

'Judy, Judy, ever the martyr.'

'What is that supposed to mean?'

'Just the truth. You're happy to sit around all day, keeping house, minding Beth. You like to pretend nothing has ever happened, nothing's ever gone wrong, and then when something out of the ordinary happens, boom! Apocalypse.'

Judith's voice was barely audible. Fury leaked over every word. 'You are despicable, Chris. Despicable. There's no other word for you.'

Chris and Judith argued on, back and forth, their words a rolling buzz, punctuated by a hand slammed on a hard surface, a plate, maybe, thrown at the wall. Voices from another world, behind a fluttering voile curtain, they drew us into their adult orbit and we didn't know what to do. It felt wrong to be eavesdropping, felt like breaking some code of behaviour that bound us.

'Let's go inside,' Daniel whispered, even though Chris and Judith couldn't possibly have heard us. 'We can finish the game later.'

Mrs Sullivan called over the wall. 'Daniel? Are you there?'

'Yes, Mummy. We're just playing Monopoly.'

'Did I hear shouting?'

I answered, more ready than Daniel with lies. 'Just the radio!'

'Well, dinner's ready. We're eating early today because Mary has to be up for the first train in the morning.'

Obediently, Daniel turned to leave. 'I'll see you tomorrow,' he said. 'We can swim again.'

⬦⬦⬦

Later that evening, Gemma and I were having our dinner. Omelettes again. It was too warm for a proper dinner. We were just finishing when there was a knock at the open kitchen door.

Judith.

'Can I have a quick word, Gemma? It won't take long.' She looked at me. 'Megan, honey, would you mind giving us a few minutes, please?'

I retreated to the dining room, but even from there I could still hear Judith. She sounded measured, steady. Controlled.

'Gemma, I'm sorry that I have to say this to you, but I need you to leave my husband alone. He's not worth ruining your life over, and he's the father of my child. I don't want any more drama and I don't want to upset your mother or your daughter, but if I have to I will. Stay away from him.'

Gemma was still sitting at the table when I ventured back to the kitchen. She was staring at something on the wall. She turned to me as I entered, altering her features into a semblance of a smile. 'There you are! Will we have dessert?'

38

The street lights were orange capsules and they hummed in the hush of night. The light at the canal bridge wasn't working properly and it flickered, emitting a crackle of electricity each time it tried to right itself. The locks had been opened earlier, and below where we leaned on the metal handrail, the water plunged, black and gushing, into the narrow channel where the barges passed through.

Stan's barge had moved further along the canal, towards the bridge at Portobello. The water was shallower there, Daniel said. Sarah told me that when she was a child there were many more barges than there were now. She said we were lucky to have been able to get onto Stan's boat, because so few of them travelled the canals any more. The concrete bollards for mooring boats were vague heaps carved in the darkness, the ghosts of ancient ropes tied around them.

We were night swimming. Daniel and I had wanted to use the pool, but Beth and Stevie won out, and we had gone to the canal. It wasn't worth fighting over. Beth and I had reached a truce of sorts, borne more out of the proximity of our shared living spaces than any real desire to be friends again. Her words had angered me deeply, her insults of my mother unforgivable. It struck me that she hadn't insulted her father in the same way, something I noted when she'd approached me, stealthy as a cat, earlier that day.

'Friends?' Her hand held out to me in reconciliation. Two plaited bracelets looped her wrist, blue and yellow. They were new.

I had turned away. I didn't know how to be friends with someone who hated my mother.

She touched my shoulder, forced me to turn to her again. 'Seriously, Megan, this is crazy. I live here. We can't not talk.'

'You called my mother a whore.'

'I know. I'm sorry. I was angry.' She fiddled with the bracelets. 'We all say things we don't mean when we're angry.'

'I don't.'

'Well, I do. And most people do too. They're just words, Megan. I didn't mean any of it.'

'But you said it like you meant it. And you didn't say anything horrible about Chris.'

'But there aren't any words like that for men.'

'That's not fair.'

'It's just the way it is.'

I hesitated. It wasn't good enough for me, but Beth was right. We lived too close to each other to be fighting. It made everything uncomfortable, and on top of that I had to hide it all because how could I explain the roots of our disagreement? Where would I even begin to unravel it all if my mother asked me?

Reluctantly, very reluctantly, I took Beth's proffered hand. She squeezed mine, smiled.

I wasn't convinced, but there seemed to be no other option. For now. This wasn't going to be forgotten. I would take it out later, examine it again, think it through.

A spurt of light as Stevie lit a cigarette. He dragged on it deeply, before passing it to Beth. I heard him trying not to cough. Beth's nonchalance with the cigarette was impressive. She held it between her fingers, elegant in her insouciance.

'Come on,' she said. 'Let's swim.'

'We should have brought a radio,' Stevie said, taking the cigarette from Beth as we walked over to the lock.

'Why?' asked Daniel.

'Because, stupid, we could listen to it,' Stevie said, rolling his eyes. 'What else would you do with a radio? Eat it?'

'I'm not stupid.'

'Yes, you are. Actually, I think I'm going to get one of those *I'm With Stupid* T-shirts and wear it every time I'm with you.' Stevie laughed, but I saw how his eyes flickered towards Beth, his anxiousness to impress her.

'Leave him alone!'

My own voice surprised me, magnified as it was by the empty silence of the night. 'Stop being such a bully.'

Stevie pulled on the cigarette again. 'Fuck off, Megan.'

I pushed him. 'Why don't you?' We glared at each other.

Beth stood in front of us. 'Guys, guys. Stop it. Do you want to fall in there?'

We clambered onto the lock. The water was black at our feet. Behind us, where Beth pointed, the canal gushed at its most dangerous point, where it refilled after the lock was closed. The wooden lock was painted black and the paint peeled in places. Someone had written with a compass or something else equally sharp, *Johnno loves Babo*. It was old now, the letters uneven and jagged. I sat down beside the letters, took my sandals off and kicked at the dark canal water.

'Who are they?' Daniel asked me as he ran his fingers over the lettering.

I shrugged. 'No idea.'

'We could write our names here,' he said.

I pulled away. 'What, write *Daniel loves Megan*?'

He laughed. 'Dan loves Meg.'

We both laughed.

'What are you two giggling at?' Stevie asked, standing apart from us.

'Come on, let's just swim.' Beth pulled off her T-shirt and her shorts, kicked her flip-flops off and threw everything onto the bank. 'It's such a waste of time to fight.' She eased herself down beside us.

'Tell your boyfriend that,' I said. 'He's always starting it.'

'He's not my boyfriend,' Beth whispered. 'He's just my friend. You're my friend too, right?'

I didn't answer.

She flicked the still-lit cigarette end into the canal. It sparked in the air.

'Hey, don't do that!' Daniel said, catching Beth's arm. 'The ducks will eat it and it could kill them.'

'Sorry, Dan,' she said, shrugging.

'You shouldn't ever throw things into water. It's so bad for the fish and the ducks.'

I had seen a lot more than a cigarette butt in the canal. Before the clean-out last Easter, there had been a shopping trolley, traffic cones, two bicycles and huge amounts of other rubbish, slimy and pond-weed-darkened, clogging the waterways with their sheer volume.

A splash diverted us. Stevie was in the water. He stood up immediately, clutching his foot. 'Ow, ow!'

Beth slid gracefully in, swam over to him. 'What's wrong?'

Stevie dropped his foot quickly. 'Nothing. Just stood on a rock. It's a bit shallow.'

'Are you guys coming in?' Beth floated on her back, her hair drifting around her shoulders. She tipped her head back, brought her feet up in front of her. She reminded me of a mermaid.

'Do you want to get in?' I asked Daniel.

'Don't know.'

'Me neither.' Despite the warmth of the night, being by the dark canal had lost its appeal. I decided in that moment that this was it. No more night swimming down here. Life at night at the canal was nowhere near as appealing as it was in the swimming pool. From now on, it was the pool or nothing. I loved its clean water, the privacy the overgrowth afforded. It felt like being in another world entirely, a quiet world far from prying eyes. The canal was too open, too exposed. Anyone could see us.

'Do you want to go to the pool instead?' Daniel asked.

'Yes! I was just thinking the same thing.'

'What about those two?'

'Leave them. We can go on our own.'

'When do you want to go?'

'Now?'

'Okay. But let's give it a few minutes first, and then we can just say we're leaving.'

From the water, Stevie taunted us. We ignored him.

'He isn't always like that,' Daniel said.

'Isn't he?'

'No. He's much worse when you're around, and definitely worse when Beth's with us.'

'Why?'

'Mummy says he's jealous because I have you next door.' Daniel rubbed at a spot on the wood. 'He's actually much nicer to me when we're at home.'

I doubted it. Stevie had always been like this as far as I could tell: loud, demanding, selfish. Everything Daniel was not.

'The other day, as we were leaving Mass –'

I cut across him. 'Do you like Mass?'

He stared at me. 'What do you mean?'

'I mean, do you actually like going to Mass?'

Daniel scratched with his thumbnail at an ancient piece of chewing gum that was stuck to the peeling, flaking wood. 'I don't mind it.'

I thought of the times I'd been to Mass – twice with Daniel's family, a few times with Hannah. The enormous church, the radiators that rattled in winter and never provided any kind of heat. The priest's voice magnified by the microphone that hissed and crackled whenever he leaned in too closely. The babies crying, the children fidgeting, the dip and swoop of murmured, communal prayer. Sometimes, I wanted to go, to be a part of the herd that thronged the path to the church on Sunday mornings, on holy days. Other days, I was glad we didn't go.

'You can come with us if you like. Any time. Mummy'd be so happy to bring you.'

I shook my head. 'I don't think I'd be allowed.'

Daniel gave up picking at the gum and leaned back against the wooden lock. 'Do you believe in God?'

In school, we learned all about God. His endlessness. His never beginning in the first place. His capacity to love all his children, even those who sin. 'Maybe.'

He looked panicked. 'But you have to! It's not just about going to Mass, Megan. It's about your soul.'

My soul didn't worry me too much. God had many more souls to preoccupy Himself with. Mine was doing just fine. There were so many dead souls, so many dying ones to keep God busy for a very long time. 'I thought you weren't going to be a priest.'

'I'm not! It's just so Mummy doesn't have to suffer. She's already worried enough about Stevie going to hell for being bold. I can't add to that.'

I nudged my best friend. 'I'm only messing.' His profile, outlined by the inadequate light of the streetlamp, was softened by his smile.

'Hey, did Gemma hear you leaving?'

'No, I was quiet.'

I thought of the scene behind the mottled glass bathroom walls the first night we swam in the pool, the wobbly flicker of candles, the heavy scent of lavender. The whispers.

I wanted my mother to be happy. I wanted her to have someone to take care of her, someone she could be with without having to lower her voice, without having to sneak around and meet under the safety of darkness. I liked Chris, but Gemma couldn't have him, not properly. Even if he was free, he'd always be Beth's father and Beth had to come first. Sarah always said that. The child comes first.

Beth floated, a siren of the night. Her wet skin gleamed, her hair the colour of marble. 'Come on, Dan! Get in the water. You too, Megan.'

'Daniel's afraid, aren't you?' Stevie teased.

Anger tripped over itself inside me. 'Shut up, Stevie! Leave him alone. He never does anything to you, but you're always horrible to him.'

Stevie laughed, that low mocking sound I'd come to hate. 'Fuck off, Megan. Stop fighting his battles for him.'

Daniel leaned forward. 'I can fight my own battles, Stevie.'

'Then why is your girlfriend always standing up for you?'

I turned to Beth. 'See? This is what he's like.'

Beth was treading water. 'Come on, stop fighting. You're ruining everything.'

My face burned. 'I'm not ruining anything. You just don't want to stand up to Stevie.'

Her voice quieted to a hush of whispers. 'Why can't you leave him alone?'

I was only nine, but I could see even then that Beth was one of those girls who would always stand up for a boy. She would forsake her friends, be unreliable and flaky, if a boy was in the picture. Daniel touched my arm. The stillness of the night swelled around us. To the left the moon had reappeared, a barely there fragment of silver in the indigo sky.

Daniel got to his feet. 'Come on.'

I stood up too. 'We're going home,' I called out to Beth.

She stopped whispering to Stevie. 'Oh come on, Megan! Stay. This is fun.'

'No, we're leaving. See you later.'

The swimming pool was waiting for us and I couldn't wait to

slide into the night-cooled water. In the pool, we had cover and shadow. We had space and silence and no one ever heard us. We could swim, dive, jump, whatever we wanted to do. Here, we were exposed, our skin rusted by the streetlights, too far from home for comfort.

Daniel put one foot in front of the other on the narrow lock. On one side, Beth and Stevie outdid each other in their efforts to impress. On the other side, far beneath us, the water surged. The old black paint under our soles was flaking, the wood in need of replacing. Later, that was the detail that stuck most firmly with me. The flaking paint. The old wood. Johnno and Babo and their long departed love.

Daniel slipped. It was that simple. It happens to everyone, almost every day. We slip. We lose our balance. We wobble. It's something that barely registers, most of the time. He reached out to steady himself but grabbed air instead of wood. He swung his eyes briefly towards me, his face blurred with fear. Arms windmilling, he fell backwards. I saw myself reach for him, but of course it was too late. His scream rang out in the tar-coloured night. It lingered in the dark air long after he hit the rushing black water and vanished.

A terrible darkness closed over my head and for a moment I couldn't see. I screamed for Daniel, the sound of my voice swelling like thunder. It alerted Beth and Stevie, who were suddenly beside me, pulling at me. Beth's hands on my face, forcing me to look her in the eye, most likely to tell her what had happened. Stevie, having already guessed, tried to climb over the lock and get down to where his little brother had disappeared. The whole time, all I heard was my own voice, shrill.

Beth mouthed soundless words, and her gestures to Stevie seemed ponderous and slow as Stevie tried to clamber down to find Daniel. I watched his fingers scrabble against the wood, paler than my arm, freckled at the knuckles, and much bigger than I would have thought. More like a man's hand than a thirteen-year-old boy's.

And where was Daniel?

I couldn't see him anywhere. Black poppies bloomed in front of my eyes, and I thought I was going to pass out. But then Beth screamed, her finger pointing, and the world suddenly burst into sound again.

Daniel had surfaced, some feet downriver from where he had fallen. I saw the back of his T-shirt, the white stripes vivid in the blackness. I called his name, relief flooding me. I told him it was all right, that we'd get help. I told him Stevie was coming to get him, even though Stevie's efforts had stalled and he stood helplessly, shouting at his brother. I told him anything at all, anything just to keep him from going under again, just to keep him conscious. I saw that recently, on television, where a person kept telling someone who'd been shot that help was coming. It had kept the person alive.

Except Daniel didn't respond. He just stayed there, his face in the water, his body twisted at an awkward angle. He didn't move, but I kept on calling, telling him to hold on. Help was coming. He'd be fine. Help was on its way.

The arms around my waist were unfamiliar, the voices not instantly recognisable. Stan. Stan and Barbara. No glasses of orange this time. They pulled me to my feet, then led me off the lock. Stan tried to get down to Daniel but he couldn't. He told Barbara to go back to the barge and get a rope. She did, then stood out on the road, hoping to flag down a passing car, but it was too late and no cars drove by.

AUGUST

39

Everything changed. Quietened, cooled. Even the heatwave seemed to lose some of its intensity, or maybe we were just so used to its grip that we ceased to notice it. The days emptied themselves. One by one they slipped by. I barely noticed. The Olympics ended. Beth wanted to watch the closing ceremony and I sat with her in our front room, the window pushed open to let in the air. I still couldn't tell you what we saw. Beth didn't talk much and I didn't say a word. Talking was difficult for me in the aftermath. There just wasn't anything to say. All that needed to be said faded into nothing beside what had happened. I had Beth around me all the time now and all I wanted was to be away from her. Stevie too had faded, retreated behind the garden wall. Occasionally, I heard the thwack of a leather ball on the stone wall. I imagined I heard him leaving the house after dark, to night swim alone, but really I didn't think too much about Stevie.

I hid in Gemma's attic when she wasn't painting. I didn't even care about the ghosts. I touched all her things, all her art books, her canvases, her brushes. I removed the tango watercolours from the wall and laid them on the floor, changed around their order, poured water over them and made the paint even blurrier. I squeezed paint tubes and left snakes of colour all over her long worktable. I even opened her trunk, sweeping the embroidered cover to the floor, clicking the latches, lifting the heavy lid. The hinges creaked with age and lack of use. Visions of uncovering secrets, lifting shrouds on the past, finding letters, photographs, albums of pictures crowded my head, but I let the lid slip from my fingers and slam shut. Much as I wanted, needed, to learn, I couldn't do that to my mother. Grief makes us foolish, but I wouldn't allow it to make me mean. Gemma kept things from me for a reason. Some day she would tell me, and I had to accept that.

Something fluttered to the floor from between the pages of a book I picked up. Two photographs. A younger, shinier Gemma with a pale baby me, a man with dark hair and a striped shirt. Felipe. He too was gone, God only knew where. I opened the trunk again, dropped the photo back on the pile and let the lid fall.

I wandered the attic, my jittery fingers touching everything. I read articles about *Los Desaparecidos*. The ones who never came back. Old now, they were filed in an ancient spiral copybook, wedged among heavy art tomes, yellowed, peeling away from the pages that held them. Red marks, faded to a shade that was less than red and closer to brown, circled around certain paragraphs, certain names. Most of the pieces were in Spanish, but I tried to read them anyway, my inability to decipher the strange words somehow comforting me. Gemma's secrets were surely there, under my wandering fingertips, waiting to be uncovered, held up to the light. Shouldn't all this have been in the trunk? Mysteries slid under my curious touch, so many things to look at, understand, know. I only grazed the surface. Gemma's stories, which were my stories too, only different. Told in a different time, from another perspective, they made up part of my fabric, but not all of it. My own imagination had been quelled, by my fear of upsetting my mother, by my apprehension of wandering too far into the dark, but now, leafing through pictures from newspapers, magazines, thumbing original photographs, seeing the photos of women and their placards, their headscarved heads held high, their mouths open, I could hear their cries, could feel their pain, for surely it was the same pain I was feeling. Loss, despair, sadness. And I joined with the women, *las abuelas*, as the pictures identified them, and their sorrow was mine. There's no end to suffering, Mrs Sullivan was fond of saying, because it's only through suffering that we will come to know God. Well, I wasn't sure if that was true or not, but there's something universal about grief. Gemma knew it and I knew it too. I was closer to knowing Gemma's truth, and it would reveal itself to me when the time was right.

Standing on Gemma's chair, I looked out the skylight, out onto the tiled roof with its chimney pots stacked against the sky, and all the other similar roofs and chimneys, and it was as though they weren't there. I played Gemma's records, but nothing that reminded me of anyone but my mother. Simon and Garfunkel. Carole King. Joni Mitchell. All the quiet, slow American music. No rock and roll. Nothing noisy, nothing with a beat or psychedelic guitars. Just the simple sounds of folk music, spilling like water over me as I wandered my mother's attic room. The ghosts left me alone, must have sensed something in me that kept them at bay. There weren't words for how I felt, so I didn't bother trying to find any. There was just a black glacier lodged within me and nothing would move it. Light slipped into corners and out again as the sun moved across the sky. Then I thought of how Daniel would have corrected me. *We're the ones that move. Earth revolves around the sun, not the other way around.* But it didn't matter any more, and anyway, I preferred to think that we were still and the sun did the moving. It was easier to accept that we had no power at all and everything that happened to us was out of our hands.

Because if we did have a say in how things were, then I had played my part in Daniel's death. Daniel's death. It was impossible to say it, even more impossible to accept it. But I had asked him to come with us, each time we went. Night swimming. Night swimming, as though anyone swims at night. As though we should have been doing anything but sleeping. The night wasn't for children. Night-time was for grown-ups, for adults. It was their time to do what they needed to do, away from the eyes and ears of snooping children. It was a time for martinis and white wine, for candles in jars, records on the turntable, whispered conversations. We had no place in the night, yet we had taken one anyway, carved out a special niche just for ourselves. And look what had happened.

There were no remonstrations from Gemma, or from Sarah. They said not a word, because I had taken all the words for myself. All those recriminations, all the what-ifs, the if-you'd-only-listen-and-do-what-you're-tolds. I had taken them all and stuffed them deep inside me. I probed them, like a sore tooth, like an exposed nerve. I didn't want to, but I couldn't stay away. They tasted bitter, like blood, or lead, and they jangled in my ears, but I had to look at it all, see it in the platinum summer light.

Sarah and Gemma left me alone to do what I needed to do, and they waited for me, with hugs and kisses, with hot chocolate and soft blankets, warm laps, and tissues to dry my cheeks.

I thought about it, over and over, like a home movie stuck on replay. The flaked paint. The silent slip of Daniel's foot. The look on his face in the millisecond before he fell. The fear that leaped out at me and my own frozenness. I imagined reversing it. How I'd have held onto his hand so that he couldn't fall, how I'd have refused to walk on the lock, insisted on staying on the canal bank. Or, even better, how I'd have said no to night swimming in the first place.

Swimming teaches you endurance, Beth had said the day we swam in the river. Green light had shone through the overhanging trees, the shadows on the water's surface wet and dappled. Two kingfishers had zipped past, little more than a dazzle of perfect blue. A dragonfly had landed on the water between Daniel and me, and we had stood, as still as statues, watching circles widening on the surface around its tiny form. Chris had held our hands, even though we could all swim. He hadn't wanted to let go in case the river carried us away. Endurance. I'd have swapped endurance any day to have my friend back.

I'm sorry, Daniel, I said to him in my mind. I'm sorry. I should have saved you. I should have grabbed you as you fell, pulled you to safety. Given us both a fright that we would talk about for years afterwards. *Remember the time you almost drowned? Remember you slipped and I caught you? What would we have done without you?* And my friend and I, the friend of my childhood and I, would laugh in horror at what had nearly happened. We would have learned our lesson and stayed away from the night.

40

'I wonder how she'll cope?' This was Gemma's observance, a day or two after Daniel's funeral, *she* being Mrs Sullivan.

Daniel's mother had strength I hadn't understood, hadn't appreciated. She said she didn't need to worry about Daniel, now that he was with God. God would keep him safe until she joined him again. Daniel was waiting for his mother, she could feel it, and it kept her strong.

Mrs Sullivan organised the funeral with a swiftness that surprised Sarah and Gemma. She spoke at length with the parish priest, who called to see her the afternoon after the fall and sat with her for the rest of the day. Mrs Sullivan knew exactly what hymns, readings and prayers she wanted for the funeral Mass. As though she'd been planning it for ever. She asked me to read a prayer for the safe repose of Daniel's soul. She'd even written it herself. I didn't want to, but Gemma encouraged me to. It's what Daniel would want, she said. You were his best friend. He'd do it for you.

But Daniel had been a better person than I. More patient, kinder. He didn't bail on me at the first appearance of an American, or spend time wondering what else he could be doing when he was with me. I wasn't deserving of him and I didn't deserve to read a prayer for the repose of his soul. I said this to Gemma. We were sitting on the big armchair in the attic. Heat and sadness had sapped our energy, and I sat on the arm of the chair with my bare feet on my mother's lap.

Gemma disagreed. 'Daniel loved you. He probably didn't even notice that you were spending a lot of time with Beth, and he wasn't the jealous type, so it wouldn't have occurred to him to be angry.' She rubbed her knuckles on my cheek. 'He was your friend.'

'But I didn't want to play with him all the time. And now I can't play with him ever again.'

I swiped at tears, angry with the anger within me, overwhelmed by the pointlessness of being sad because nothing, no amount of tears or crying, would bring Daniel back. Grief is a waste of time, I was quickly learning. There's no point to it, except to make ourselves feel something, anything, in the aftermath of tragedy.

'Wait here a minute,' Gemma said, lowering my feet as she got out of the chair. She came back after selecting a book from her pile of art books. Leafing through its glossy pages, she quickly found what she was looking for. 'Look, here, have a look at this.' She placed the book on my lap and sat down again.

What exactly she wanted me to look at I couldn't see. The picture lay across two pages of the heavy art book, a mass of knife strokes and thumbprints, colour exploded all over the canvas.

'What do you think?' Gemma's hand on my arm.

Nothing in the picture made much sense. Colours swirled. Blue for sadness. Black for death. Red for blood. Gemma had schooled me early in the basics of art appreciation. 'I don't know what it is.'

'Look closely. Here, look at this.' My mother's finger traced a broken line, a white mass. A horse. A house. Fire, or was it the setting sun?

The picture absorbed my attention. We hadn't done this in quite a while, my mother and I; not since before the Americans arrived. We hadn't sat with a book of paintings and looked at them, figuring out what the artist was saying. Because the artist was always saying something, Gemma said. Always. No one painted just for the sake of it. Art had to mean something.

'Is it Picasso?'

Gemma shook her head. 'It's Yeats. This is called *Grief*. I thought it might help you understand how you feel.'

I looked at her. Topaz light slanted into the room from the

skylights. The fan whirred in slow revolutions, barely disturbing the heavy stillness of the heat, which tipped itself into every corner. The attic door was open and from downstairs I could hear Sarah's sewing machine. The world carried on as it always had. No regard for Daniel. No recognition of his absence.

My fingers ran over the outline of the white horse, the riot of sunshine or fire, the pleading people. What was their loss? Who was their Daniel?

And even though Yeats' grief did little to relieve mine, for the time that I sat with my mother, her book heavy on my lap, her arms circling my shoulders, I was able to put my sadness aside for a moment. Not forget it, not remove Daniel from my thoughts, but allow my mind to move beyond the groove of grief I had been stuck in since that night.

For a couple of weeks after the fall, my mother and I sat thus each day. The time was not appointed, the clock unwatched. Sometimes it was a painting, others a verse of poetry. A few times it was a record, circling out of sight. It was hard to know what to do in the face of death, harder still in the aftermath. One evening the previous winter, Sarah and I had listened to a radio report about funerals in China. The people had to cry, wail, roar. They shouted out during the ceremony, banged drums and cymbals. We had turned down the volume on the radio, so great was the wave of riotous grief coming at us. I understood it now, though; the bloodletting of sorrow, the venting of heartbreak. We sat around in dazed silence, afraid of talking in case we might say something that could cause further sadness. Hours with my mother in the shelter of her attic, her books on our laps as we traced the history of grief through others' interpretations. Did it help? Perhaps. People had grieved for their dead since time began and would continue to do so until the end of days. We were just following the pattern.

And I saw how it could be. Minutes like these, where Daniel

would retreat, allowing other things to flood the expanse in my head. And maybe with time, possibly, Daniel would still be there in the night sky of my mind, but like stars, occupying some space, instead of being the whole darkness.

41

A thunderous rain fell with jarring suddenness. It was a shock, at first. I hardly recognised the rain as it slammed against the windowpanes and slid like mercury under the opened sashes, soaking the floors. From the kitchen, I watched as it flattened the flowers, knocked unripe apples off the tree, soaked the khaki grass. Sarah's terracotta pots filled and overflowed. Spiders were driven from their hiding places in the crevices of walls. It lashed for three days, the skies grey and full of menace, the heat sucked from the air. The deckchairs, abandoned on the lawn, flapped their sodden canvas like defeated flags. The patio furniture sat in a puddle of water on the flooded paving. The bougainvillea was plastered to the handrail, half its blossoms washed away.

We went hunting for warmer clothes, for sweaters and cardigans that had been packed away. I pulled on the unfamiliar garments, unused to having my arms covered, my legs encased. The rain, biblical as it was, distracted me.

The rain eased into a fine mist after a few days, and this hung over the darkened sky. It sparkled when the sun tried in vain to break through. On the radio they said this wet spell was only a break and to enjoy it while we could. The heatwave was coming back.

✧✧✧

Mrs Sullivan persisted with her absolute belief that Daniel was at peace. 'He's in a better place,' she said to me about a week after Daniel's funeral. I sat in their kitchen, my denimed legs hanging from the stool I was perched on. A plate of biscuits occupied the space between us, but I didn't touch them. Digestives. Daniel's favourites.

Candles dotted the house, in varying stages of life. By each was a prayer, or a photograph, something connected to Daniel. Mrs Sullivan had increased her daily allotment of prayer, it seemed. The Lord is always listening, she told me. Always, and we must be prepared.

I envied her. It seemed to me that she had found some peace in Daniel's death, some way of accepting the unacceptable. I smiled at her when she spoke of him. It would have been cruel not to. Daniel's sisters had shrunk into the shadows of their house. Stevie stayed out all the time, with his friends, with Beth, or maybe just on his own. Their mother depended on me now for company and I was happy to oblige. I wondered aloud if Mr Sullivan would be found now. Mrs Sullivan shook her head. 'He doesn't want to be.'

✿✿✿

My mother went back to her painting, filled her evenings with classes. She took on extra work as a guide in the National Gallery and even began to talk of returning to college in the autumn, to finish her studies. Gemma had done her foundation year and was already in second year when I was born. At the end of second year, students could apply for a diploma in sculpture, fine art or design. Gemma had planned on studying fine art, and one of her professors had advised her to come back after I was born. She hadn't, but now, in the aftermath of everything that had happened that summer, Gemma was thinking of returning. She met with the professor, Dr Doyle, who was willing to accommodate her circumstances, she told Sarah and me later, and give her credit for work already done.

'Maybe I'll teach art eventually,' she said. 'Properly, in a school or a college.'

'Then you must go back,' Sarah said.

'How will we manage?' Gemma asked, biting her lip.

'We'll manage,' Sarah said. 'We always do.'

And Chris? Gemma didn't seem to slip out as much any more, and my own curiosity about the affair had lessened. Maybe it was Judith's visit that day, maybe it was Gemma realising that Chris was never going to be fully hers. She didn't discuss it with me, of course, and I'm not sure even now if she knows how much I was aware of. Chris came and went, sauntering to the bus stop some mornings, walking into Trinity others. But I kept watch anyway. From a distance. Just in case.

✿✿✿

The weather forecaster was right. The heatwave did return. In some ways, it was as though no rain had fallen, and we were back to watching the amount of water we used and being careful outdoors. But it was different too. The madness, the changes, the insanity – all that had been swept away in the rain. Mrs Doherty next door no longer lay around reading, eating sandwiches with her husband on blankets in the garden. The doctor across the road put his shoes back on, except at the weekends, when the surgery was closed and he was free to wear sandals again.

The women still gossiped. The heatwave had changed none of that. No doubt they blamed Gemma for Daniel's death. If she'd never had me, he wouldn't have gone to the canal. Or something like that. We closed our ears to gossip in our family. It was what we did.

And the Americans. What can I say about them?

Judith emerged, stronger and more determined than she had been before. The woman who had told my mother to leave her husband alone made a decision. I heard her one day, talking to Chris. I was watering the pots on the deck, using dishwater siphoned from the basin in the sink.

'We're leaving. Beth and I. We're going home.' No emotion, nothing. Just a flat statement.

'I can't go.'

'That's the point. You can stay here. But we're going.'

Chris said something I couldn't catch. Judith snorted, derision making her voice edgy.

'For fuck's sake! Are you insane? No, wait, you are. You're absolutely insane.'

There was steel in Chris's voice. 'I'm not.'

'You're right. You're not insane. *I* am. I must be, to have put up with you for all these years. My God.' Judith laughed, only it didn't sound like proper laughter. 'My God, I uprooted our daughter, took her away from her life back home, so that we could maybe start over, and what do you do?' I imagined Judith throwing her hands up, shaking her head. 'You do it all again. And with that poor girl, too. You had no right, Chris. You had no right.'

Did she mean Gemma? Was that who the poor girl was? Why would anyone describe Gemma thus? My mother was at that moment, while I stood in the sunshine watering plants, on her way into Kildare Street, to put her name down for two years of study. She had put on her denim dress after breakfast, the one she'd bought in the Dandelion, brushed her hair till her arm ached, strapped on her red sandals and left in a flurry, nervousness making her jittery. She'd put on her silver bracelets, her earrings, but she wore them in a distracted way, as though they were no more important to her than the dress or shoes. She was doing the right thing by going back to college, I knew it. Nothing much would change with Gemma studying. She might be around less, but Sarah and I would be waiting for her when she came home. No, Judith couldn't have been talking about my mother. Was there someone else Chris had been night swimming with?

'I think I love her.'

Judith laughed, a mirthless snort. 'Love? Please! You don't love her. You don't love anyone but yourself.'

'No, that's just how you see me.'

Judith's voice dropped, but I heard her anyway. 'Go fuck yourself.'

They moved away, further into the house. A vague murmur of voices, a door closing.

Footsteps behind me. A swing of white hair. Beth. She eased herself into the space beside me, held up a hand in greeting.

'How've you been?' she asked.

I shrugged.

She sighed. 'I know. I'm the same. I know he was your friend all your life, but I really liked him too.' She put her chin on her knees, wrapped her arms around her legs. 'He was so nice and I miss him.'

I didn't want to talk about Daniel. I really, really didn't want to talk about Daniel. My thoughts whirled, dervishes in my addled mind, and I was exhausted. It was bad enough thinking about him all the time. Talking about him only added to it.

'Have you seen my mom?'

I lied. 'No.'

42

Judith and Beth were moving home. Judith wanted to go to New Mexico, where her parents still lived, but Beth put her foot down. New York or Dublin. End of story.

'I know what I'd have said if she gave me that choice,' Sarah said to Judith over a cup of tea in the garden. They didn't seem to know Beth and I were on the deck above them. The tops of their heads were visible, circles above the circle of the table they sat at. They reminded me of draughts on a board.

'I know, but this is a big thing and I need her to feel that at least one of us is considering her needs.'

A glance at Beth, but she was absorbed by the jigsaw we were piecing together and didn't appear to hear a word of the conversation below us. The puzzle was a difficult one that Sarah had unearthed earlier in the attic. Two thousand pieces and a map of Europe. Now that Gemma was going back to study, the attic would be used by all of us again. It would still be Gemma's, but Sarah and I had each claimed some space for our things. Change was afoot. Judith and Sarah had started walking, a routine they had established in the aftermath of Daniel's accident. Maybe it would have started anyway, but each evening my grandmother and Beth's mother took to walking for an hour. The evenings were shrinking perceptibly, that slow darkening of the summer skies happening earlier and earlier. The heatwave lingered, but less so.

'Chris will have to find somewhere else to live, you know that, don't you?' Sarah placed her cup carefully back in its saucer. 'It wouldn't be right for him to stay on here. I'll find someone else to rent to.'

'Of course he'll have to find someplace else. That's his problem.

Not that it should be too big an issue for him; he knows enough people here to help him.'

'Good.'

'He's not a bad man, you know?'

'Hmm?' Sarah said, looking incredulous.

'No, he's not. He's just selfish.' A short laugh. 'Seduced by his own beauty.' A pause. 'I'll miss you, Sarah, you know that?'

'And I'll miss you. I really will.' She put her hand on Judith's arm. Judith covered Sarah's hand with her own and they stayed that way until Judith began to clear away the tea things and they both went indoors, Judith promising to show Sarah some cookbooks she could keep if she liked.

It was that time of day, with the last light before the sun goes down falling on our faces and arms, making our skin look as though it were on fire. With Judith and Sarah's conversation at an end, I returned my attention to the activity in front of me.

Mid jigsaw, Beth announced that she wanted to watch television. 'Are you coming?'

I slotted a particularly tricky piece into its groove. 'In a minute.' A segment fell to the ground and I picked it up. Part of Czechoslovakia. Near Romania, where Nadia was from. Another country behind the Iron Curtain. I pondered the Curtain, as I frequently did, and all those lives lived behind it, under the control of someone else. Invisible power. The most dangerous kind. Were their lives lived in colour, or was everything black and white?

Gemma cut across my contemplation of secrecy. 'How are you getting on with that?' She stood, framed by the doorway. A strand of bougainvillea drooped over the wooden railing and she pulled at it. Despite the dwindling summer, the interminable heat, the plant showed no sign of fading. In fact, it was positively robust, in full perfect bloom.

'Fine.'

'Where's Beth?'

'Gone in to put on the telly.' The border between East and West Germany was a heavy black line. East was pink on the map, West green. I rummaged for Checkpoint Charlie in the box. Shouldn't that have been on the map too? Maybe there wasn't space.

Gemma nodded towards the house. 'You should go in with her.' I knew my mother wanted me to have company, was worried that I'd be lonely. Gemma knew loneliness, had walked its crooked paths and winding ways. She didn't want that for me, but she needn't have worried.

'I will in a minute. I'm just finishing this part.'

✧ ✧ ✧

The potted plants partially obscured me. Chris and Gemma must have assumed I had gone indoors. They sat on the wooden stairs, Gemma one step above Chris. Gemma leaned back on her elbows, her hair fanned on her shoulders. In the pumpkin-coloured light, her white top was orange, her tanned skin the colour of almonds.

Chris turned around to face my mother. 'It could have worked, you know.'

'Don't be ridiculous,' she said, her voice sharp.

'I'm not,' he replied, sounding sulky now, like a small boy.

'Chris, your wife is leaving you and taking your daughter with her.'

'But you and I could still be together. Couldn't we?'

'No. It's too much, all of it.'

'Please, Gemma. That's not fair.'

Gemma's hand on his arm. The tinkle of her silver bangles. The softening of her voice. 'No. It's too huge, too much. I can't tell you that I'll do what you want or be who you'd like me to be. I have a child, and she comes first.'

My spirits lifted when she said that, and I knew everything

would be all right. I would get through this blackness I'd been stuck in since Daniel's death, everything slowed to a crawl. Sometimes, it felt like I was wading through water, wanting to go faster but not being able. My mother understood. She would carry me through.

'I still don't see why we can't just be together. It's not as though no one knows about us now.'

Gemma's voice like a knife. 'No one knows about us. Besides Judith, no one knows, and that's how I want it to stay.'

'Why?'

A slow shake of her head, her hair moving on her shoulders. 'Because, Chris, it's just too much. It's all wrong, everything.' Gemma flung her arm wide. 'The timing, the place. I live with my *mother*, for God's sake! Megan comes first, and she has to. I'm all she has.'

'What about her father?'

'Stop it. Stop it this minute.'

'But you're perfect for me.'

Gemma turned to face him. Her unblemished profile, outlined by the dying sunlight. Chris touched his fingers to her mouth. She caught his wrist, held it, rubbed his hand against her cheek, then twisted away.

Chris, his fingers under her chin, tried to turn her face to his again. Gemma resisted. 'Look at me. Please, Gemma. Just look at me.'

She acquiesced, but reluctantly.

Chris moved his fingers to her hair, winding a strand into a corkscrew. 'This is what I want to remember. Okay? If we can't take it further, then I want to be able to have moments like this to think about.'

'What, when you're old and grey and feeble, you mean?' But I heard humour in her voice, saw a smile lift the edges of her mouth.

He laughed, elbowed my mother, put his hand on her hair again. 'You're great. And I'll miss you more than you will ever know, believe me.'

'I'll miss you too.'

'You're right for me.'

'I'm not. I'm not the right person for anyone, except maybe my child.'

'Children grow. They grow up and then they leave.'

'Which is why we have to take care of them while they're with us. I don't want Megan to turn around in twenty years and think that I didn't do everything I could for her. You're the same as regards Beth.'

Chris looked ahead. 'I know.'

Gemma shook her head. 'Then don't say you'll abandon her for me. I couldn't live with that and you couldn't either, no matter how you feel right now.'

Chris threw his head back and laughed. 'My God. The martyrdom!' But his laughter held no mirth. 'The Irish martyrdom.'

Gemma stood up. 'Don't be such a child.'

Chris got to his feet too. He reached out and pinched Gemma's cheek. 'Let's not fight. I don't want any more fighting. I've enough of that in my own life.'

Gemma caught his hand, threaded her fingers through his, touched her lips to his knuckles. Neither of them spoke for a moment.

'I'm in love with you.'

Gemma looked down, didn't let go of his hand. 'Please. Please don't.'

'But it's true. And if you're honest, you'll say the same thing.'

'Maybe, but I can't.'

'You're perfect for me.'

'But our timing couldn't be worse. Really, Chris.'

'But this doesn't just happen. In life, this isn't something we run into many times.'

'I can't. I'm sorry, but I can't.'

'Timing? Is it just about timing? Really?'

Gemma dragged her hands down her face, exhaling as she did so. 'Isn't everything?' And I knew she wasn't just talking about Chris. She meant something else entirely, but she let Chris think that it was just about him.

Chris shook his head. 'What's that they always say? The right person at the wrong time is the wrong person.'

'I haven't heard that one before, but there's a lot of truth in it.'

'Will you think about it? Just think about it?'

Beth appeared at the kitchen door. 'Megan, are you coming in?' She spotted Chris at the foot of the stairs. 'Oh, hi, Daddy!'

Chris twisted his torso around to look up the steps. 'Hey, baby girl. What y'all up to?' A wave at me. 'Hey there, Megan.'

'Nothing much.' Beth turned to me. 'Are you coming?'

Gemma stood, advanced towards where I sat, obscured by plants. She held her hands out to me, supplicant. 'Have you been here long, Megan?'

'I suppose.'

'Did you hear me talking to Chris?'

'You weren't whispering, were you.'

She looked back at him, then put her hand on my face. 'We'll talk about this another time, okay sweetheart? For now, go inside with Beth. She'll be gone soon and you'll have all the time you need for jigsaws.'

Reluctantly, I put down the piece of puzzle I was holding. The geraniums in the pots glowed so brightly in the fading light that they looked as though they might burst into flames at any minute. A pig squealed over the wall. Sarah said that the piggery was going to close soon. Too many complaints. About the noise, the stench. Their owner had told Sarah he was going to keep hens instead, and sell eggs. A cleaner business altogether, he'd said. Equally noisy, though, Sarah said. The following summer, with no heatwave, we would hear the clucking of hens, their early morning squawks, see their feathers blown on the wind. By then, my mother would be finished her year of study and would be readying herself for the next.

But that was all a long way off. When you're nine, six months is an eternity, a year even more so. Slowly. Change was better when it happened slowly.

I followed Beth indoors, leaving my mother with Chris. With one last look back I saw the last of the sunlight slip over the garden, coating everything in its tangerine light.

My mother and Chris stayed outside, until eventually I forgot they were there. Beth and I sat on the couch with the television on and the lights off. The programme we watched filled in the gaps in the silence for us. I was too tired to speak. Events had hollowed me out, and the peace and quiet that came with watching people compete in team games while wearing foam suits was enough. We even laughed, quite a bit as it turned out, and it was strange to hear our laughter in the quiet house. It pushed some of the shadows back into the darkness, allowed me to imagine, just for a moment, the possibility of moving forward.

It wasn't much, to be honest, but it was something. A start.

43

Before Gemma resumed her studies, she and I were in the attic, clearing out some of her things. Already, it was more organised. After fixing the old bookshelves, Jim had put up several more long shelves and a bookcase at Sarah's request, and had painted the attic walls and ceiling.

The new shelving was a marvel, row upon row of plain wood running the entire length and breadth of the walls, which Gemma had stained in various colour washes. On it, we stacked boxes of paints and brushes, blocks of paper, baskets of inks, pastels, pencils. Carefully, we placed art books, huge tomes, spines straight, dust jackets immaculate. Gemma's artwork went in special boxes, her current pieces stacked neatly on her huge table. As we worked, a record whirled on the player. John Lennon. A parting gift from Chris before he moved out. He had taken his records with him. I wouldn't miss them – The Doors, Jimi Hendrix, Pink Floyd – all the noise of rock and roll and the summer.

Judith and Beth were leaving soon. Going back to New York in time for school to start. Judith was going to get a job teaching music. I hadn't even known she could play an instrument, but here she now was, unfolding her talents to us. It was as though Chris had taken up all the energy in their family, his needs, his brilliance, his ideas. No room for anyone else to venture forth. Yet now Judith was taking her own steps, away from his gaze.

I'd sat on the wall with Stevie one evening, eating ice-cream wafers. Mrs Sullivan was praying indoors. His sisters played quietly with dolls on the grass behind us. Ever aware of Stevie's need to needle me, I was tense, ready to drop off the wall and go home, but he was fine. He was starting at a new school in September. Boarding school. Dismissively, he said it was his grandfather's old school. They were letting him in because of family connections. 'That, and money too.'

'Why are you switching schools?' The ice cream had made my lips freeze. I wiped my mouth with the back of my hand.

'My mother says a change will do me good.' He snorted. 'She thinks that if I start shoving people around a rugby pitch that I'll behave myself when I'm at home. Use up all my energy in sport. She hasn't a clue.'

I brushed crumbs from my shorts. It was a change, being affable towards Stevie, but Gemma said he needed a friend. Stevie already had friends, the boys he went fishing with and played football with, jumped the cinema queue with, but Gemma said we all needed to be good to him.

The record sleeve was cool to my touch. I ran my fingers over John Lennon's face, which was obscured by clouds. Behind me, his piano music spilled out into the warm room. Above me, the sun shone through the open skylights, illuminating the millions of dust motes that we were unleashing with our cleaning and tidying. Jim's shelves were filling rapidly, the floor suddenly bigger, wider, emptier.

Gemma's trunk occupied the middle of the floor, large, draped with the handstitched quilt. Over the course of the summer, Gemma's trunk had loosened its grip on my curiosity. Even the ghosts were less of a threat now, maybe not a threat at all. Daniel was a ghost now too, and who could be scared of Daniel? Maybe that's all Gemma's ghosts were, remnants of other people, other lives, drifting around the space they could no longer occupy.

'Are you going to open it?'

I turned. My mother had her hands on her hips, painting shirt flapping open. Gemma gestured towards the trunk. Her bangles jangled.

I faltered. Part of me wanted to open the creaky clasps, delve deeply, bring light to all those dark spaces. Another part of me didn't mind if it never happened. Pandora regretted opening the jar. Only hope was left. But hope wasn't always a bad thing. It left us with something to strive for. 'I don't know.'

'You can, if you like.'

The leather lid was scuffed when I slid the quilt off, betraying the trunk's age. The fading patchwork fell soundlessly to the floor, leaving the trunk exposed. The ornate key in each brass clasp turned easily, as they had the last time. They opened with a click when I pushed the brass buttons. The lid creaked, the only sound in the hushed attic. I half expected a flotilla of ghosts to sail past me, berating me for spying on my mother's secrets.

'Go on,' my mother said. 'It's time I told you.'

'Told me what?' I asked, even though, really, I knew. 'If you want, we can do it another day.'

Her voice was soft, but I knew when my mother had set her mind to something and this was one of those times. 'No, Megan. We can do it now.'

44

The photographs of him weren't in albums. Gemma had kept them in envelopes, each one printed neatly with her calligraphy pen. Dates, places, names. There were letters too, wrapped in bundles with blue ribbon. Sarah's warnings echoed in my ears: never read another person's diary or their letters. Under the photos and the piles of correspondence were drawings. Some pen and ink sketches, some watercolours. I noted several charcoal drawings of my mother. Three unmounted canvases bore heavy oil paint in vivid colours. Two or three spiral sketchpads with creases on their covers. Newspapers, yellowed and fragile with time. Posters, creased down the middle. Tapes of songs, their Spanish titles scripted in an unfamiliar hand. There was so much more than I had skimmed the first time I dared to open the trunk.

'Felipe's things.'

It wasn't until I spoke that I realised how dry my throat was. My words came out raspy, stilted.

'Everything here is.'

The wooden boards were hard beneath my knees, but I didn't mind. I trailed my fingers through the trunk as through water in a tank, touching only the barest surface of things. Where to begin when given access to what one has always wondered about?

Gemma made that decision for me. She pulled a large sheet of paper out from where it was wedged under a paperweight. Another drawing, this one in pen-and-ink: Gemma leaning back in a chair, a rocker, smiling at the artist.

'Did he draw this?'

She sighed. 'He did.'

I gestured towards the piles of drawings and paintings. 'And these?'

'Most of them. Some are mine, but most are his.'

Gemma dropped the sheets on the floor beside her and reached back into the trunk. More pictures, more of Gemma, but some too of other things. Flowers, mountain ranges. Jungle. Alpacas and llamas, their eyes lidded and staring. There were photographs too, big black and whites, bold in their statement. Men underground, headlamps attached to their hard hats, sacks stacked around them. Children running from soldiers. Women holding babies, their faces in a twist of sadness. People hunched over the salt flats, scooping white salt into metal buckets. *Los saleros*. A man in a black beret, flanked by other men. I knew him, from the poster on Gemma's wall. Che Guevara.

'What are they doing?' I asked my mother, pointing to a photo of the miners.

'They're striking. These signs are in Spanish.'

'What do they want?'

'An end to corruption. The right to join a union. That sort of thing.'

'Where are they?'

'Bolivia.'

The picture of the Andes. The painting of the *cholita*. The Che poster. My mother's fascination with South American politics. The Borges quote.

And the question that was most important of all to me, the one I was almost afraid to ask, but which slipped out so easily that afterwards I wondered why I hadn't asked before. 'Where is he? Is he in Bolivia?'

Gemma lifted another picture, and another. I thought she hadn't heard me, but eventually she looked up. 'Felipe wasn't your father, Megan.'

'What do you mean?'

My mother looked at me, her face so close to mine that I could see the minuscule flecks of amber in her irises. Our identical eyes. Then she shook her head. 'Megan.'

Felipe wasn't my father. Felipe had been her friend. A beloved friend, her greatest friend, but the kind of man who didn't like women, at least not in a romantic sense. Felipe and Gemma met in an art history class and became friends. Everything about him was true, right up to his return home and his disappearance. Gemma never saw him again, but she wanted to find out something about him and she was going to do it. 'Because if I don't, Megan, no one will. There's no one left who will look for him.'

This I could come back to later, unpack in the quiet of my room, think it through.

What she told me next was more difficult.

It came out in a rush. A tumble of words, falling over each other in a desperate scramble to be heard. My mother unburdening herself after almost ten years of secrecy.

My mother's story and, subsequently, my own story, untangled itself around me in the heat of that late August morning, while the sun made patterns on the floor and seeped into the cracks and fissures between the wooden boards. Listening to her was like listening to a tale about someone else, other people, other families. Spaces opened up between my mother's words, then were filled in with what she had to tell me. It was difficult to listen to her. I was too hot, and the mention of Daniel planted him into my head again, distracting me.

It was complicated.

But in the end it was very simple.

Daniel's father was my father.

This is what my mother told me. It hadn't been planned. Nothing like that ever is, Gemma said, as she leaned her back against the attic wall. Like a baby, or a very young child, I crawled into the gap between her legs, leaning against her. She stroked my hair as she spoke and her voice sounded far away, as though she were speaking to me from another room, her words tinny and distant.

It was like listening to a tale from a book, something filled with dark adrenaline. Questions tumbled through my brain as we sat there on the attic floor, with sunlight spilling down the walls and across the floorboards to where we sat, the steamer trunk open beside us, the ghosts merely a hush in the stillness of the late morning warmth.

'It was the most ridiculous occurrence,' Gemma said. 'Unplanned, stupid, wrong.'

'Why wrong?' I asked.

'Because it was,' she replied. 'My neighbour. Married. Two decades older than me. Ridiculous. And yet,' she said, turning my face to her, her fingers soft under my chin, 'look at what I got out of it.'

Gemma met Mr Sullivan walking home one night. He had been working late; she'd been at a party. Somehow, they ended up sharing a bottle of wine in the garden flat and one thing had led to another. My mother used that phrase. *One thing led to another*. As though the simple act of meeting on the street after hours needed no further explanation, as though running into your neighbour was a good enough reason to end up with a child.

I wasn't judging my mother. I wasn't yet old or cynical enough to do that. Later, I would develop the necessary skills to throw her actions back in her face, but even when I did, years hence, Gemma was invariably calm in the face of my fury. If it didn't happen, I wouldn't have had you. It's that simple, she would say. One slip and I got you, and nothing you say, nothing you do will ever change my mind about that.

Sarah didn't know, Gemma said. Sarah was allowed to believe the Felipe fable; indeed, it was Sarah who had first assumed that Felipe was behind it. Gemma didn't correct her mother, because it was one thing having a baby by an activist artist who was murdered for his political beliefs, even in the Ireland of the 1970s. But a brief interlude in the garden flat with a married neighbour, well, that was cause for total condemnation. I wouldn't have been allowed to keep you, Gemma said, tears springing in the corners of her eyes. I almost didn't as it was, but if the truth had come out there'd have been no way I would ever have been able to hold onto you. My baby girl, she said, her hands soft on my cheeks. My most beloved, precious, baby girl.

And even though there was so much more to say, so much more to ask her, I let my mother hold me, and I didn't mind that she cried over me and whispered. She said: I love you so much. She said: I'm sorry for this mess. She said: Everything will be fine.

Daniel was my brother. This was the most obvious realisation from my mother's admission. My grief, huge and unmoving, was somehow further magnified at this, the catastrophic loss of him reawakened all over again.

Too much else lay in my path – to be picked over, sorted through, put into perspective. I needed time, and at nine, I had so much of it. The future lay open, a book with blank pages. There would be more time to ask Gemma, other occasions such as now, when we would sit together, my mother and I, and we would talk. There would be time too, when I was older, to find traces of the father I didn't know. When I was older, and Gemma was finished her studies. During a future summer, not quite as long or as dramatic as the one we were helping to draw to a close, we would venture, my mother and I, into the unknown, and we would go and find him.

But that was a long way off.

'Why did you wait so long to tell me about him?'

Gemma shrugged, displaying the palms of her hands. Paint had collected in the lines along her skin. Her nails were short. Artist's hands. 'I wanted to find the right time. And maybe I thought that if you never wanted to know, then maybe I wouldn't have to tell you.' She thumbed the remaining tears on her face. 'But after what happened to Daniel, I figured there was no way out; you needed to be told the truth.'

Sarah called our names, but still we lingered. My story, my ghosts, bowled through my mother's attic and I was aware of a change within myself, a slotting together of pieces of the puzzle I hadn't up to that point even realised were missing.

I drew in a lungful of the attic's hot air. My head rested on my mother's shoulder. This. This was all that mattered.

Epilogue

Summer ended quite abruptly, as it turned out. Judith and Beth left at the end of August, taking their boxes and suitcases with them. Sarah and I had dinner with them both the evening before they left. Judith made *carne adovada,* with big chunks of pork cooked in chilli sauce. Her last meal to be cooked in Dublin on the small stove. Judith said the dish was better served with black beans, but she cooked rice because it was easier to buy. I asked Gemma was she coming with us, but she shook her head. Too much to do, she said. Plus I have my class in the gallery.

To be honest, Judith hadn't invited her.

Sarah and I waved Beth and Judith off the next day. Brad came to collect them in his car. He tossed their suitcases and boxes into the boot as though they were toys. He didn't mention Chris, and neither did Judith. We waved till our arms hurt and the car had disappeared down the road.

'Well!' Sarah said, her arm around my shoulder. 'That's that.'

Quickly, it seemed as though the summer had never happened, except that Daniel's absence still left a wide gash in my days. A long time would pass before I accepted that he wouldn't be back. It was difficult, but childhood brings with it its own resilience. Traces of Daniel lingered: a ladybird struggling over grass; a moth banging its way around inside a lampshade; the copper sheen of a chestnut, just out of its spiny case. He was everywhere that autumn. All I had to do was look. Mostly, it made me happy that he was in so many places, but oftentimes it filled me with a sadness that seemed to seep from my very skin. Do you know this grief? It sits like a glacier, mostly hidden. Then drop by melting drop, it begins its slow emergence.

Swimming teaches you endurance. I had no choice but to endure, and I waited for the sadness to exhaust itself. It wasn't easy, but I did it. And I thought of Gemma's ghosts, of my father. If ghosts stick around for long enough, they'll travel with you eventually.

Sarah had wondered aloud to Gemma if Daniel's death would bring his father home, but Gemma dismissed such a notion out of hand. 'Why would they want him? He'd only leave again, anyway, and they're better off without him.' She looked at me as she said that. I wasn't sure if I agreed with her, but I let it go.

✿ ✿ ✿

With autumn came cooler days, shorter evenings. Sometimes, sitting indoors while wind and rain raged outside, it was almost as though the heatwave had never happened. Our summer clothes had been bundled up and packed away in boxes on the new shelves in the attic. Old patterns had been resumed, old habits refusing to go away. The pool was left to its own devices. Maybe the water evaporated, maybe it stagnated. I never swam there again. The house remained empty for the rest of my childhood, each year falling further into disrepair.

Sarah and I settled into a routine. I went to school, making the journey alone for the first time, though I liked to think that Daniel's ghost kept me company on the walk. While I was gone, Sarah made curtains, hemmed skirts, knitted, and did whatever she needed to do to keep our household afloat. Gemma went to her lectures, and we waved her off in the mornings, her old bike clicking as she pedalled, her clothes billowed by the breeze. She didn't care what anyone thought of her. She was happy, the basket on her bike stacked with books, a bag of brushes and pencils on her back. Sarah said she had no idea how we'd get through the next few years and she wasn't going to be bothered by worrying about it. I knew we would be fine because we always were. My small family didn't sit back and rely on rosaries and novenas to get us through. We did it on our own, and we minded each other along the way.

I didn't ask Gemma about Chris. There wasn't anything I could really say that hadn't been said or thought. As far as I knew he was in Trinity, but where he lived and what he did was unknown to me. Judith sent an occasional letter to Sarah, always brief, the details light and chatty. Music classes going well. Beth happy in school. New York was hot or freezing, always at the extremes of temperatures. We read of Thanksgiving, Christmas, other celebrations, but little else. It was as though Sarah were someone Judith had met on a weekend away, with whom she stayed in touch out of politeness. Sarah always responded with something short and warm, which she allowed me to read over her shoulder as she wrote.

I missed Beth. I missed her outlook on life, her puzzlement when confronted with anything that could be construed as an obstacle. For Beth, life was for living and obstacles were just something to be blown through. Her fearlessness had chipped away at some of my reservations and, who knows, maybe it was because of her that I was now stronger in some ways, less fearful of what lay ahead.

I missed Judith's food too. All those concoctions that became familiar with tasting and testing: her blue corn, her stacked enchiladas, the quinoa and *sopapillas*, chilli with everything. I didn't mind going back to eating lamb chops and stew, potatoes and vegetables without adornment, but I had tasted what was different and I was unable to forget it. It was a tantalising hint of the future, of all that lay ahead. I was in no hurry to get there, but it was nice to know it was waiting.

But always, there was the other.

I can still see it now, after all this time, all these months and years that have been folded and stacked into great piles behind me, so many years that it's hard to believe. It is the barest whisper of sound, a glimpse of what could have been. The hesitant track of insect feet across the back of my hand. The jungle heat of a metal-roofed hideout on a summer's day. An ant tumbling over discarded crumbs. The navy ink of a swimming pool on a moonless night. Dragonflies alighting on a summer bloom. The silent beating of butterfly wings in a glass jar, under a sky so bright, so blue, it hurt your eyes to look at it.

Acknowledgements

Many thanks are due to everyone who helped and supported me in the writing of *Night Swimming*:

Adrienne Gill, who years ago read an enormous draft of what eventually became this book.

Bettina Knipschild, for early reading and astute observations on the text, as well as a supply of home baking!

Vanessa Doherty, Tracy May Fung, Brid Brogan, Philippa Buckley, Pat Buckley, Barbara Allen, Toni Hickey, John McCarthy, who variously read, advised, printed, praised, encouraged and helped in myriad ways.

Bill Core, for being a permanent source of sound advice and common sense.

My colleagues at Muckross Park College, for their support and encouragement.

My friends and extended family, for buying my books, coming to events and for generally being there.

Many thanks to all the writers I know who help and support each other, give feedback and provide blurbs for covers – it is indeed a community I am honoured to belong to (and can't quite believe I do!).

Janet Fitch, for transatlantic support.

Sophie Grenham, who is a true champion of Irish writers.

Margaret Bonass Madden, without whom the Irish book scene would be a very lonely place indeed.

Julia Kelly, Rachael English and Claudia Carroll, for reading and for their kindness.

Catriona McCarthy and John Riordan for the photos.

Special thanks to everyone at Mercier, especially Patrick O'Donoghue, for picking my book up; my editor Noel O'Regan for his phenomenal skill for finding all the mistakes in the text and improving on what I've written; Alice Coleman for the cover, Deirdre Roberts for the publicity, and John Spillane for getting the ball rolling.

My agent, Caroline Montgomery, for sticking with me and providing me with countless Skype sessions, where we spend more time laughing than actually discussing writing.

My brother, Alan, who has always had faith in me and makes me pursue what I believe in, and my sister-in-law, Sarinya, and her unrivalled ability with food.

My father-in-law, Mel Schrier, for helping promote me.

My parents, Ted and Yvonne Finn, for endless patience and wisdom and encouragement and support. There will never be enough pages to thank you fully!

My children, Emily and David, the best children ever born!

My husband, Mark, who always puts my writing first. Thank you.

And finally, to all the readers out there who buy books, read books, talk about books, attend readings and events, and give writers a reason to keep writing.